HOLD YOUR FIRE

HOLD YOUR FIRE

FIRE

Stories Celebrating the Creative Spark

Alicia Cay, Brian Corley, CJ Erick, Jace Killan,
Kat Kellermeyer, Kevin J. Anderson, Kitty Sarkozy,
Kristen Bickerstaff, M. Elizabeth Ticknor,
Mary Pletsch,Melissa Koons, Mike Jack Stoumbos,
Neil Peart, October K Santerelli,
Raphyel M. Jordan, Rebecca E. Treasure,
Shannon Fox, Tanya Hales, Wayland Smith

EDITED BY LISA MANGUM

AN ANTHOLOGY TO BENEFIT THE DON HODGE MEMORIAL SCHOLARSHIP

WFP
WORDFIRE PRESS

EBook ISBN: 978-1-68057-175-2
Trade Paperback ISBN: 978-1-68057-174-5
Hardcover ISBN: 978-1-68057-176-9
Library of Congress Control Number: 2020951430

Cover design by Janet McDonald
Cover artwork images by Adobe Stock
Kevin J. Anderson, Art Director

Published by
WordFire Press, LLC
PO Box 1840
Monument CO 80132

Kevin J. Anderson & Rebecca Moesta, Publishers
WordFire Press eBook Edition 2021
WordFire Press Trade Paperback Edition 2021
WordFire Press Hardcover Edition 2021
Printed in the USA

Join our WordFire Press Readers Group for
sneak previews, updates, new projects, and giveaways.
Sign up at wordfirepress.com

CONTENTS

Introduction: The Fires of Inspiration　　　　　vii
Kevin J. Anderson

SPLENDID MIRAGE: THE SEEKER'S TALE　　　1
Kevin J. Anderson & Neil Peart

THE FIRE SERMON　　　17
Mary Pletsch

ONE-HIT WEBSTER　　　35
Brian Corley

THE DOOR　　　50
Kristen Bickerstaff

THE BURREN OF MARS　　　68
CJ Erick

WHITE FEATHER　　　85
Shannon Fox

INTO THE VALLEY　　　98
Wayland Smith

THE LAST WAKING PRINCESS　　　107
Kat Kellermeyer

THE FIRST PROBLEM　　　123
Alicia Cay

MI JACULPO　　　139
October K Santerelli

ONE FOR HUNGER, TWO FOR JOY　　　149
Tanya Hales

THE HUNTER AND THE HUNTED　　　165
Raphyel M. Jordan

TAKE ME FOR A RIDE　　　181
Mike Jack Stoumbos

HYDE PARK　　　197
Shannon Fox

BOW DRILL   208
Jace Killan

DREAM GIRL   224
Kitty Sarkozy

WHITE SAILS AND STORMY SEAS   231
M. Elizabeth Ticknor & Rebecca E. Treasure

CHECK YES OR NO   245
Melissa Koons

DON'T IGNORE IT   267
Tanya Hales

About the Editor   271
If You Liked ...   273
Other WordFire Press Titles Edited by Lisa Mangum   275

INTRODUCTION: THE FIRES OF INSPIRATION

KEVIN J. ANDERSON

Hold your fire
Keep it burning bright
Hold the flames
'Til the dream ignites

Those are lines from "Mission" by Rush, a song that is very close to my heart. Neil Peart, who wrote those words, was one of the greatest drummers and most profound lyricists of all time—and yet the song is about how he himself was amazed and humbled to see great architecture, works of art, literature, and motion pictures.

We each get inspired when we see masterpieces that we couldn't imagine creating ourselves. I have always been inspired by music, particularly progressive rock (in particular, Kansas, Styx, the Alan Parsons Project, and Rush). As a nerdy kid in high school, when I was much more interested in Middle Earth and the sandworms of Dune than in the homecoming dance, I drew inspiration from epic songs about dystopian worlds, necromancers, spaceship expeditions to black holes, sailing ships and starships, aliens stranded on Earth.

I couldn't sing, couldn't play any musical instrument, but I could *write*, and I transformed that inspiration from music into stories (which grew increasingly better as I practiced).

After I graduated from college and got a full-time job, Rush released a new album, *Grace Under Pressure*. To my ears and my imagination, it was a science fiction tour de force that serendipitously aligned with the ambitious first novel I was developing, *Resurrection, Inc.* I listened to "p/g" (as Rush fans affectionately abbreviate *Grace Under Pressure*) countless times, and the songs and lyrics directly shaped my story and characters. "Distant Early Warning," "Red Sector A," "Afterimage," "The Enemy Within," "The Body Electric," "Beneath the Wheels"—so much so that when I eventually sold the novel to Signet Books, I included an acknowledgment: "To Neal Peart, Geddy Lee, and Alex Lifeson of RUSH, whose haunting album *Grace Under Pressure* inspired much of this novel." (Yes, I actually misspelled Neil's name.)

As a naïve and optimistic twenty-five-year-old, I autographed copies to the members of Rush and sent them to Mercury Records, hoping that someone might read it.

Neil Peart did, and he wrote me back, saying that he had enjoyed the novel. "You have gone so far beyond anything I have experienced in lyrics that the dedication seems unmerited. Never mind—it's still a very nice thing, and I'm proud of it."

From that, we struck up a correspondence and friendship that lasted more than thirty years. We wrote a short story together in 1993, and I surreptitiously managed to work snippets of Neil's lyrics into many of my novels, including Dune books, my Saga of Seven Suns (which Neil particularly enjoyed), and others.

He occasionally reciprocated. After reading my novel *Lifeline* with Doug Beason and our next book *Timeline* (the title was eventually changed to *The Trinity Paradox*), he wrote the song "Dreamline," one of the most popular tracks on the *Roll the Bones* album. There are also multiple Seven Suns references in their *Snakes and Arrows* album.

Our greatest cross-pollination, though, came with *Clockwork Angels*, the last studio album from Rush. Neil had an idea for a sprawling concept album, a steampunk fantasy adventure, a coming-of-age tale in a fantastical world, and he brainstormed the story and the world with me. He sent me the lyrics as he wrote each song, and I loved the story of the domineering Watchmaker, the ruthless Anarchist, the Alchemy College, pirates and airships, the Seven Cities of Gold ... and the amazing mechanical Clockwork Angels.

After all that, I would have been inspired to write something of my own, but it got even better when Neil asked me to write the novel version of the album. Published in 2012 and beautifully illustrated by Hugh Syme (Rush's cover artist), *Clockwork Angels: The Novel* hit the *New York Times* bestseller list and has won or was nominated for several awards.

Inspiration didn't stop flowing, though. Because the story was so visual, we adapted it into a graphic novel from BOOM! Studios, and Neil himself narrated the audiobook, the first time he had ever done so.

After such a remarkable creative experience, we talked about doing a sequel, noting several interesting characters we wanted to revisit in short stories. We had ideas, but I was reluctant to do just a collection of scattered tales. I wanted something to bind them together, but I didn't have that spark. Not yet.

Enter more musical inspiration, through Matt Scannell, lead singer and front man for Vertical Horizon, and a close friend of Neil's. When Neil introduced us, Matt and I hit it off immediately, and he invited me and my wife, Rebecca, to Vertical Horizon concerts, including one stadium event in Colorado Springs. Before the show, we joined Matt for some conversation, and he pressed me whether Neil and I were ever going to write more in the Clockwork universe. I explained our smaller ideas, but we just didn't have the big one yet.

During the concert, Matt played "Save Me from Myself," a

song that consists of several dramatic stories from the news all interconnected through a focal point of a man's personal tragedy. As I listened to that song live, the idea suddenly clicked, and *Clockwork Lives*—my favorite of all my novels—was born right there in the stands of SkySox Stadium.

Would I ever have come up with that twist without hearing that song? Maybe, but it likely wouldn't have been the same. Would I have written *Resurrection, Inc.* without having the inspiration of *Grace Under Pressure*? Maybe, but it would have been an entirely different novel.

I am pleased to include one of the stories from *Clockwork Lives*, "The Seeker's Tale," in this anthology.

I draw on music for my inspiration just as flowers drink in sunshine. My muse has a soundtrack, a very loud one. Other writers draw on poetry, on paintings, on natural beauty, on staring at the waves of the ocean. Anything can light the creative fires.

Neil Peart died in January 2020 after a long struggle with brain cancer, but every time I play one of my favorite Rush songs, he is still there, inspiring me.

> Life is just a candle
> And a dream must give it flame.
> —*Neil Peart*

SPLENDID MIRAGE: THE SEEKER'S TALE

KEVIN J. ANDERSON & NEIL PEART

I had a dream, or perhaps the dream had me. I don't know which came first, or which was stronger—I won't know until the story ends.

An unending quest becomes a reason unto itself, a journey that means more than any destination. And I learned how to pass that dream on to others, even if I did not succeed for myself.

I grew up in a lakeshore village, Opal Lake, which was nestled in the foothills with the rugged mountains visible beyond. Farther still, I had heard of the unexplored Redrock Desert, but the desert and the mountains were so distant they might have been a different world entirely. I didn't bother much with daydreams then; I was busy enough with my everyday diversions. I would catch frogs in the tangled marshes or take a paddle boat to scoop mudfish, which provided more sport than food.

When I was fourteen years old, an old man with one missing foot changed my life, ruined my life. He infected me with an unattainable dream, a fever of the imagination. "Tell me, Cabeza," he said to me as he sat on a weathered tree stump on the lakeshore, "ever heard of the Seven Cities of Gold? Ever know anyone who's seen them?"

Old Fernando hobbled around with a crutch, swinging his footless leg beneath him; he wove frog traps from dried reeds and occasionally caught mudfish or crabs to sell. Mostly, the old man liked to talk.

"Seven Cities?" I asked. "I've never even seen one city."

"Not just any city, Cabeza." Fernando leaned forward, no longer interested in the reeds he was idly weaving. "Cities of *gold*. Lost cities. Towers and walls so beautiful they hurt your eyes when the sun shines on them."

"Gold? Here in Atlantis? You must mean in Albion—cities built by the Watchmaker? He makes all the gold."

The old man made a rude noise. "Not that kind of gold! And I don't mean any place like Poseidon City either. You don't think we were the first people to live here do you? The Elder Race of man built those cities, all seven of them, deep in the Redrock Desert on a high mesa rising above a sparkling lake. They're so far away and so unattainable that no one has yet found them." The old man shook his head. "Although I tried." His voice became clogged with tears. "How I tried for so many years."

"But you never found them?"

He shook his head and looked down at his unfortunately abbreviated foot. "I gave it my best attempt, and alas I'm no longer able." He raised his eyes. "You, though ... *you* could find the Seven Cities. Wouldn't that be more glorious than splashing in the mud and feeding marsh gnats?" To emphasize his point he swished his palm around his face, scattering the tiny blood-sucking insects.

I glanced at his stump. "Is that how you lost your foot?" One of my friends told me that a swamp alligator had bitten it off, but none of us really knew.

He nodded slowly. "Most grueling ordeal of my life, dragging a bloody stump for four days out of the desert, using only a mesquite branch for a crutch."

"So, it wasn't a swamp alligator then?"

He scowled at me. "There aren't any swamp alligators in the canyons of the Redrock Desert." He gazed toward the foothills. "Beyond the mountains, far outside of civilization, you will see landmarks and miracles. There's a shrine up in a slickrock grotto, a pool of purest water that seeps through time itself, a sacred place for the Elder Race. Any man who drinks of the water is said to become immortal. It was called the Fountain of Lamneth."

I had never heard of the Fountain, nor the Seven Cities for that matter, but I didn't have extensive schooling ... and his enthusiasm was infectious.

Fernando set his reeds aside to lean closer. "I thought they were just silly myths at first, but every legend has a kernel of truth. *Someone* must have seen the Fountain of Lamneth at one time.

"I tracked the markings, traveled through a wilderness so deep that it didn't even remember the *idea* of human footprints. I saw rock writings, petroglyphs that told an ancient story and gave directions to intrepid dreamers like myself." The old man's eyes were shining, and his voice took on a greater intensity. I couldn't look away.

"At the end of a narrow, high-walled canyon, I climbed from one shelf to another on the slippery red rock. I could see the smooth grotto above, a beckoning doorway with a trickle of the purest water. The Fountain of Lamneth—it had to be! The rock wall was sheer, but I found handholds and hauled myself up using all my strength, arms, legs, fingers. It was precarious—but my whole life was precarious. I was all alone in that slickrock canyon, months and countless miles from the nearest human being.

"I was exhausted by the time I reached the ledge, lifting myself up on my elbows, barely holding on. I raised my head over the lip just enough to see that beautiful hollow surrounded by emerald vines and a carpet of lush moss. The drip of fresh water was like music, and I saw the pool shimmering like a moonstone mirror. The Fountain of Lamneth—one sip would grant me immortality. It was perfect. It was a miracle!

"Then a boulder broke from the side of the crumbling cliff, and I slipped, taking more rocks with me as I scrambled for any kind of handhold. I cried out into that endless empty wasteland where no one could hear me.

"I should have died in that fall, but somehow—a blessing and a curse—I was uninjured ... except for my foot. A boulder had smashed it clean off from my ankle. I managed to tie a makeshift tourniquet before I fainted.

"By the time I woke, much of the bleeding had stopped, and I had nothing to do but go on or give up—and I could always give up later. I gazed one last time at that lost canyon, the high unattainable grotto where I had seen only a hint of the Fountain ... Some other seeker would have to find it.

"I dragged myself through the canyon and found a broken branch for a crutch. I followed the canyon to a larger wash and followed that wash until I met a stream, followed that stream to a larger stream, and finally a river. I kept going downhill out of the mountains until I came upon a village."

Fernando looked up, his eyes shining as if he had been transported to another world. He waved more gnats from his face. "You're young and strong, Cabeza. *You* could find the Fountain of Lamneth, or even the Seven Cities of Gold." He reached out to grasp my arm. "You can do it—no one else can."

I answered with a nervous laugh and told him that I had to go do my chores. But I didn't know how to resist those exciting stories. I didn't sleep at all that night or the next. On the third night, when I finally dozed off from sheer exhaustion, I dreamed of gleaming towers, majestic cities with walls of gold, architecture that made even fantasies ache.

I knew I had to find the Seven Cities. I had been infected.

When I told my parents I intended to set off for the Seven Cities of Gold, they forbade me in the strongest possible terms—which is a very good way to inspire a teenager. In secret, Fernando told me everything he remembered about his route, about the intervening mountains, and the Redrock Desert. His stories painted a jumble of spectacular images in my head.

I secretly packed supplies, food, rope, packets of alchemical firestarter ... and a great deal of encouragement from the old man with one foot. I could see the mountains on the horizon, and I knew the Redrock Desert lay beyond them. I would find the Seven Cities of Gold—and the Fountain of Lamneth, too, for good measure.

I sneaked away from home one night and trudged off into the dark, following the constellations, which seemed to lead me directly where I needed to go. By the next morning, though, my confidence had already begun to flag, but I knew that a quest is not something one undertakes lightly. Reaching my goal would require more than a half day of effort, so I stuck it out. Sore feet would be the least of my concerns.

But sore feet became sore legs and a sore back. My pack weighed as much as a boulder and I discarded all the luxuries I no longer considered necessary, bit by bit along the way. It took me five days to cross through the foothills up into the mountains —and I had not even begun the real journey through unexplored territory.

In two weeks, I saw not a single soul. At first, the solitude was exhilarating, then frightening, then simply oppressive.

As I wandered, occasionally I would look up in the sky and see a chugging steamliner plowing across the winds, delivering cargo to the mountain villages or scattered lake towns. But the airship captain flew too high to see me even if I tried to signal him. I walked onward, climbing and descending, following the fading vapor trails of steam the airships left in the sky.

I ran out of food. Since I had grown up in a comfortable

village, I had few survival skills. I didn't really know how to hunt, and I certainly couldn't defend myself if I should come upon a giant bear.

I ran out of firestarter on the night of the first snowfall, and I huddled under my thin blanket, shivering against the bone-breaking cold. I cursed my poor planning and my gullibility. And I hadn't even reached the Redrock Desert yet! I was a fool.

The next day, trudging onward with numb feet and doubled vision, I topped a ridge and looked down into a cleft of rock, saw sheer cliffs with stairstepped quarries, mine shafts, even the terminus of a steamliner supply rail. A mining town built into the cliffs!

I nearly collapsed at the sight. I had not eaten in days. My throat was parched, my clothes tattered, and my satchel of belongings nearly empty. I reeled like a drunken man toward the quarry and the cottages built of stone. Three miners hurried out to catch me as I fell. "You look as if you've been chewed up by the world," said one.

"And then spat back out," said another.

They carried me to an inn where they gave me water and hot broth and bread that tasted like ambrosia—not that I've ever tasted ambrosia. The miners gathered around, all of them intent. They gave me a mug of mountain spirits, which made me dizzy.

"Where are you from, lad?"

"What are you doing out here?"

"What's your name?"

I lifted my large head, which was shaggier than usual after my tribulations. "I am Cabeza de Vaca from Opal Lake, and I am on a quest to find the Seven Cities of Gold."

The miners drew back, some chuckling, others amazed. "You've been out there, then? You've been to the Redrock Desert and come back?"

I hesitated only a moment, unwilling to admit my dismal failure. "Yes! Months of staggering around lost, but searching. All the things I've seen." I shook my head. "I can't even describe."

"Try," said one of the miners, and they all leaned close to listen.

So I told them what they wanted to hear. Remembering Fernando's descriptions, I talked about fantastic rock formations, stone windows, petroglyphs, and a mysterious grotto high in a canyon wall that held the Fountain of Lamneth.

"The Fountain?" one of the miners cried. "Haven't heard that one in a long time!"

Seeing the enthusiastic reception to my words, I told them even more.

The mining village was called Endoline, and the men and women worked a rich vein of alchemical minerals, extracting sunstone, bloodstone, dreamstone, green sulfur, fire opals, and many other rare substances, all of which were shipped by steam-liner to Poseidon City for trade, mostly to Albion.

The Endoline miners tended me, cleaned me up, gave me fresh clothes, and let me rest there until I was more than recovered. When I regained my strength, the people were eager to re-supply me, stuffing my pack with a far more practical inventory of survival goods.

"Will you be going out again to find the Seven Cities?" they asked. It seemed important to them that *somebody* continue the search. "And when you find them, will you come back here and tell us?"

"Of course," I said. "I promise."

They advised me about the mountains and the desert, definitely more accurate directions than old Fernando had been able to provide. And so, with more caution than the first time, I set off toward the great mysterious expanse beyond the mountains.

I lasted five days.

The desert was an inhospitable place, but I forced myself to go into the canyons that Fernando had talked about. Towering walls of rust-colored rock were marked with dark stains that I could not decipher. My feet were sore and my spirits were low. I was tired of being alone, but I had not yet found what I was looking for. I made up my mind to continue for one more day, because my food would not last longer than that. Then I would have to make it back to the mountains, or I'd perish out there, lost and alone.

In the distance I saw a large chiseled design on the side of a mesa, a pattern that looked like a flying owl clearly drawn by the hand of man, but so distant and so high that it had to have been carved there by the Elder Race. What mortal could have achieved something like that? I shaded my eyes and stared longingly at the distant cliffside and the rugged intervening terrain—and I knew it would take me several days to reach the base of the mesa. I did not have the food, or the stamina, to make it, and so with one last longing glance, I turned around and made my way back....

Reaching the mountains, I followed the lines of roads until I found another mining village, this one named Broken Cliffs. Again, they welcomed me with astonishment. I staggered into their town. "I've been to find the Seven Cities!"

And the people gathered around me. "The Seven Cities of Gold? You come from the Redrock Desert?"

"Yes," I said and told them how I'd wandered the uncharted landscape, the grand designs I had seen on the slickrock cliffs. "A message from the Elder Race for seekers like me. I didn't reach the Seven Cities this time—but I will return."

My story fired their imagination, and I began to realize the value of what I was providing. I rested in Broken Cliffs for weeks, waiting for a cold snap to pass. The villagers were happy to replenish my supplies, give me warm blankets and wool clothing, and they also offered me vague directions and advice.

I set off again....

I repeated the same scheme, over and over—for years. I ventured deeper into the Redrock Desert, always searching, going as far as my supplies and my blisters would allow. I became familiar with the various mining towns, which were much easier to find than the Seven Cities.

When I eventually returned to Endoline, I was delighted to find that the villagers remembered me. They had continued talking my tribulations from the first time, and they had added fanciful perils, glorious visions, and remarkable discoveries that exceeded even my ability to describe. Then, as I returned to Broken Cliffs, Chalcedony Wells, and Quartzline, my own story preceded me. The *fact* of my quest had revitalized dreams in the Seven Cities, awakened curiosity and a sense of wonder in those who led painfully uneventful lives. What was wrong with that? I felt proud to give them such inspiration.

At one point, five years into my quest, I realized it was more efficient just to wander the mountains from one mining town to the next, telling my story without the bothersome step of arduous desert explorations. By then, I was familiar enough with the landscape that I could describe my adventures convincingly without having to suffer further. It was far less taxing that way.

Eventually, I returned to my old home of Opal Lake, a grown and hardened man full of adventures, ready to be received as a hero. I was disappointed to learn that old Fernando had died years earlier, as if relieved to have passed on his dream to me. The people of Opal Lake remembered me as the boy who had run off and never come back. My parents were glad to know I was all right, but they had grown accustomed to life without me.

I spent nights in the village telling stories by a bonfire at the lakeshore. I described the Seven Cities of Gold, and I told them I had found the mystical Fountain of Lamneth, but declined to drink of the magical water, so as to maintain my hold on humanity. The people of Opal Lake needed the second-hand adventure, for they would never experience anything similar for themselves.

My mother tentatively asked if I intended to stay, and the crowd of listeners fell silent as the bonfire crackled. I looked at her and shook my shaggy head. By now I had grown a beard. "Someone has to find the Seven Cities of Gold, and I am determined that it'll be me. *Somebody* has to explore the world."

The villagers applauded me as a hero. They gave me the supplies I needed—food, fresh clothes, newly shod boots—and I departed, leaving only my stories behind.

At first I set off toward the mountains, but when I was out of sight, I circled back and headed instead toward the coast. I had more important things to do in Poseidon City.

After all my years of questing, I had built up a vivid imaginary picture of what the Seven Cities of Gold looked like, but I really had no comprehension of what a "city" was at all. Opal Lake barely qualified as a village, and even the mining towns of Broken Cliffs, Endoline, and Chalcedony Wells had no more than a few thousand souls.

Poseidon City, though, was a cacophony of people, vehicles, smells, shadows, and streets—and an expansive audience hungry to hear about my epic journey. These everyday people sorely needed a dream of lost marvels.

I had spent enough time in the Redrock Desert that my face was weathered, and people said that my gaze had an odd quality of *distance*. Remembering what I had seen in the eyes of old Fernando, I cultivated an edge of exotic wariness, a hint of driven madness.

Since I had been infected by the quest, pushed to the far

fringes of nowhere in search of that splendid mirage, I wondered just how much truth there had been in Fernando's tales. What if he hadn't actually lost his foot from a fall after glimpsing the Fountain? Maybe his foot had been amputated after something as mundane as an infected cut? But who wanted to hear that story?

I'd suffered through enough starvation and thirst in my search for the Seven Cities, and I much preferred to spend an evening in a tavern with a drink and a friend—preferably many friends, and preferably friends who would buy the drinks.

Poseidon City had ale far superior to anything in Opal Lake or the mining towns. With its countless workers, weary men and women who rarely, if ever, set foot outside the city, there was an infinite landscape of taverns and listeners. Apart from the stream of sailors who frequented the dockside inns, most of the taverns had regular customers who did not visit other drinking establishments. Therefore, I could go just a few blocks away, pull up a new bench, call for a tankard of ale, and tell the very same adventures to an entirely different audience. No one would ever know the difference.

My heart swelled when I saw their intent expressions, when they glanced toward the windows and considered mysteries that had never previously crossed their minds. I was doing a good service. Even though my stories were not true—well, very few of them at least—I didn't consider what I was doing as *lying*. I was entertaining. I was *inspiring*. And if I could give these lackluster people a sense of wonder for the mere price of a tankard of ale—or two or three—then it was a good thing by far.

Once I learned which taverns were most lucrative, I began to dream aloud about my next expedition to the desert. I vowed that if I could just go farther, if I could just endure longer, I would find the object of my lifelong quest. Then, as my next step, I would forlornly look at my empty money purse and request funds for supplies so I could head out into the emptiness again and find that great dream of human history....

I made a fair amount of money that way, and I could have purchased fine clothes and jewelry, but my dusty tattered clothes served my purpose well. Before entering any new tavern, I would find a safe place to stash my ever-growing hoard, so that I once again appeared penniless.

I wandered from place to place, talking about my goal, my tribulations, my need to find grand and mysterious places. By now my personal legend had grown. Tavern patrons talked about my quest even when I wasn't there.

But I had completed the circuit of likely drinking establishments, and I could no longer stay in Poseidon City and remain convincing. So, I used some of the generous contributions to buy actual supplies and booked passage on a cargo steamliner that took me out to Endoline again (no use walking all that way). I spent another week in the mining town, telling the stories I had honed in Poseidon City before venturing out.

With a full belly, warm clothes, and plenty of supplies, I set off in a different direction, winding through a new set of canyons on an unpredictable course, going wherever the desert and my feet would take me. Maybe I was caught up in my own story. I found more cliffs, more slot canyons, even other petroglyphs, mysterious symbols of squiggles and arrows.

After a few weeks out there though, I'd had quite enough. During my year in the city I'd grown better at talking than walking. Muscular thighs had given way to a rounded gut, so I looped back into the mountains, found another mining village, one I had not visited for two years, and plied them with my stories, telling them how I'd seen the Seven Cities in the distance, but hadn't been able to make it there before my supplies gave out.

My quest had become legendary, though it was clear some listeners had begun to consider me obsessed and mad. I stayed in the mining town for only a few days before heading off to another village in the foothills, where I told the same stories.

Eventually I returned to Poseidon City, having let the audiences lie fallow long enough. My most receptive crowds were in the dockside taverns because sailors were always new. Crews came and went, and most of the local listeners were tired of hearing about Albion or their absurd myths about angels beneath the sea. They had never heard my tales of the Seven Cities or the Fountain of Lamneth, though!

One day, before the taverns opened for the evening crowds, I came upon a place called Underworld Books. I wasn't much of a reader, preferring stories told from one person to another without the intervention of written words. But the proprietor of the bookshop seemed to have explored more exotic worlds than I had. She knew exactly what I might be looking for, even though I didn't know myself. She watched me from the door of her shop. "I know what you lack. You are a seeker."

I smiled, scratched my shaggy beard. "Ah, you've heard my story, then." I extended a large hand. "I am Cabeza de Vaca, the man who will find the Seven Cities of Gold."

"That is your intent, but you lack a map. I have maps. I have exactly what you need."

I was doubtful. "If maps existed to find the Seven Cities of Gold, then someone else would have found them by now."

"There are maps from different worlds," said the bookseller. "Some accurate, some not, but all could be useful, since the Redrock Desert doesn't change much from universe to universe."

I suspected she had cultivated this tantalizing tale to lure potential customers. Still, I realized that if I carried maps—as props—my own story might be more believable. I patted my tattered trousers. "I have little money. I'm a weary traveler who generally lives off the land."

"I think not." She frowned at me. "And I think you would be a much more effective seeker with my maps."

Maybe she glimpsed the sack of coins I kept hidden under my shirt, but I knew she told the truth. So I purchased the maps at a price that I thought was too high, but the bookseller's penetrating gaze seemed to peer right through me, and she would not lower her price.

I marveled at the maps she provided; they would indeed be quite beneficial, for not only did they sketch out the rough topography of the desert, they also showed the intervening mountains in greater detail, the roads, the mining villages, even some population clusters that I had not visited before, places that had never heard my stories. All in all, a good trade.

Eventually, I set off to the wilderness again, telling everyone I would continue my quest until I found the Seven Cities, and they all bought me another round of drinks.

With the maps I could travel deeper into the desert, go places I had never seen. This time, I felt the quest more strongly than I had experienced since I'd listened to old Fernando spin his tales on the muddy shore of Opal Lake.

The maps also showed me easier ways into the desert, and by now I had gotten more proficient at choosing my supplies, and I also knew how to locate rock potholes that held rainwater or hidden springs surrounded by tamarisks, so I could actually stay out there longer.

That time, I ventured deeper into the arid wasteland than I had ever gone before, and finally I saw a shimmering mirage, something I had never expected to find. A gleaming expanse of a distant lake that lay like a moonstone mirror at the base of an enormous mesa that rose from the desert like an island in the sky. Exactly as the legends had foretold! The Seven Cities must be up there, the Elder Race separated from base mankind in their high fortress.

I froze like a starving man holding a spoon of food up to his mouth, afraid to take that first delicious bite. It was there, within a day's journey—two at the most! I could traverse the shallow lake and climb those cliffs. I could find the Seven Cities of Gold at last.

But what if the cities were a disappointment when I found them? What if the gold was tarnished, the majestic cities no more than abandoned huts that were crumbling into dust? Maybe it was better that I didn't risk that.

After all, my dream was perfect as it was.

Because it was late in the afternoon, I camped. The sun set behind the mesa, and red rays sent a firestorm of flares reflecting from the broad lake in the distance. That night I slept restlessly and dreamt of the finish line, the long unfulfilled quest that had sustained me for my entire life.

What would I do with myself if I finally found my goal?

Next morning, I packed up my camp and headed into the sunrise on the trail ahead, *away* from the mesa, leaving the prize in the shadow behind me.

No, I was not ready to find the cities—not yet.

Long afterward, I kept telling my story to many people who listened breathlessly, and the tales grew in the telling, thriving like a garden. My search itself became a thing of legend—and that was something I chose to perpetuate, because it was good for *them* to have their legends too, to have their unattainable dreams which I could provide. In my mind, that was a far more satisfactory experience than actually finding the Seven Cities.

Life is but a candle, and a dream must give it flame. Who was I to extinguish the flame?

About the Authors

Kevin J. Anderson is the bestselling science-fiction author of 165 novels. His original works include the Saga of Seven Suns series;

Spine of the Dragon; the Terra Incognita trilogy; and with Brian Herbert, he is the co-author of 15 novels in the Dune universe. He has written spin-off novels for *Star Wars*, DC Comics, and *The X-Files*. His first novel, *Resurrection, Inc.*, was inspired by the Rush album *Grace Under Pressure*, with lyrics by Neil Peart.

Neil Peart was the drummer and lyricist of the legendary rock band Rush and the author of *Ghost Rider, The Masked Rider, Traveling Music, Roadshow, Far and Away, Far and Near,* and *Far and Wide.*

Anderson and Peart coauthored the steampunk fantasy novels *Clockwork Angels* and *Clockwork Lives,* as well as the graphic novel adaptations of both, and the story "Drumbeats."

Neil Peart passed away January 2020 after a long battle with brain cancer.

THE FIRE SERMON

MARY PLETSCH

I don't even like cigarettes, but I light one anyway. I flick my thumb to mimic a lighter, and the tip of the cigarette bursts into flame.

I wonder if this alley has security cameras. If so, I wonder if the person watching them could tell that there's no lighter in my hand.

I tilt the cigarette downwind, letting the breeze wash my long-sleeved silk blouse in tobacco smoke. It's hot today, even with the wind. I wish I could wear short sleeves, but I don't want my scars to show.

Will anyone notice if I don't take a drag on this cigarette? Best to be safe. I take a few puffs, grimacing, knowing if I keep up this front too long I might actually get addicted to the damned things. I drop the cigarette and crush it with my foot.

I should pick it up and put it in the canister thoughtfully provided nearby. Flame courses through my veins and sets my heart pounding with alternate possibilities.

The canister is meant to hold cigarette butts. The liner is fire-resistant. The canister itself, though, is made of rugged plastic.

It might still burn.

The contents of the garbage can beside it will *definitely* burn. Paper bags with half-eaten muffins, napkins, paper cups ...

My fingers grow hot. Underneath the cloud of tobacco smoke I can smell my hair beginning to singe.

Deep breath. Cool thoughts.

I walk out of the alley, turn the corner, open the door of the coffee shop, and step inside.

I am not sure I belong with this writing group. I've been a member for five months, and the disorganization still irritates me.

Shareef, yet again, has nothing to share this month because *he's been busy.* He works in my office and he's always busy. To his credit, he provides thoughtful analysis on everyone else's work. I should be happy with that.

I should be.

Rua, yet again, has provided us with three thousand words of fan fiction.

Kimiko, yet again, has refused to edit something *unpublishable.*

And I, yet again, sit there, seething. The constant bickering pisses me off and starts me sparking. I'll have to write all night to calm myself down. I wonder why I even bother with this group.

Am I really this damned lonely? Is this what it's come to?

I don't date. Don't have kids. I avoid close friendships. I say it's of my own choosing, but I don't know how true that is. My *choice* is made with extenuating circumstances.

I hate that I'm like this. I shouldn't *have* to cope with a constant desire to burn things. Nobody else does.

Injustice makes me angry.

My gut roils. My hands itch. I can feel my skin tightening with heat. I keep thinking about the garbage can in the alley.

I can't stay. I'm too frustrated and that's too dangerous.

I stand up. Turn around.

Come face to face with a girl with lank black hair that needs a good combing. A moment later, I inhale the skunky scent of weed.

Ugh. I guess that's legal here now, but I don't want to smell it. It's obnoxious; one more pushed button I have to try to ignore.

You want to smoke? I'll give you smoke.

Wrath and hunger are a united voice shouting in my brain stem. Logic is a cool warden keeping the lizard brain in its terrarium. There's a part of me that's always found burning garbage cans unsatisfying. That part wants to know what it might be like to set fire to something more consequential.

This is a person. *Not tinder.* A person.

You can't turn someone into a pillar of fire in the middle of a Coffee Moose.

Look at her, and tell a story about her. Tell a story and burn it slowly. Keep the flares at bay with a story and a slow burn.

I look at the girl again. What kind of person is she?

She looks about the same age as Kimiko, who's in university, but Kimiko is all cute collegiate in her pricy branded sweatshirt, while this girl ... I can't tell if she's poor or just doesn't care. Perhaps the second. The gold bracelets on her right wrist look real. She's wearing a tee and jeans that aren't like the deliberately distressed clothing they sell in the mall. Those little blackened holes in her clothes are made by sparks.

"Uh, is this the writing group?" she stammers.

"Yes," I say. Sizing up our new member has distracted me from my frustration, and my hands are no longer burning. I offer one instead. "Welcome. I'm Kenna."

She shakes my cool hand, and I wonder what she sees when she looks at me: middle-aged, sensible blouse, pressed slacks. We couldn't be more different.

Then sparks jump between our palms.

Instinctively, I press my hand hard against hers to snuff the fire.

She sniffs. Her eyes grow wide.

I don't react. I've had forty years of not reacting in a way that others can see. My heart is pounding as I release her hand.

Can't be.

In a lifetime of looking, I've never met anyone like me.

"Folks, this is Agni, from my English Writing course," Kimiko says, ignorant of my life-altering revelation.

Kimiko's words break the spell. Agni pulls up a chair, pulls out a sketch pad, and starts doodling. I sit back down and pretend to skim notes on Rua's story.

I sneak peeks at Agni's art while we workshop Rua's and Kimiko's stories. Agni is drawing a dragon wreathed in a crown of flame.

Shareef and I will have our turn next week. Kimiko invites Agni to submit something too, and I know what she's doing. Shareef is going to be *too busy* again. Agni agrees. We all give her our email addresses.

I wonder if I'll hear from her.

I don't hear from her. Not personally. Perhaps it's my own fault. I don't reach out to her, either, though I know I should.

What I get from Agni is the same thing that everyone in the group gets: a short story submission entitled "Some Like It Hotter."

Kimiko is going to say the story is unpublishable, and she's not wrong. Serial killer stories tend to be a hard sell. Worse, Agni makes a novice's mistake. She dwells on the gruesomeness of the murders rather than making her protagonist compelling.

I'm fascinated anyway.

Because Agni is writing for a very specific audience. An audience of those who know what it's like to feel the urge to burn.

I wish she hadn't chosen this boring detective as her point of view character. This should be a story for an audience that has looked at passersby on the street and imagined the pyre, smelled the smoke, and gritted their teeth and pressed their hands against their own arms and let the heat tear through their clothes, through their skin, down to the bone where there's no more pain. An audience that has held the fire inside them until their eyelashes burn away and their skin blackens, lifting away from the muscles beneath.

What if we didn't hold back?

I'm afraid to dwell on the wild excitement flaring inside me, so I take another look at my own submission. *Princesses and Thieves* is a perfectly serviceable fantasy, and last night I had been happy with it. Today, not so much.

The best thing I can say about this story is that it's *okay*. Solid beginning. Definitive ending. Suspense. Action. Laughs.

This isn't a story. It's a checklist.

Frustrated, I skim the folder labeled "Kenna's Writing" for an alternative. One particular document catches my eye. Its name is a description, not a title: *dragon*. I have a sudden, vivid recollection of Agni's sketch. I click and read to remind myself where this document came from.

Hah. I'd cut it out of an early draft of *Princesses and Thieves*, where the princess and her sidekick attempt to steal the royal crown back from a dragon. I had scrapped the dragon because I was devoting too much of my word count to the dragon's point of view, and I'd replaced her with a generic ogre warlord. A scoundrel who wouldn't tempt me to waste limited space with detailed rhapsodies of fire.

I *like* those rhapsodies. I love the part where the dragon faces down the heroes. "I was born to burn," she proclaims, "and burn I will."

I wonder if Agni would enjoy it too.

This concept appeals to me far more than *Princesses and Thieves*. It's not like my usual submissions, but does that matter? I'm not trying to sell this story, and I don't care what most of the group think of me.

What's the worst that could happen?

I could write a crappy story.

So what?

I start typing away on the *dragon* file, and I do what I wish Agni would have done in her submission. I abandon all pretense of the princess as protagonist. I evade all temptation to dwell overlong on the crispy skin and bubbled fat of bodies retrieved from burned-out houses. I don't flinch from the horror of villages razed to the foundations, but I do tell a tale of a dragon who turns a kingdom to ash because she was born to burn, and because she can.

I call it "The Fire Sermon."

It's a good night. A good day follows. No smoldering hands at work. No dreams of flame at night.

Two days later, I get a private email from Agni.

I'm nervous about my first workshop. Do you want to get together for coffee and talk about our stories before we meet with the whole group?

Underneath is her cell number.

I don't believe she's really anxious, but there are things that I won't put into text. Particularly on computers, where nothing is ever really deleted. The incorporeal web of data and light is more permanent than an epigraph chiseled in stone.

There are some things I don't even say out loud. Words can change the way people think about you.

I've always hated this, all the thoughts and feelings I don't dare voice, and the tension of cloaking them under enough layers of fiction that I can plausibly deny they came from my heart. Someday I just want to *write what I feel*, no metaphors or allusions, no fear muzzling my deepest truths. Ironically, "The Fire Sermon" has been the most honest thing I've ever written.

Yes, I want to talk about it. Not in a Coffee Moose, where other people might overhear. But there's no way to put *let's go somewhere private* onto the internet in a way that won't seem suspicious to outside eyes.

The texts I send are blandly agreeable. I accept the invitation. We pick a place—the same Coffee Moose—and a time—6 PM—after I'm done with work.

No hypothetical investigator would know the subtext when I type *I loved the real hero of your story.*

When I arrive, Agni is already there, waiting for me. She comes up to me while I order a coffee. I notice she doesn't smell like weed today. She smells like ash and blackened logs.

Drinks in hand, I suggest we walk and talk. Agni agrees. Once we're out of the coffee shop, I mention how some things shouldn't be spoken in earshot of others.

"Yeah," she agrees. "Sometimes it's just hard to hold back, you know?"

Do I ever.

"You don't smell like tobacco," Agni says abruptly.

"And you don't smell like weed," I counter.

"But I still smell like something burning. You don't. You don't smell like anything at all."

I blink. "I ... It's been quiet lately. The fire, I mean."

"It *does* that?" Agni pounces on my words. "Goes out, I mean?"

From her words I guess that hers is a constant low boil at the best of times. I remember feeling that way when I was her age.

"I'd never say *goes out*," I reply. "More like a low smolder. But I can manage it long enough to go to work, do chores, sleep at night."

"I have to burn a *lot* to concentrate in school," Agni admits. "Or smoke a lot. I can sedate myself to the point I don't want to set all the idiots around me on fire, but then I don't want to do anything else, either." She looks at me. "You're obviously getting through life without spending every day getting so high you lose the urge to burn. How do you manage it?"

"How I manage it," I repeat automatically. It sounds like the most boring discussion I could imagine. How to blend into society while keeping everyone at a distance? I don't *want* to talk about how I manage to hide what I am. What we are. I want her to keep blazing brightly, that weird, off-kilter spark that she is.

"Yeah," Agni says. "I mean, you must've burned something a lot bigger than dumpsters and abandoned buildings."

A chill runs down my back. "You've burned an abandoned building?"

Her expression turns quizzical. "You haven't?"

I feel ashamed that I am not cool enough to have ever had the nerve to set a building on fire. Oh, I've wanted to.

"I was a farm kid," I say, by way of explanation. "I made huge bonfires."

"So what's the biggest thing you ever burned?"

"Tractor." I'm proud. "An old rusted-out hulk that my grandfather had abandoned in the bush. Took me almost a year to finish. When I was all done, it was just a big oval of melted metal."

"You can focus your fire hot enough to melt metal?"

"Like I said, it took a year of practice." I pause. "Actually, I think I learned a lot from that. Focus, like you said. Control."

"Control," Agni repeats with a frown.

"Like this."

I reach into my purse, pull out a cigarette, hold it up in one hand, and snap my fingers with the other. The tip bursts obediently into flame.

"Wow," Agni says. She seems impressed, which surprises me, because I could do this easily at her age.

"It's about meeting my needs without drawing attention to myself. Some of it is burning small things. Like candles, incense, or these cigarettes that I don't actually want to smoke." The urge to burn something larger crawls over my skin, itching. "Most of it is about keeping myself distracted by writing stories."

"That's why I draw as well as write. It's easier to draw while other people are talking. Keeps my hands busy while my brain concentrates on reality. With writing, it's easier to lose yourself inside your characters' heads."

Which is exactly the point. When I'm tired of staying in control—when my patience is wearing thin—I can escape into someone else's life. Someone else's problems.

Or I can escape into the life of someone who can let their fire free without fear of real-world consequences. They're my characters. They'll only suffer the consequences I'm willing to give them. Of late that's been precious few. It's my fantasy, after all. My dream.

"Hey, you've got a car, right?" Agni says.

"Yes."

She grins. "Because I know this run-down old barn outside of town. Eyesore, really. They should knock it down before it falls down."

The image hits me with almost physical force. I can smell the sweet scent of blazing wood, see the colorful chemical-tinted flames, feel the heat on my face.

I want it.

I want it more than anything.

It's beautiful.

There were things I never thought I would dare to try. Things I never dreamed I could be.

The barn's main beam collapses. I watch a thousand sparks fly toward the moon, glowing like fireflies.

Beside me, Agni smiles. "Imagine what we can do together."

As expected, Kimiko hated Agni's story. So did Shareef, who's more squeamish than I thought.

I was surprised they seemed to like mine. Rua said I should consider writing young adult fiction. I don't remember much else. My mind was elsewhere, thinking about what I was going to do with Agni after writing group was over. Thinking about a condemned house out near the county line.

Going out with Agni is thrilling. Exciting. Riding around on the back roads, looking for abandoned buildings, feeling like I'm a teenager again.

The feeling might be more suited to someone Agni's age, but I can't shake the vehement belief that I was robbed of this sensation when I was an actual teenager. When I was ashamed of my need to stay home on Friday nights, burning things in the shadow of the bush lot instead of going out with kids at school. With the friends I was afraid to have, lest I lose my temper.

I'm tired of playing it safe. In my writing. In my life. I'm tired of trying desperately to pretend I'm just like everyone else. I'm tired of writing things that people think a woman like me *should* be writing.

Most of all, I'm tired of stories created solely to bleed my energy and keep my fire at a low smolder.

I don't stay up all night writing to exhaust myself until I'm worn-out enough to sleep without dreams. Now, I stay up all night because I'm inspired.

I tell stories of djinn and wyrms and daemons.

I write about what might happen if I lived my truth openly.

I write the kind of stories I want to share with Agni.

Except for nights like this one, where I don't write anything at all. Agni and I are out dancing on the razor's edge between late last night and early this morning, dressed all in black, looking for things that will burn.

I can't take my eyes off the structure in front of me. "Are you sure?"

"We'd be doing the owner a favor. Get rid of this, and it'll be easier to put up condos or whatever on the site."

It's an abandoned convenience store. The windows are broken. The brick walls are covered in graffiti. Yet it seems different than collapsed barns or condemned farmhouses.

Perhaps it's because it's in town. I can see the huge empty parking lot of a shopping mall across the street. There are other businesses beside it: a dentist's office on one side and an auto repair shop on the other. I've parked my car in front of it. We stand on the sidewalk, and a truck drives by on the road behind us.

I feel as though igniting this building will mean crossing a line. Part of me can't wait to see what's on the other side.

The other part of me can't ignore the undercurrent of trepidation running beneath my excitement. "Maybe we should just head back to the municipal dump."

"We've been to the dump twice this week, and honestly, garbage is boring. I mean, we've both been burning garbage all our lives, right?"

I hesitate. "Have you been reading the local news at all?"

Agni shrugs.

"People are starting to notice that there are an awful lot of suspicious fires lately."

"So you're saying you want to quit," she says skeptically, like one addict to another.

"Not *quit*. Just lay low until things quiet down."

"Is that who you want to be? The kind of person who's living some kind of half-life, pretending to be someone you're not? Thinking about how you're *supposed* to act instead of how you *want* to?" Agni's words sting because they're true. "Come on. You and me, we can burn anything we want."

She's right. I've been so cautious my whole life, hiding what I am, that I've ended up not really living at all. Not until she came along.

I answer her question with a wave of my hand.

A tongue of fire rises up on the other side of a cracked and dusty window.

Agni grins and joins in, raining sparks until the roof shingles combust.

It's breathtaking to watch.

Someone shouts nearby. Time's up. "I guess we should leave," I say reluctantly.

"There's no proof we did anything. We're just walking by, right?"

I hesitate. Despite the gap in our ages, I listen to her. She's the one who inspired me to live my dreams.

"Come on, Kenna," Agni wheedles. "Half the fun is watching the show."

I'm not sure I agree with her. My pleasure is in the act of creation. The release I feel when a flame I made starts burning. I don't think my creations need an audience.

Then, to my horror, the door of the convenience store swings open from inside. Two figures stagger out. I can't tell how old they are in the dark, but the taller one has his arm around the smaller one, who's wrapped in a tattered plaid blanket.

The taller person looks back over his shoulder. "Markie!"

Are they local teens looking for a place to party? Addicts, seeking a spot to use? Are they homeless people who wanted somewhere dry and quiet to sleep?

Does it matter?

Our glorious fire is growing so very big. Smoke pours out of the broken windows. There must be all kinds of combustibles inside. Trash, old carpet, maybe a mattress. Flames dance to their own tune, a low, sensuous hiss.

"Markie!" the person in the blanket cries.

The taller man lifts the front of his T-shirt over his nose and mouth as he walks toward the door.

I don't know what to do.

Call 911? The police will want to talk to me for calling it in. I don't want that kind of attention.

Stop the man from going back into the building?

Go in myself to search for Markie?

Ask Agni if she can snuff this fire?

My head turns to Agni. Why did I never think to ask her if she can control her flames once they're lit? If she can extinguish the sparks she's created?

Agni smiles at me.

Raises her hand.

Snaps her fingers.

The plaid blanket ignites.

The person inside it screams, high and shrill, and throws the blanket away. I still can't tell if it's a woman or a child. They're thin, and they hop around, shrieking, before they remember to stop, drop, and roll on the broken asphalt in front of the shop.

Agni is laughing.

I stare at her, like part of me can't understand what's happening.

From the corner of my eye, I see motion at the door of the

store. The taller man is back with his arms around the shoulders of a man in a brown jacket. I'm guessing this is Markie.

"Take your shot," Agni purrs.

"What?"

She looks back at me. Her smile is gone. "I *said*, take your shot."

I don't know where to begin explaining to her that I'm not going to burn *people*. Especially not people who've never done me harm. People whose lives are already hard enough.

"Too slow," Agni says, and raises her hand again.

You and me, we can burn anything we want.

She's been an inspiration to me—right up until this moment when I realize I don't want what she wants after all.

I grab her arm. Yank her hand and her attention away from Markie and his rescuer and the slim person panting on the ground, watching the blanket burn. "No!"

Agni's eyes spark fire.

Heat sears my skin, burrows down into flesh. I know this sensation. When I was Agni's age, and the flame within became more than I could handle, I would focus my fire and burn lines into my skin. A vow that if I absolutely had to hurt someone, it wouldn't be someone innocent.

Agni's sparks lash my entire body. They sting my ankles and burn holes into my clothing. But they're nothing next to the deliberate scars that I seared into my arms myself. Either she's not really trying or she's so surprised that she is failing that she can't focus well enough to light my clothes.

I'm angry, of course, that Agni would attack *me* of all people. And I'm curious, too. I have better self-control than she does. I bet I could burn her in a way that would hurt.

"What the *hell*," Agni spits. She struggles, but I hold firm to her arm.

"Agni, you need to stop." I hate that I sound like a parent lecturing a teenager. We're supposed to be equals.

"Nobody is going to miss those people," Agni argues. "Nobody cares what happens to them."

"You don't know that." What's more chilling is that *she* doesn't care. I don't know how to argue against that.

"Don't you want to see how far we can go?"

A rising wail in the distance focuses my attention. "The fire trucks are coming."

"So?"

"You're in university. You're going to throw that away for ... what? Spending the rest of your life moving from city to city to stay ahead of suspicious fires in your wake?" I hate that I have to frame this argument in terms of self-interest, but maybe that will break through to her. "Ahead of suspicious *deaths*?"

"Better that than spending it like *you*." Agni tears her arm out of my grip. "I'd rather die than get old *wishing* and *hiding*."

It hurts because it's true. I wasn't happy when I was pretending to be the person I thought I should be: so bland that nobody would notice me. I can't go back to that life.

Yet I won't fall headlong into Agni's life either. My talent doesn't give me a license for needless cruelty.

"Go back to your fiction," Agni sneers. "You don't have the guts to make it real."

A fire truck comes around the corner, splashing us in lurid red light.

"You don't get to tell me what to do." Agni lifts her hand as if to wave at the firefighters. Her eyes are fire. Her smile is ice.

I may not be responsible for what Agni does, but I can't stand back and watch her hurt people, either.

I take aim. Not at Agni herself.

At the gold bracelets on her wrist.

"I won't let you do this." It's hard not to release my anger. Particularly when that lizard voice inside me is raging that Agni has brought this on herself, and it would serve her right if I lit her up like a Roman candle. It takes all my willpower to keep my focus.

I snap my fingers.

"Stop it!" Agni claws at her burning left wrist with her right hand. "I ... I'll burn you!"

I'm not afraid. She already tried. Her anger is wild, impulsive, and unfocused.

"No. You won't burn me, or those firefighters, or anything else in my city. Because if you do, I'll find you."

Then I turn around and walk back to my car.

I can hear her howling behind me. Part of me expects my car to ignite, or the fire truck to explode. But nothing happens. I climb into my car and start the engine, and I can see Agni in the middle of the road, staring at the melted circle of gold wrapped around her wrist.

Agni doesn't come back to writing group. Doesn't email or text.

Two months later, I ask Kimiko if she's heard from her. Kimiko tells me that Agni dropped out of school. Nobody knows where she went.

I don't know what to feel about that.

Relief, that I don't have to make good on my threat?

Anxiety, that she might start burning things—or people—somewhere else?

I scan the news, looking for signs of Agni. There are no stories about firebugs that I can find, but not every suspicious fire makes the headlines.

She's not your responsibility.

Still, I can't undo what she's done.

Back in my apartment, I meditate on a single candle flame.

Agni was supposed to be my inspiration. She'd taught me to accept what I am. She'd opened my mind to a world of possibilities.

But just because something is possible doesn't mean I truly want it. Or the consequences it brings.

It's time for me to figure out what I really want. I watch the candle until an answer comes to me.

I want to make this world better for having lived in it.

I can't do that by setting random fires just because it feels good. I take a deep breath. My nighttime excursions were thrilling, but they're also over. I think I can be at peace with that.

What will I do with my fire now?

I snap my fingers and light all the candles in my apartment. Then I sit down at my computer.

In a far-off land, there lives a dragon who loves to burn. She's defeated the knights who tried to destroy her, but now she's all alone in her cave. She wonders, *What place is there in the world for someone like me?*

I'm writing it for me, but I'm also writing it for the kid that Agni used to be. The kid I used to be. For all the kids with no words to talk about their concerns, and the kids who believe that everyone they know would reject them if they tried. I'm writing it for anybody who feels like nobody else would ever understand the fire in their blood.

I think that when I'm done, I'll find a way to share it.

About the Author

Mary Pletsch attended Superstars Writing Seminars in 2010. In the years since, she has published short stories and novellas in a variety of genres, including science fiction, fantasy, and horror. "The Fire Sermon" is based on a nightmare about the destructive aspects of creative inspiration and the ability to use art (writing, drawing, crafting, building, designing) to channel that energy. She lives in Ottawa with Dylan Blacquiere and their three cats. Visit her online at fictorians.com.

ONE-HIT WEBSTER

BRIAN CORLEY

I'm sorry, kid; it's out of my hands," the muse drawled in his West Texas accent. He was the type to wear aviator sunglasses inside at night and was a good six foot four when he wasn't sitting down. He absentmindedly stroked his dark beard as he rocked back and forth in a creaky wooden rocking chair that always happened to appear whenever he did. It barely fit in Matt Webster's crackerbox of an apartment, and Matt usually ended up sitting at an odd angle on the couch to accommodate it.

"So, you're on strike?" Matt asked. "That's funny." He set his guitar back in its stand.

"I'm not trying to be funny," the muse replied.

Matt tried not to panic. Maybe the old demigod was just pulling his leg. It wouldn't have been the first time. "You mean to tell me I've been calling you here for the better part of five years, and now that I have my shot at making it big on Music Row, you're on strike? The song is due by 11:59 tonight!"

Music Row was the heart of Nashville's entertainment industry, and every major label mover and shaker had a spot in the area. It was a songwriter's dream to get a call to submit a song, and Matt was living that dream. At least he thought he was. With his muse on strike, it was starting to feel more like a nightmare.

The muse shrugged and adjusted the hem of his jeans over his custom-made cowboy boots. He cocked his head like he did whenever he was about to say something profound. "Union rules are tools for fools, but schools for a jewel like me."

"What?" Matt asked.

"You better not take inspiration from that," the muse said.

"From those lyrics?" Matt shook his head. "Not hardly. They need *work*."

"Heh," the muse chuckled. "I guess they do. Just saying I'm a union man."

Matt ran a hand through his stylishly unkempt brown hair and exhaled as he threw himself back against the cushion of his ratty old couch. He'd found it next to his apartment's dumpster the day he'd moved to Nashville, and dreamed about upgrading to something that didn't smell like someone else's bologna. "So, why'd you even bother to come?"

"I don't know." The muse sighed. "Guess I like you. 'Sides, ain't got anything better to do. We're on strike."

"Well," Matt said, "thanks for nothing."

The muse chuckled again. "You're welcome, kid." He took off his black cowboy hat and examined its brim before setting it on his knee. "Look, what I'm about to tell you don't count as inspiration, alright?"

Matt leaned forward. He was desperate for anything he could get at this point. He only had a few hours before his deadline, and he was stuck without a song. "Yeah, okay. I won't be inspired —promise."

"You know the Parthenon over at the dog park?"

Of course he knew about the replica Parthenon in Nashville's Centennial Park. It was one of the weirdest sites in the whole dang town. "Yeah?"

The muse dabbed his head with a handkerchief before

retrieving his hat and easing himself up from his chair with a grunt. "Now, you didn't hear this from me, but you may want to give it a visit."

Matt thought about it and decided he was in the bargaining stage of grief. Grief over lost opportunity and the death of his career before it even had a chance to get started. "Centennial Park is way over on the other side of town! Can't you do anything to help me here? I don't have time to go on some wild goose hunt."

"Ain't askin' you to hunt, kid. I'm telling you. If your mind's as song-blocked as you say, there's folks over there that'll do you a deal. Oh, and don't forget to bring your guitar." The muse donned his cowboy hat and flicked the brim. "*Vaya con dios, mi amigo* ... At least go with some of the lesser *dioses*, if you know what I mean." The muse winked and vanished in a cloud of smoke. The smell reminded Matt of closing time at the honky-tonks his grandfather used to play. Back before all the smoking bans.

"Great," Matt muttered under his breath. He grabbed his grandfather's old Fender Telecaster and eased it into his gig bag. Actually, it was much more than just an old Telecaster; it was a 1959 Tele and worth a small fortune. Worth even more to Matt, though. He'd watched his grandfather play it his whole life, and the old man had bequeathed the instrument to Matt with his dying breath. He always thought it was strange his grandfather had waited until that last moment, but if he didn't know any better—and he didn't—he'd have thought his grandpa had done so deliberately.

Matt threw a denim trucker jacket over his 1979 Waylon tour shirt and headed out to his beat-up old pickup truck. He didn't have time to spare but was desperate to impress the label. Song-writing contracts were few, far, and in-between, and he couldn't screw up now.

The old beater came to life, and the radio blared Charlie Daniels's "The Devil Went Down to Georgia." Matt sang along as he eased the pickup forward. "*Fire on the mountain. Run, boys, run!*"

It was a cool spring night, and Matt drove across town with the windows cracked. He couldn't help but think about his grandfather and how he'd spent all those years playing his heart out to sparse crowds in dive bars across Texas. His grandfather was one of the best guitar players he'd ever seen—one of the best songwriters too, he thought. That said, for the life of him, he couldn't remember one of his tunes. He knew his grandfather was great, but he couldn't recall a single verse to one of his songs—not a hook or even a melody. That always stuck with him, and he felt bad about it.

Matt shut the radio off and let his mind wander, hoping it would attach to a feeling or memory that might shift into a song, but nothing came. He tried whistling a melody and drummed his hands against the steering wheel as he pulled into the deserted parking lot. It was a pretty catchy tune, he thought, before realizing it was the Charlie Daniels song he'd just heard.

"That ol' muse better be right," Matt said to himself. He grabbed his guitar and slammed the door shut. He didn't bother to lock it. The key to the door only worked half the time these days, and he wished any would-be thief luck in figuring out how to time the ignition just right in order for the engine to turn over.

His scuffed-up dingo boots beat a leathery rhythm along the sidewalk to the weird landmark. Matt always wondered why someone would build a restored version of the Parthenon in the middle of Tennessee; it'd never made any sense to him.

He sighed as he adjusted the straps of his gig bag along his shoulders and bounded up the steps to the replica temple.

Strange no one is out tonight, he thought.

He tested the colossal glass door to the Parthenon and found that it was still open—which didn't come as much of a surprise since a minor Greek deity had just recommended he check the place out.

A single bright light shone down on a man in the middle of the wide open room framed in Doric columns. He wore a blue-and-white embroidered Nudie Suit like the old country-and-western stars used to wear. The kind with all the ornate embroidery and sparkling rhinestones. The man stood on the base of the forty-two-foot tall statue of Athena and commanded Matt's full attention.

On second thought—Matt realized it wasn't a man at all. But it sure was something like one. A saccharine-smiling, sparkly-eyed, something or other with a white hat and dark boots. Sure, he looked human, but something about his presence told Matt he wasn't. He'd been around big personalities before—like that time he served Dolly Parton a pig in a blanket at a party he worked at when he was between jobs. Her laugh could fill a room like no one he'd ever been around before, but even that was nothing compared to whatever this guy was throwing off.

"Heard you have you a shot at the big time, son!" the man said. He worked a piece of gum between his teeth as if it owed him money.

"Yeah," Matt said. He wrapped his hands around the straps of his gig bag and pulled them tight across his shoulders. "I think I do."

The man hopped off the base of the statue and swaggered toward him. If Matt didn't know any better—and he didn't—he'd have thought the light followed him.

"Now whatcha got in the bag on your back? Lemme take a look-see."

It reminded Matt of the time he went to one of those big-tent revival things where a preacher from who knows where trotted down the aisle to ask him if he'd been saved. Then, not twenty seconds later, he started to whirl around the row behind him to hit up the crowd for money.

"Just my guitar," he said. "Figure I'd need it if we're going to write a song."

"Matthew Webster." The man clapped and beamed a hundred-watt smile. "You humble-talking so-and-so!" He doubled over with what sounded to Matt like the fakest laugh he'd ever heard. He even slapped his knee while he did it. "Now, I know what you got in there. Our mutual friend already told me. A '59 Tele? Can I see it? Let me see it!"

He kept walking forward, only now his arms were outstretched, making grabby hands.

Who is this guy? Matt thought. He'd known his muse for the better part of five years. They'd shared a lot of songwriting sessions together. Deep, soul-bonding sessions. Those don't just happen—you had to be vulnerable. Matt had shown the muse his soul. Surely he wouldn't steer him wrong, not in his time of need.

"Yeah, sure," Matt said. He begrudgingly slid the bag from his back and unzipped it.

"Blonde with a white pickguard," the man said. He whistled as he turned the guitar over in his hands. "Almost looks gold, don't it?"

"Yeah," Matt said. "Everyone thinks so, but it's just the in-house factory color—at least that's what my grandpa said. Pretty sure they only made them in that and sunburst."

"Mm-mm-mm," the man said. "It sure is a beaut."

"Thanks," Matt replied and reached out to take it back. It always made him nervous whenever anyone touched it. Aside from its monetary value, Matt had put in tens of thousands of hours on the guitar and guarded it with his life.

"Now, hold on," the man said. "Hold on. I understand you've come here tonight in search of a song. Is that right?"

"Yeah, that's right," Matt replied.

"And your muse is on strike?"

"Yep."

"Ain't no words a-comin'?"

"Yes," Matt said. "I mean, no."

"Ain't that a sonuvagun?" the man said and chomped away at his gum like he was punishing a lost soul, and his mouth was hell itself.

Matt started to sweat. The man in the Nudie Suit was raising more red flags than the entire Communist Party.

"Okay, boss," the man said. "I can tell you're uneasy. Let me just hand this back to you and let you hang onto it." He gingerly passed the Tele back to Matt.

The man took off his hat and dabbed his brow with a sequin-spangled handkerchief. "Now, son, I've seen 'em come, and I've seen 'em go. Listen here, young man. This town will make gods out of God-fearing men. You hear me?"

The man gazed at Matt with an openmouthed grin that let him know he wouldn't speak again until Matt said something.

"Yeah," Matt said. "I hear you."

"Let me tell you somethin', Mat-*thew* Web-*stah*! You got it. You got that X factor everyone wants to see. You just need that song!" The man made a sweeping motion with his hand and looked out into the ether. "That opening melody that sets hearts aloft. That punch line at the end of the chorus that sets eyes a-cryin'! That bridge, that gentle bridge that'll make a man rethink his whole entire life, every decision he's ever made." His attention snapped back to Matt. "How's that sound, Matt Webster?"

Matt blinked. "That sounds ... really good. That's exactly what I'm going for."

The man ducked dramatically like someone just shot off a twelve-gauge shotgun. "That's exactly what I'm going for, he says." He clapped his hands one time. "That's exactly what I'm going for!" He clapped his hands again. "Son, that's what I like to hear."

The man hunched over and waved Matt to him conspiratorially. "Now come close to me, boy, come near."

He looked Matt in the eye and dropped his smile for the first time since Matt had walked in. "Now, you may ask yourself, what is the price of such a celestial gift?"

"Fire on the mountain. Run, boys, run!" The lyrics stampeded through Matt's brain, and his heart pumped so much adrenaline through his body he could barely stand still.

"No," Matt said. "I hadn't been asking myself that. My muse and I were talking, and he said there would be someone here to help me."

The man looked wounded. "Oh, but there is. I'm right here. Your savior in bright shining sequined tailoring." He took off his hat and held his arms out wide.

Matt doubted a savior would have such a bad comb-over, but that deadline was looming large, and he was clearly in the presence of a higher power. Why not hear him out? Besides, he didn't want to anger a celestial being. Not on a Tuesday night.

"Okay," Matt said. "Let me hear it; it's time for the close. What's the price for the song?"

The man wagged his finger. "Nuh-uh-uh, not just any song." He started strutting around, flapping his arms and doing some sort of chicken dance.

Frankly, it was embarrassing to watch, and Matt found himself looking around to make sure they really were the only two people there.

"*The* song of the year," the man shouted. "A song they'll never forget. Wouldn't that be something, boy?" The man flashed his pearly whites. If Matt didn't know any better—and he didn't—he'd have thought one even glinted cartoonishly. "Don't you want to watch people rush the dance floor for that one slow dance when they hear the opening notes? Don't you wanna watch people hold each other tighter as the chorus kicks in?"

"Yes!" Matt yelled. "Of course I do! Just tell me what you want!"

The man leaned back on his heels and smirked.

Matt knew he'd just played into the man's hands, but he'd do anything—anything short of selling his soul. No, he'd make sure to keep that for himself.

The man made prayer hands under his chin. "All you have to do—"

Here it comes, Matt thought.

"Is hand over—"

Don't say "soul," Matt thought.

"That guitar."

What? Matt had been so focused on his immortal soul that he'd somehow forgotten about his one prized possession. The guitar he'd spent decades watching his grandfather play. The guitar he'd spent thousands of hours playing himself. The one thing he had left of his grandfather that connected them more than anything else.

But it was just a thing, right? This was his dream. This was a new life, potentially. It wasn't a trick. If a god said they'd do something, they'd do it.

Right? They were a god, after all.

Right.

Probably.

Matt kicked himself for not being better versed in mythology. Did gods normally keep their promises?

"Well," Matt said, "how about I just let you borrow it for a while?"

The man in the Nudie Suit doubled over with fake laughter again, only this time, he bent all the way down the floor and slapped his hand against it for effect. After what seemed like forever, he finally stood back up and wiped his eyes with the sequined handkerchief. "Now, that was funny. You sure you don't want to be a comedian?"

The man had that look on his face again. The one where Matt could tell he wasn't going to talk until Matt said something.

"Yeah, I'm sure."

The man rubbed his hands together. "Okay, then, what will it be?"

Matt closed his tear-filled eyes and thrust the guitar forward before he could talk himself out of it. He felt the weight leave his hands, and soon, heard the man strum a chord.

He blinked and stared at the floor for a moment before something caught his attention. He initially thought the man had been wearing dark boots, but those weren't boots at all—they were hooves.

He scanned slowly upward and saw that the man was no longer holding his grandfather's guitar but a set of panpipes—and he had horns on his head ... and a beard.

He looked awfully familiar with that beard. Even more so after he donned a pair of aviator sunglasses.

It was his muse.

The man laughed.

"Why?" Matt asked. "Why would you—How could you?"

The Greek god Pan stepped forward and put his hand on Matt's shoulder. He wasn't sure how he knew it was Pan; it was like the god's transformed presence informed his soul—and not in a warm and comforting way.

"Son," Pan said, "in five years, did you ever think to look up what exactly a muse is? Or more to the point—who they are?"

Embarrassment mixed with the anger and sadness broiling inside Matt. Why hadn't he researched the minor deity who had visited him periodically? It was clear from the first night that the muse was otherworldly, so why wouldn't Matt try to find out more about him?

And, maybe more troubling, why was Pan asking Matt that question right now?

"No," Matt said. "I didn't."

"Yeah, that's obvious, Matthew. It was more of a rhetorical question, to be honest. The muses are the daughters of Mneme and Zeus. *Daughters*, kid. That was the dead giveaway."

Matt didn't know what to say, so he didn't say anything. He remembered something someone once told him about being a star on stage. It's all about how you look when you're nervous. The greats look like they take the stage the same as they'd stroll into their living room.

"Aw, don't look like that, son," Pan said.

"Don't look like what? I just found out I've been tricked by a Greek god on the most important night of my life, and worse, I just traded away my favorite thing in the whole world—" Matt cut himself off. He was getting choked up, and he didn't want the man—the muse—the god, whatever, to see him cry.

"There, there, now," Pan said. "I'll admit, I pulled one over on you." He took a step back to collect himself, but still laughed. "I mean, you bought that the muses were on strike, like it was some sort of Santa's elves situation—"

"Are you telling me Santa Claus is real?"

"What?" Pan said. "No! No, son, that's ridiculous. Santa's not real."

It wasn't that ridiculous, Matt thought. He was talking to the immortal god of the wild, a guy with horns and hooves—and a stupid flute. He'd always hated panpipes, but doubly so now.

"Listen, kid," Pan said. "I wasn't lying when I said I like you. I do. Now, your granddaddy, not so much, but you—I like."

"You knew my grandpa?"

"Hell yeah, I knew your grandpap. You know that Charlie Daniels song?"

"'Devil Went Down to Georgia'?"

"Yeah, that's the one!"

"You going to tell me you gave that one to Charlie?"

"Hell no," Pan said. "No, son. That was about me and your grandpap."

"What? No, it wasn't. It was about a fiddle player."

"No, it weren't," Pan said with a lilt at the end of the grammatically incorrect sentence. "Ol' Charlie Daniels played the fiddle, so he probably felt like he made it his own with that tweak of the story. No, truth be told, I got to drinkin' one night at this old honky-tonk, and there was this band playing. They was as hot as an afternoon summer sun in Waco. And I mean to tell ya, kid, your granpap was just pickin' fire all night long. Well, anyway, I got a little jealous, as I tend to get from time to time, and before I knew it, I'd hopped up on the bandstand and challenged your grand old man to a guitar duel.

"From there, it went pretty much how the song played out except it was in Texas instead of Georgia, but Charlie probably thought that tweak made it his own too. I mean, it's a great song, so he's allowed some poetic license."

"Wait," Matt said, "Charlie Daniels was there?"

"Yeah, son," Pan said. "It was the seventies. Musicians were everywhere."

"But it's about the devil, not Pan," Matt pointed out.

"You gotta admit," Pan said. "Devil sounds better."

Matt scrunched his face and shrugged. "That's true."

"Plus," Pan said, "the hooves and the horns—eh, it could be confusing."

Matt nodded; the god had a point. "Just want to make sure I have this straight," he said. "You turned your pipes into a guitar."

"That's right," Pan said.

"Then you challenged my grandpa to a guitar duel and lost."

"You got it."

"You wanted your pipes back, so you pretended to be my muse for five years?"

"Yep," Pan said.

Matt scratched his head and exhaled a deep breath. "Talk about your long cons."

Pan shrugged. "Five years ain't that long for me, and truth be told, I enjoyed the company. Also, I cursed your grandpap after that. He could be the best guitar player in the world, but no one would ever remember a single thing he wrote or sang ever again."

"What?" Matt exclaimed.

Memories of his grandfather pouring his heart out through those strings flooded his mind. All those years of blood, sweat, and toil—for nothing. Just because one night he bested a drunk, old, goaty-looking god.

"Yeah," Pan said. "I kinda feel bad about that. That's part of why I helped you out here and there, but now it's time for me to move on."

Matt rubbed his hands over his face. "I can't believe this."

"Just the cost of doing business, kid. At least I didn't turn him into a swan or nothin'." Pan snapped his fingers. "But before I go ..." He chirped a riff across his annoying, reedy pipes and called forth thunder.

Smoke billowed throughout the temple—the same smoke that reminded Matt of those old honky-tonks he'd visited with his grandfather.

A beautiful woman stepped through the haze. Dressed in jeans and one of those understated designer jackets that look subtly amazing and cost, like, four thousand dollars. She grinned at Matt and passed something to Pan.

"Calliope, Matt—Matt, Calliope," Pan said, introducing the two. "Now, this is what a real muse looks like, by the way."

"Hi," Matt said. "Need a job?"

Calliope waggled her fingers in a wave before stepping back into the mist.

"Thanks, darlin'," Pan said.

"You owe me," her trailing voice replied.

Pan laughed, shook his head, and hooked a thumb over his shoulder. "We trade back and forth all the time. Here, take this." The god held what looked like a phone out toward Matt.

He took the item from the god and turned it over in his hands. "It's a phone," Matt said.

"It's *your* phone," Pan replied. "With a hit song loaded and ready to go. All you need to do"—the god pointed a finger gun toward him—"is hit send."

Matt opened the phone, and sure enough, there was a file loaded and ready to email to his guy at the label.

"Thank you," Matt said, but Pan was already gone.

He opened the file and gave the song a listen. It was him. His voice, his style of play—everything. Somehow, he even remembered writing it.

He collapsed to the floor and wept.

Not at the loss of his guitar—and the shared memory of his grandfather. Not at the loss of his muse—and pretty much his best friend for the past five years.

No, it was that the song was just that damn good.

It was everything he'd ever wanted.

He pressed send.

"Another hit, Webster," the voice on the other side of the line drawled. It was his guy at the label.

"Thanks," Matt said. "I was worried about that one."

"Yeah, me too," the guy said.

"Really?"

"Nah," the guy chuckled. "Not really. I knew it was a hit the first time I heard the turnaround to the chorus. Need the next one by 3:00—got a big meeting this afternoon."

"Yeah, alright," Matt said with a chuckle. "It'll be ready when it's ready." He ended the call and strummed a few chords on his new custom shop Fender Telecaster—blonde with a white pickguard, almost like his grandad's, but with a nitrocellulose finish instead of an enchanted golden sheen.

Most songwriters would kill to even chart, let alone have a song at number one. Calliope had come through with a hit, but it was the song Matt wrote the next morning that made him a household name.

Matt always marveled at how he could work on a song for weeks, then turn around and pen something better in, like, five minutes. That's exactly what had happened after the night at the Parthenon. He woke up the next morning and wrote the best song he'd ever written. No surprise, it was about the relationship between him and his grandpa.

Turns out, it had never been about Pan the fake muse, or Calliope the real one, or his grandfather's guitar. Instead, all Matt needed to do was trust himself and have the confidence to put pen to paper.

There was a hell of a lot more than one hit in Matt Webster, and he couldn't wait to earn them on his own. He grinned as he cranked up his amp and went back to work.

About the Author

Brian Corley lives in Portland, Oregon, with his dog, Brisket, and a lamp that looks like a bunch of grapes. Corley is the author of the novels *Ghost Bully* and *Space Throne*.

THE DOOR

KRISTEN BICKERSTAFF

Sometimes, on days like this, the wind told Sofia secrets. She wished Mamma would roll down the car window so she could listen. Outside, the sky sparkled with green and pink and purple, happy colors. Talking about the sparkles and the wind's secrets made Mamma sad, so she didn't say anything. But Sofia knew what the colors meant. They meant it was going to be a good day. Her dream last night had told her so.

"Mamma, why aren't we going to day care today?"

Sofia knew why, but she wanted Mamma to tell her again.

Mamma's brown eyes met hers in the rearview mirror. They crinkled with a smile. Mamma always played along. Even when Sofia wasn't *really* playing.

"Because Auntie Giulia's going to watch you from now on. Day care can't take you all day, and I'll be working late with this second job."

A thought popped into Sofia's head, a cloud passing over the sun.

"What about Bobby and Cherise?" Her bottom lip wobbled, so she bit it. She was a big girl now, six and a quarter since yesterday, not a baby. Only babies cried.

"Oh, honey, we'll find time for you to see your friends. Maybe we can have a playdate soon."

The cloud passed. The sun shone bright again.

"Oh, okay. Then I can tell them about Auntie Giulia!"

Mamma smiled at her, but the clouds had moved into her eyes now. She looked like Sofia felt when she was about to do something new that she wasn't sure about, but that couldn't be right. Mamma was always sure.

Flowers waved in the wind as their battered minivan whooshed by. Sofia hummed a little flower song. It was a happy song, celebrating the rain coming tomorrow. Even so, a tiny seed of darkness grew in her stomach. Although she would never admit it to Bobby or Cherise or Mamma, she couldn't remember exactly what her mother's younger sister looked like. The last time she'd seen her aunt had been a *long* time ago. When she was five and really had been a baby.

The minivan pulled up to a one-story blue house on a corner.

"Is this it?" Sofia asked. Orange threads of disappointment tangled around her fingers, snuffing out the purple sparks. She shook them off with a huff. *No bad colors today.*

The grass was long, and the bushes around the fence looked like Sofia's hair had after she had gone on the hayride and Bobby had pushed her into a hay bale. The flowers by the door were sad and droopy. Sofia didn't want to hear their song. It would sound like a thunderstorm.

The black shutters were shiny with new paint, though, and the outside of the house was happy-sky-blue. Much different from Nonna Claudia's house. Sofia decided this was a good sign.

"Yep, we're here," Mamma said. "Hang tight. I'll get you out."

Mamma unclipped Sofia from her booster seat. They walked hand-in-hand to the door. Sofia frowned at the flowers, wishing she could put her hands over her ears. Their song made her want to cry.

They waited forever. Just as she was about to ask Mamma how much longer, the door opened a crack.

"Giulia? It's Connie and Sofia," Mamma called out.

The door opened wider. Sofia stared at the skinny woman standing behind it.

Giulia didn't look at all like Sofia had thought she would. She was thin, her bones sticking out from under her skin like knives. Her green eyes were ringed with the dark circles, but she didn't wear makeup to cover them up like Mamma did. Her long, black hair hung in a tangled mess, not in a neat braid like Mamma's.

The worst part, though, was something only Sofia could see. A dark cloud clung to Aunt Giulia, sliding over her arms and torso, slithering down her legs, chaining her to the ground.

Sofia balled her hands into fists so the darkness couldn't reach her fingers. She snapped her blue shoes tightly together, making herself a smaller target. She wouldn't be scared. Mamma needed her to be brave.

"Come in," Giulia said. Her voice sounded like she hadn't used it in a long time.

Giulia retreated into the shadows of the house, and Mamma nudged Sofia to move forward.

"Go play out back, Sofia," she whispered. "I'll be back before bedtime. I love you very much."

Her mother smiled, but blue waves gathered around her, the ones that meant she needed a hug.

Sofia sighed. She couldn't pitch a fit now.

"I love you, too, Mamma."

She looked down. The darkness had snuck an inch closer to her sneakers. With a little gasp, she ran away from her aunt, the center of the darkness, and further into the house. She would be brave again in a minute.

She ran past a messy stack of boxes toward the sliding glass door that led outside. Instead of going into the backyard, though, she crouched behind one of the boxes. Sofia told herself she was just gathering more information about this mysterious aunt of hers, even as gray tinges of guilt bubbled under her sneakers.

"If you have any questions, just call me," Mamma said to her sister.

"Connie, I already told you, this is a bad idea," Giulia grumbled. "You should have Mamma watch her."

"No, she's too busy teaching her cooking classes. Giulia, she's only six—"

And a quarter, Sofia corrected.

"She's a good girl," Mamma continued. "She's got quite an imagination. Just get her started on a game of pretend, and she'll be entertained for most of the day. Make sure you're watching her, though. Don't just leave her in front of the TV and go back to your room."

"I'm not incompetent, Concetta."

Mamma ignored that and placed a hand on her younger sister's shoulder the same way she did when Sofia was hurt or scared. The soft light of her love radiated toward Giulia.

"Listen, Giulia, the company will be good for you. I know you're still in a bad place, but it's been eight months. It's time to start living again. Scott would have wanted—"

"Stop it," Giulia interrupted in a rough voice. She turned away from Mamma, crossing her bony arms tightly against her chest, holding her dark clouds close. Streaks of angry red appeared like lightning. "Just ... stop. I don't need life advice from you of all people. Worry about your own shit. You've got plenty of it."

The red lightning struck out and hit Mamma's blue waves. Sofia's lower lip wobbled again, and she bit down hard. Why was Mamma leaving her with this lady? She was *mean*.

The blue waves crashed around Mamma. Sofia hunched in a tight ball, afraid Mamma would drown. But Mamma just took a deep breath ... and another.

The waves calmed, retreated. The love light returned, shining stronger than ever.

"Giulia, please just watch Sofia for me," Mamma said. "It's only temporary, and I think this will be good for you. For both of you. I'll be back at nine."

Afraid Giulia would catch her listening, Sofia slipped outside —and gasped.

Compared to the shadowy hallways of Giulia's house, the backyard was a paradise. Flowers of every color bloomed. Happy flowers, not sad like the ones out front. They danced in the wind and sang a cheery song, and Sofia bounced along in time.

If Bobby were here, he would say there was no such thing as singing flowers. Cherise would pretend to hear, but Sofia would know from the strained look on her face that she couldn't really. Only Sofia, always Sofia, heard and saw these things.

But there, in the middle of the yard, she saw something strange, even for her: a frosted glass door. It wasn't connected to any walls or gates; instead its thick wooden frame was planted in the grass like a tree. It looked brand-new, the white paint gleaming in the morning sunlight. The glass was decorated with a design that looked like vines, showing glimpses of a green yard beyond the door. A painted wooden sign hung from the top of the frame from a piece of twine—*Escape Here.*

And it *glowed*. The light was so bright, Sofia had to squint.

The door to the house opened, and Aunt Giulia stepped outside, shading her eyes. Sofia crept toward her. She very much wanted to ask about the door, but she didn't want Giulia to yell at her.

Her aunt wasn't looking at her, though. Giulia's tired eyes skimmed the flowers and the grass and the fence. The dark cloud still hovered around her, drifting this way and that. It stretched to the ground, pulling and pulling. Sofia couldn't believe her aunt hadn't fallen under all that weight.

"A-a-auntie Giulia?"

Giulia started, then looked down at Sofia. Gray and blue edged the dark cloud.

"Yes?" She looked at Sofia the way Mamma looked when an unfamiliar dog came too close.

I won't bite, Sofia almost said.

"Why is there a door in the yard?" Sofia didn't mention the light. She didn't know if Giulia would get nervous like Mamma did or tease her like Daddy used to.

Giulia sank into one of the nearby lawn chairs. The cloud wavered, then darkened.

"It's a door to another world," she said.

Sofia perked up. This was what she had been waiting for: an adventure.

"What kind of world?" She peered at the door. It shone back at her, the light dancing around the wooden frame. The silver doorknob sparkled, begging her to touch it.

"Um, a magical world, filled with fairies and dragons and stuff," Giulia said, the words spilling out in a hurry.

"*Stuff?* Are you just making this up?"

Sofia hated when people said things they didn't mean or teased her about the special things she saw. Daddy used to do that, before he left. *Why don't you go look for those fairies or whatever under your bed? I'm in the middle of something.* It made her feel silly and small ... and *different*. She didn't want to be different. Different meant being alone.

Sofia plopped down on the grass. She pretended to study the long, waxy blades while she secretly kept an eye on the door.

"I don't believe you," she declared.

Giulia fought the urge to groan. She wasn't good with kids. She had never been good with kids. Scott had always wanted them, but she ...

Grief's hot knife pierced her heart, turning time into molasses. She sat in its agonizing spell, unmoving, until she finally dragged her mind away from the memories.

Don't think about it.

How did she make the door sound believable? Even when she had been as young as Sofia, she had never really believed in magic.

Tesoro, look, watch the cards. Hear the secrets they tell, Giulia's grandmother would say as she flipped playing cards onto the kitchen table.

They're just cards, Nonna Rosa. They can't say anything, Giulia would always reply. But she couldn't stop looking at the cards.

If you listen right, they will, Nonna Rosa would insist with a wink. She tapped a long, red fingernail on the Queen of Hearts, a patient smile on her face. *It's in our blood, my mother from her mother from her mother. You just need to listen.*

Then Giulia's mother would shoo her away and tell Nonna Rosa to stop playing at being an old *strega,* a witch. Giulia had secretly agreed with her mother, a rare occurrence. If her grandmother's cards were right more often than not, well, she was just good at reading people.

Scott hadn't thought like that.

I wish I could have met your grandmother, he had said wistfully when she'd told him about the cards. *Folk magic is supposed to be the strongest, especially when it follows the family line.*

She had shoved him, rolling her eyes. *You can't actually believe in this stuff.*

His white teeth had flashed in a grin, then he'd wrapped his arms around her from behind, her back pressed against his chest. She had curled her hands around his forearm and dropped a kiss on his warm brown skin.

We'll get you believing yet, my lady scientist. Like your Nonna Rosa said, witchiness is in your blood. I'll find a way for you to see it.

The door had been Scott's latest attempt to prove there was something beyond what they could see, after moonlight meditation and incense and a thousand other things had failed to produce any results. A portal, he'd called it, a threshold to cross to change the way they perceived the world.

She would have gone along with it, humored his immovable belief that there was something *more* out there. But ...

The knife stabbed her again.

Giulia glanced longingly at the shadowed depths of her house. She wanted to lie down, to sleep, to retreat into her dreams where Scott waited. Anything but sit outside and drown in her loss.

Sofia looked at her with Connie's dark brown eyes, still full of innocence and wonder. Giulia wasn't the only one who had been dealt a bad hand. She got out of her chair and sat next to Sofia in the grass.

"How do you know the door is magic?" Sofia asked.

Giulia looked over as well, her gaze lingering on the sign. *Escape Here.*

"My friend has seen it," Giulia whispered, trying to sound like Scott when he talked to little kids. Sofia's eyes lit up at her tone. "When you walk through that door, your whole world changes. You'll be able to see things if you have magic eyes."

"Magic eyes?" Sofia gasped. "Oh! I have those!"

Giulia's lips twitched up. Connie said her daughter had an active imagination.

"Then you already know. In this very backyard," Giulia said in a low voice, as if sharing a very important secret with Sofia, "there are hundreds of fairies and magical creatures just waiting for a little girl who can see them. Sometimes they can look just like ordinary objects, like leaves or flowers."

She certainly didn't want her niece to complain when the

fairies and magical creatures *didn't* appear. She was already grasping at straws.

"I can do that." Sofia lifted her tiny chin. Giulia saw so much of Connie in her in that moment, ready to jump headlong into the next adventure. "Can I try?"

"Go ahead," Giulia replied. "Just remember that you have to come back through the door when you're ready to return to the real world."

The little girl frowned. "Wait. You aren't coming with me?"

"I can't go with you," Giulia said. Her chest constricted, pressing the air from her lungs. "I ... I don't have magic eyes."

"Oh." An inexplicable sadness crept into Sofia's eyes. "Maybe you'll learn. And then you can come with me. It would be nice to finally have someone else who could see."

"Maybe," Giulia said, "but not today. Go ahead. Have fun."

Giulia got up, awkwardly patted Sofia on the head, and retreated inside, to her bed and her dreams. Where Scott was still alive, and she wasn't alone.

Giulia's phone buzzed on the dresser. She slapped it into submission. Stupid alarm, why had she set one—

"Crap, Sofia!" she cried, bolting upright.

Giulia rushed out of her room and down the hall. Visions of Sofia trapped under a bookcase, taken by a wandering child predator, or bitten by an escaped dog filled her mind. Her heart pounded against her ribs, threatening to break free. Giulia peeled around the corner, her socks slipping on the hardwood. She barely missed the stack of boxes filled with Scott's art supplies, then threw open the sliding door to the backyard.

Please be there, please be there.

She jerked to a stop, gulping in breaths of fresh air, hands on her knees. Quiet, it was too quiet.

No, no, no ...

Someone giggled. Giulia scanned the backyard and saw tiny bare toes sticking out between the purple blooms of the sage bushes that lined the back fence. She sighed with relief.

"Sofia!"

The giggling stopped. Sofia popped up out of the bushes. A purple sprig stuck out from behind her ear, tangled in her curls.

"Oh, Auntie Giulia, you should come play! The door is the *best*! It makes it so much easier to see everything. And you have the friendliest bushes!"

Sofia ran across the yard, making sure to veer through the door and closing it carefully behind her. Grinning, she skipped over to Giulia.

A kernel of pride blossomed inside Giulia. She had done this. She had made Sofia happy.

"That's wonderful, Sofia," she replied, the gentleness in her voice surprising her. "I'm glad you're having a good time. Let's get you some food."

Every day for a month, Sofia had run through the magical door in Giulia's backyard. It was so much easier to see, to hear, to *know* when she used the door. Her special dreams came almost every night now. She drew pictures so she could remember them, and sometimes she showed the pictures to Aunt Giulia.

The first time, Giulia had smiled that tiny, barely-there smile, and the cloud around her shrank a little. Last Friday, though, the day after she had handed Aunt Giulia a new picture, Aunt Giulia had started acting weird.

The picture was of Giulia with a sword, facing down a crowd of trolls trying to pull her off a hill. In Sofia's dream, Giulia fought up the hill all by herself, and she wasn't giving it up to some stupid trolls. There was one really mean troll with glasses and a chipped tooth. Sofia's picture showed Giulia about to slay him. She was pretty proud of that.

Giulia had smiled when Sofia gave her the picture, and she had pinned it to the fridge with the others. She'd even brushed Sofia's curly hair away from her eyes, her touch soft and less awkward than it had once been.

Sofia had spent the next morning back at day care since Giulia had a "big meeting" at work. When Giulia had picked her up that afternoon, her aunt was even quieter than usual. The cloud wasn't darker, but it was edged with yellow. Uncertainty. Sofia had caught her aunt studying her when she'd thought Sofia wasn't looking.

Later, Sofia found her pacing in the office. She had taken the drawings off the fridge and spread them out on the desk, the yellow growing stronger.

You gotta stop talking about these dreams of yours, kiddo, Daddy used to say. *People are going to think you're ... odd.*

Sofia had given the drawings to her aunt because she thought her aunt would like them, but maybe there was some grown-up thing about the pictures that she didn't see. She opened her mouth to ask Auntie Giulia why the drawings had made her yellow, when the doorbell rang, followed by five quick raps on the door.

Sofia and Giulia shared a look over their empty lunch plates; only Nonna Claudia knocked that way. Bright streamers of yellow flared around Giulia.

Uh-oh.

"Go outside, Sofia. I'm sure Nonna just wants to hear how my meeting went."

Giulia left the kitchen. Sofia glanced at the door, then crept to the edge of the kitchen and peeked out. Just to make sure Nonna wasn't here about the pictures.

"Mamma, good to see you," Giulia said. The cloud was much

thinner now, but still edged with yellow. It didn't pull toward the ground anymore.

"How did the meeting go? You never call me back," Nonna Claudia said. Orange sparks frizzled on her short gray hair and across her eyebrows.

"It's, uh, fine. Don't worry about it," Giulia said, her hand still on the door. Her shoulders were up like a cornered cat's. Nonna Claudia didn't seem to notice, pushing past Giulia to enter the house.

"They are keeping you full-time, yes?" Nonna Claudia prodded, her accent stronger than usual. Mamma called that Nonna's "riled" tone.

Giulia sighed. "Yes, Mamma. I got it all figured out. I'm starting classes in a couple of weeks."

Nonna Claudia patted Giulia's cheek. "Good, good. You look good, *carina*, better than before. It's good to have things to do, yes? Concetta was right to bring the girl here."

Sofia didn't like being called "a thing to do" or "the girl," but she knew that was just how her nonna talked. The love light appeared on the edges of Giulia's cloud. Sofia felt warm, from her toes to the tippy-top of her head. That light was for *her*.

"I've loved spending time with Sofia," Giulia replied. Her shoulders straightened, as if she had made a decision. "Has she ever told you about her dreams?"

Nonna Claudia snorted and rolled her eyes. "Silly little girl dreams. You used to have them all the time."

"I did?" Giulia leaned back, her eyes wide. "Don't you think it's ... odd? That some of Sofia's dreams seem to come true?"

"She's just a quick thinker, like you. Reads people, situations, connects the dots," Nonna said, flapping her hand. "Don't you start talking about true dreams and magic. Sound just like my mamma with those damn cards. It's crazy talk. Sofia has to learn, just like you did."

Sofia's heart tumbled down, down, down until it hit the floor.

Blue waves washed down her legs, over her sneakers. *Silly. Odd. Crazy.* She crept outside to the one place she felt like she belonged. Where she didn't feel alone.

"Sofia?" Giulia asked over their bowls of mac and cheese.

"Mmm?" Her niece stirred her noodles half-heartedly, staring at the bare fridge.

It had been a couple of weeks since Giulia had taken Sofia's pictures down so she could study them more closely. Giulia hoped she hadn't accidentally hurt Sofia's feelings. The girl seemed quieter. More withdrawn. Especially after she had found out that Giulia was starting work again next week.

Giulia would still watch Sofia three days a week and most evenings. She wouldn't admit it to Connie, but she was happy she still had time to do so. Sofia was an easy kid to love. She reminded Giulia of Scott, with her ability to believe in something with her whole heart.

But Sofia hadn't seemed happy since she'd heard the news.

"Have you had any more of those dreams? The picture dreams?" Giulia asked.

Sofia looked down at the table as she twirled her spoon. "Umm ... no?"

Giulia reached across the table, taking Sofia's small hand in hers. She wouldn't have thought to do so just a few months ago.

"Sofia, I hope you know you can tell me anything. I've missed hearing about your dreams and what you see outside."

"You don't think I'm being silly?" Sofia asked in a small voice.

"No, of course not," she said, hating the pain in Sofia's voice. Her niece looked up at her with the big brown eyes that saw too much.

"So why did you take my pictures down?"

Giulia looked at the fridge. Careful, she had to be careful. Not just with Sofia—with herself. Her mind had skirted around the issue for days, not wanting to look closer but unable to let it go.

"I wanted to look at them more closely. The one you gave me last week—"

"The troll one?"

"Yes, that one." Giulia paused, trying to find the right words. Not just for Sofia. For herself. "That troll you drew with the glasses and the chipped tooth reminded me of my coworker. He was mean to me in a meeting I had the next day."

Freaking Dyer, trying to get her demoted to part-time so he could clear the way for one of his favorites.

"He tried to push you off your hill?" Sofia asked, eyes alight with interest.

"Yes, actually, he did." Giulia smiled. "But I didn't let him."

Sofia clapped her hands together, that sunny smile back on her face.

"Just like my dream!" she said.

Giulia felt like she was walking on ice that could shatter at any minute.

"Yes, like your dream," she said, the words dripping from her lips like molasses.

Nonna Rosa spoke to her, words from just before she'd passed away. *Concetta's little one is precious. She is marked for good things. I've seen it in my cards. Just like you,* tesoro.

"Sofia, is it always like that? Do your dreams always ..."

"Come true? Only the special ones," Sofia answered.

"How often do you have these special dreams?"

"Oh, all the time now. Since I started playing with the door."

A crack ran through the ice.

That damn door. For weeks now, Giulia had dreamt about it. Sometimes Scott walked her up to it, his hand warm and strong and *alive* in hers as he asked her to open it. Sometimes Sofia stood beside her, smiling up at her. Sometimes she was alone, pulled by whispers from the other side of the frosted glass. Whispers of something she had known once, long ago. *Silly little girl dreams. You used to have them all the time.*

"Aunt Giulia?"

Giulia realized she was staring at the sliding door.

"Yes?" The word seemed to come from very far away.

"Come with me. Through the door," Sofia said. "It's easier to show you than to talk about it."

Complete trust glowed in her niece's eyes. Innocence, too, even after she must have been called silly or strange or whatever else by people who didn't understand, who thought she was just playing pretend.

Those other people hadn't seen the drawings of Sofia's special dreams and matched them up with events that happened later. Those people didn't hear her talk about how the flowers said a storm was coming, then have a surprise thunderstorm pour down rain hours later.

Those people didn't have dreams of their own. Odd dreams. Dreams of things she could never explain or admit to anyone, not even to Scott.

Hush, Giulia! You keep talking like that, someone is going to lock you up! Her mother's voice, a fuzzy, half-remembered warning.

Another crack through the ice, spiderwebbing out from the first.

"Yes, I think I'd like that," Giulia whispered.

Giulia helped Sofia off her stool. Sofia took her aunt's hand in hers. A small thing, but such moments had helped Giulia keep her head above water the last few months, helped her think about tomorrow again.

They walked into the backyard together and stopped in front of the door. Giulia looked down at her niece.

"What now?"

Sofia pursed her lips and tilted her head this way and that. "You should open it," she said. "I think you need to open it for it to work."

Giulia reached out, her fingers trembling. She dropped her hand and rubbed it against her jeans to hide the shaking. *This is silly. It's just a door. Just another of Scott's flights of fancy.* She saw glimpses through the glass of bright flowers running along the back fence.

So why did it feel like she couldn't get enough air into her lungs?

She looked down at Sofia to ground herself. Her niece smiled again. She looked lighter, freer than she had the past few weeks. Giulia wondered how much taking the pictures off the fridge had weighed on the little girl, made her feel alone, different.

"It's almost gone, you know," Sofia whispered.

"What?"

"The cloud that hangs around you. It was there for a long time, but it's been shrinking every day. I can barely see it now."

"What does that mean?"

Sofia shrugged, the blithe movement of a six-year-old completely confident in herself once more.

"I think it means now is a good time to try the door," Sofia replied. She looked up, but Giulia had a feeling she wasn't looking at her, but instead at the cloud. "I think Scott would have wanted you to try."

Giulia's vision blurred, but the knife didn't come.

"I think you might be right," she whispered.

She reached out again and grasped the doorknob.

She opened the door.

The ice broke, and she fell through it.

Colors, everywhere. So many colors they almost blinded her. Everything was louder, brighter. The wind rustled through the sage bushes, and Giulia swore she heard whispers. Overwhelmed, overstimulated, she sank to her knees and closed her eyes, putting her hands over her ears.

Am I crazy?

A small hand grasped her shoulder.

"Auntie Giulia?"

Suck it up. Put on a brave face for Sofia and figure out the crazy later.

She forced her eyes open. The colors were still there, bright sparkles in the air. A strange pink mist hovered above the sage bushes. A strong white glow emanated from behind her. But with Sofia's hand on her shoulder, they were manageable now, less frightening. She blinked and looked at Sofia. And started to cry.

Her niece radiated soft, warm light, like a tiny star. Giulia knew, somehow, without having ever been taught how to see this way, what that light meant. It was love.

Bright sparks of purple flared and faded, then flared again, like fireworks, all around Sofia. *Bravery,* a voice inside Giulia whispered, one that sounded very much like her grandmother.

Giulia looked down at her hands. They were covered in a faint gray mist, remnants of the cloud Sofia had described. But as she watched, the wisps started to glow with that soft, warm light, too, echoing Sofia.

"Auntie Giulia, are you all right?" Sofia asked.

A spark of purple burst into the air, near Giulia's engagement ring.

Scott, I wish you could see this.

"I will be," Giulia whispered. Suddenly, for the first time in months, she believed it. She clasped Sofia's hand in hers. "Now, show me how to look with magic eyes."

Sofia beamed.

About the Author

Writing since she could pick up a pen, Kristen Bickerstaff has always loved exploring the worlds and characters that live in her head. By day, she's a content marketer and freelance writer/editor based in Dallas. By night, she dreams of magical worlds and crashing spaceships. Learn more about her current projects and other published works at kristenbickerstaff.com.

THE BURREN OF MARS

CJ ERICK

From the top of the ridge, with the Martian night approaching, the Burren Project looked to Doria like interconnected green canyons spreading over the ancient plain of Elysium Planitia, as if the surface of the Red Planet had fractured and emerald vegetation had sprouted from the cracks.

Ravishing. It was everything she'd hoped it would be.

But sadly, the Burren Project, her project, was failing.

"Sandstorm's ten kilometers away, Doria." Sheela McCoshen's voice over the pressure suit's comm link was calm but urgently insistent. A smudgy red line rose from the western horizon, turning a slice of the darkening sky an angry rust color.

"Ten-four, Sheela. I'm on muh way."

She powered up the hydro-vac excavator and drove down the face of the ridge toward the gray metal box that was the main vehicle hangar. The wind whispered over the sloped hood and windshield with the faint hiss of thin dust. The red smudge climbed the sky like a Martian hand poised to capture them.

Two years earlier, the sandstorms were only a nuisance, a whisper of wind that filled the sky with fine dust, micron-sized particulates that coated everything and blocked the sun. But since the American terraforming project had been drilling into carbon dioxide deposits in the planetary crust and intentionally releasing the gas into the atmosphere, the storms had gotten stronger and more frequent. They called it the "transition period," when increased atmospheric pressure created chaos and turbulence in the sun-wind cycles. It will settle down, they said, especially after the plant life began to convert the CO_2 into oxygen.

And those conditions would prove her colony design to be superior to the dome projects blistering the plains all over the equatorial zone of the planet and protecting the five hundred souls currently on Mars.

Instead of domes, Doria envisioned canyons of life, inspired by the great Burren of western Ireland, protected by a meter-thick canopy of transparent polymer, letting in the light, keeping out the dust, and allowing her and the others in her mighty team of five to control the inflow of CO_2. They would grow their own food in a self-sustaining biosystem and expel glorious oxygen into the air, just like the terraformers wanted.

But if they couldn't work faster, they would run out of funding, and the Great Burren of Mars would be just another wacky idea destined to die there in the red dirt. Humans would be confined to metal domes for a very, very long time, looking at the beautiful Martian sky not through miles-long, crystal-clear skylights but through small porthole windows and video screens.

Metal domes, where she and her team would have to live if they failed.

Doria's assistant project manager, Sheela, met her as she stepped from the hangar air lock into the square, drab gray dressing area, seven feet high and wide. The ever-present smell of decon chemicals followed her from the lock and lingered in the room. Sheela's eyes explored hers as she helped Doria shrug out of her safety suit.

"I'm fine," Doria said. "It takes more than a little Mars quake and subsequent sandstorm to worry me."

She was pleased to find that her words were sincere. Tough spots made one tougher, hadn't her grandfather told her that more than once?

"Aye," said Sheela, "but you were due an hour ago, and this storm came on faster than we were thinking. Hungry?"

"Aye, famished. I stayed to get the third cut on Channel 15 before this storm hit. How bad is it?"

"Very, looking at the satellite view. It's a good thing the HVEs are safely in the garage."

Doria's safety suit, now deflated, looked like crinkly white pajamas made out of oddly flexible printer paper. They checked it for any pink blush, the suit's built-in warning system for integrity damage, and found a thumbnail-sized spot where her shoulder blade had rubbed on the HVE seat. She'd have to ask Nuala, their equipment handler, to paint a patch of coating there before she could go out again.

They left the dressing room and headed toward the common living area. The hall was a square tube about seven feet tall and wide, a tight fit for two women walking side by side, and a real tight one for the only man on the team, Kellen Talmadge. He said the passage made him feel like a beach ball trying to blow through a heater duct.

"Shannon make it back?" asked Doria.

"Minutes before you did. Safe in the second HVE hangar. Said the quake shook her teeth a bit, but no cave-ins."

"Good. There was a bit of settling in Channel 15, but for a minute I thought I'd need a pull out. I was deep in, so that would have been dodgy."

"I keep telling you to hook up the safety grapples, don't I?"

"Aye, aye. You're right, Sheela. I'll do it."

As they walked to the small meeting room that doubled as the cafeteria, Kellen waved them in to the electronics room, or the "Comm Closet," as he called it.

"Messages from Ares Dome Five," he said, passing his massive hands over the control pads on the situation desk, a used communications center that looked like something from an old 2020s space film.

A voice recording came over the speaker system, female with a slight Chinese accent. The recording sounded real and not AI-generated, interrupted by the inevitable crackling and hissing of surface-to-surface radio transmissions during Mars's frequent storms.

"... winds never ... kilometers and rising ... barriers down ... all personnel inside immediately ..."

The garbled message repeated, generic statements about storm intensity and possible damage and warnings to move all personnel and equipment under protective cover.

They listened a third time, then Doria signaled Kellen to stop it. The room seemed small enough that they could hear each other's hearts beating.

Doria mentally ran through her contingency plan. "We need to check the roof seals. And the solar grid. I'll start with Channel 1."

Sheela said, "I'll have Nuala inspect the west channels, but we have too many kilometers to check visually. We'll have to rely on the sensors."

"I'll keep monitoring transmissions from Ares Dome. And I'll track the storm intensity and radar information," Kellen added.

"You're a saint, Kellen," said Doria. "Looks like we may be hunkering down for a few days, if this storm is anything like the last one."

Damn, more time lost in the trenching. More days behind schedule, and not from lack of planning. Mars just wouldn't cooperate.

Doria descended the synth-metal staircase into the green wonderland that was Channel 1, their maiden dig, the one nearest her heart. Two years after covering it, installing artificial supplemental lighting, and filling it with breathable air, it felt like a virgin Irish forest cradled in the hands of God.

The channel was sealed and stabilized with polymer cement, and then covered with the clear polymer roof, the three-inch-thick skylight that would allow precious sunlight in and contain the even more precious air, water vapor, and mineral nutrients. Since Mars's sunlight energy was less than half of Earth's, UV lighting had been installed all along the walls to aid photosynthesis of the flora, powered by solar panels and windmills on the surface.

These were all the ingredients required to turn the deep chasms into the reality of Doria's vision, fertile green oases that would provide the basic needs for a growing colony—food, energy, oxygen, and joy. Previous failures within early lunar and Martian colonies had proven the final item on that list—joy—to be just as important as the others for the explorers' health.

After inspecting the half-kilometer of roof and testing the air quality with a handheld meter, Doria climbed the stairs, followed the gray passages, and joined Sheela in the Model Room, a square room little bigger than the Comm Closet, with walls painted a pleasing pale green by Nuala and Shannon. In the center of it was a scale model of their entire project, the INAC—the Irish National Ares Colony.

The model looked so much like the place Doria had designed it from, the Burren of western Ireland. Flat gray plateaus sheltered green channels where lush vegetation flourished, protected from winds, cold, and extreme radiation. It was a network of connected, meandering emerald oases on the barren, sterile plain. A land where life thrived between the rocks of a brutal, windswept, inhospitable landscape. A beautiful duality of hardship and nurture, brilliant color and stark monochromatism, successful abundance and grim scarcity.

"If you're lookin' for the best design to enter in that Mars contest, Doria," Grandpa Vaughan had said, looking out over the gray rolling hills of the Burren one day after they'd spent the better part of a windy wet Saturday hiking to get there, "then think about this place 'ere, blessed by God. Lash her with rain, torture her with wind, freeze her with bitter cold, or parch her with sun-searing drought. And she just keeps goin'. The miles and miles of green crevasses between the hard rocks, the lovely green springing up every year like it don't care what goes on around, like magic is in the ground. Aye, the world is changing too fast for us old folks to keep up with, with the climate change they call it, the ocean risin'. But through it all, the Burren endures. She endures, lass. Think about that."

Her grandfather had died less than a year later of a respiratory ailment, but his last words to her had been about how proud he was of her going off to the New World, to Mars, and taking a bit of Ireland with her. It meant so much to him. His green eyes had lit up in his ruddy face when she'd showed him her designs.

A wee bit of Ireland to stand against the God of War.

But the vision was half-complete. Only fifty percent of the proposed channels had been trenched to the depth of forty meters and covered, and only half of that pressured with breathable air. The going had been tougher than they'd expected, trenching through areas of volcanic rock, then crossing pits of sand and dust so fine and light that the HVEs would sink up to their roofs.

The rapid movement of Sheela's hands on the controls drew Doria from her reverie.

"So far, the pressure readin's are all green," Sheela said. "But we are seeing a bit of surface loss on some of the sky barrier."

"More than the expected slough rates?"

Sheela shook her head. "Less. The polymer is doing well, despite the higher than expected radiation exposure."

I'm dancing around the real issue here, Doria thought. She said, "The land subsidence, the cave-ins. We're running into them more and more often. Like the whole valley is falling underneath us."

Sheela said nothing at first, but her eyebrows curved downward. "We've expected delays and problems," she said. "We've built these things into the schedule."

"Aye, but the spare resources are goin' down faster as we go. We should be moving quicker now, not slower."

Sheela was about to reply when Kellen leaned into the room, his face knotted with worry.

"The message from the dome," he said. "It's now a distress signal and call for assistance."

Sheela spoke Doria's thoughts. "A breach?" A worst-case scenario for the dome designs, but what else could have happened?

Kellen shook his head. "Not yet. From what I gather, the wind's digging the foundation from under the structure, undermining it."

Sheela sighed. "We always thought their design was too weak. The pilings were not deep enough, and not nearly enough of 'em."

"Did they formally request our assistance?" Doria asked.

Kellen nodded. "They've sent requests to all the nationals in the area."

"The Europeans have enough of their own problems," Sheela said.

"And the South Koreans are too far away to respond quickly," added Kellen. "They may not have even captured the transmission."

"Call Shannon and Nuala to the conference room," Doria ordered Kellen. "We need to plan our response."

Kellen nodded and left. Sheela headed down the hall, and Doria followed.

When everyone had gathered, Sheela started with the most obvious problem. "If they have a breach, we're in no shape to bring them here. We'd need at least two months before we can start moving in more colonists."

"We don't have it. The fool Domies brought too many people in before they were ready," said Nuala. "Pressure from their investors to win this race. Get here and get set up first. Their arrogance is going to cost them."

Doria held up her hand. "We must respond to this request, and immediately. We have two excavators and one track-crawler to transport dome citizens. That's only twenty passengers per transit."

"What about their transports?" asked Kellen.

Sheela answered. "From what we know, they have only a few two-man, heavy-duty pods, used for scientific research. They'd planned to stay in the dome during sandstorms."

"Another serious error in judgment," said Kellen.

"Yes, but not unreasonable," said Doria. "Their assumption was that all crises would have to be handled at their facility, since there would be nowhere else to go. Leaving was never going to be an option."

"So they should stay there and handle it, right?" said Shannon.

"And many of the leaders will, if it comes to that," said Doria. "But they'll want to evacuate all the children and as many of the others that can't help their efforts. Twenty children, roughly, and another hundred not directly involved in the repairs, just using up air and resources."

Grumbles and headshaking.

"If they come here, they'll just be using our air and resources." Kellen muttered.

Doria said, "So we help them fix their balloon so they don't have to evacuate. But if we fail in that ..."

Like we've failed too many times here ...

"We have enough air generation to handle it," Sheela said. "But they'll have to bring their own food and as much water as they can."

"Kellen, help us load as much of the concrete as we can carry," said Doria.

"We've only enough to finish lining Channels 11 through 15, Doria."

"I know," she said. "But I think we're going to need it. And the UV lamps."

"Veer ten degrees right, Sheela. You're getting a bit close to Channel 12 on your left."

Kellen's emotionless voice in Doria's earbuds was torn by static and grew worse as they crept closer to the dome facility of the International Martian Exploration Project. That was expected but, in the blindness of the storm, unsettling.

Sheela, being the better operator of the two, led the convoy of two HVEs along the convoluted surface of the Elysium Planitia, with Kellen tracking and guiding them by radio from the Comm Closet. The winds were over ninety miles per hour, well over the sixty miles per hour maximum winds they'd registered before human terraforming.

They'd chosen the low-elevation plains area to build their project to benefit from the denser atmosphere, but it worked against them now, the wind rocking their machines and filling the sky with a wash of billowing, relentless red. Sheela's HVE was barely visible just fifty meters ahead of Doria.

"I see the channel," Sheela responded. There was a pause. "Or what's left of it. It's nearly filled in with dust."

Doria's heart ached. All that work to dig it out totally undone in a few hours. They'd made a point to cover the trenches as they'd gone, but there were still several miles of channels in various stages of digging. If they weren't heading to repair the dome—and evacuate it, if necessary—they could be installing temporary covers over their channels.

All of it would fill in. All the man-hours and fuel used, with no results.

That would be it, really, wouldn't it? Their sponsors would see this as a weakness in the plan, a failure, and withdraw funding.

Maybe it wasn't meant to be. Maybe it was a misguided vision after all, and she was just another hardheaded Irish woman who wasn't willing to wake up and smell the bangers and fried tomatoes.

She imagined her grandfather standing on a ridge overlooking the Burren, and in this daydream, her parents were there also, and her sisters and brother, all preteens bouncing from stone to stone, like giants leaping across the tiny green microcosms that flourished between the glacier-wiped granite. She'd wanted nothing more than for her siblings to join her on Mars, nurturing the green spaces just like the ones they loved in Ireland, making this a place for all people, not just her Irish kin, to live in beauty instead of the prison of a metal bubble.

And then she remembered something else her grandfather had said to her that day when the whole family was there.

"You're just like this place, lassie. You're tough as the rocks, and you endure, just like she does." He'd always thought of the land as a woman. She didn't know why.

She raised her hands from the HVE's control pads and stretched the tension out of them, then keyed the radio.

"Speed it up, Sheela. We gotta get this metal bubble fixed so we can get back and protect our Burren."

Sheela's HVE accelerated in front of her, pulling away and almost out of sight in the red haze. Kellen's broken voice sounded in her ears.

"Meters ... straight in ..."

And then Sheela's voice cut in. "I see it! Just a little right. Follow me, sister."

Within fifty meters, the glow of intense floodlights cut through the murk in front of Sheela's HVE, and a dark gray wall rose up from the red ground. The outer bell of the elliptical dome rose straight up from the foundation before curving over to meet the ground in a near-perfect circle.

Workers in blue pressure suits labored within the circles of light, like cartoon characters bounding in great leaps in the light gravity. One of them waved them to the left with two hand lights.

A voice crackled in Doria's headset. "Welcome, friends. Follow the lights, please. Thanks for coming."

They didn't know this was costing Doria and her team everything they'd worked toward for three years.

"Roger," said Sheela, who had slowed and turned her HVE to the left.

About a hundred feet around, the dome's curve reached the trouble spot. The ground had fallen away from the dome's lip. Wind whipped around and under it, eroding the sub-base. Eventually, all the fill dirt and rock would be gone, leaving the vertical pilings exposed, like a house on stilts. And those stilts were not designed to carry the entire load. The section of the dome would collapse, which would breach the shell, causing an explosive release of breathable air, damaging the dome further and injuring people inside and all the workers nearby outside.

Doria keyed her mic.

"This is Doria Vaughan. Who's in charge?"

A male voice responded immediately. "This is Assistant Director Warren. I'm handling this situation."

"We're here. What do you need us to do, Mr. Warren?"

"The quakes loosened the rock around the pilings and shifted the subsurface plates. We need you to help backfill where the foundation has blown out."

The quakes. Another unexpected by-product of the terraformers extracting water, ice, and CO_2 from medium-depth deposits.

Doria called back, "It will just blow out again, sir. You need to stabilize the pilings until we can backfill with quick-set concrete and rock support."

"Listen to her, Mr. Warren," Sheela chimed in. "She's a hard-headed structural engineer."

Sheela and Doria backed their vehicles up to the network of pilings, metal piers that plunged tens of meters into the ground. At Sheela's direction, the workers linked the HVEs to the pilings via heavy cables. Sheela and Doria inched the machines forward until they applied stabilizing tension on the pilings, keeping them from tilting down into the expanding pit where the fill material had eroded away.

Then Sheela and Doria used the HVE's snorkels to excavate massive, mushroom-shaped holes at the base of the pilings to form stabilizing footers. The holes were filled with their concrete, nearly all of it.

And then they waited. The concrete was miraculous, but it still required four hours to harden while technicians bathed it in intense UV radiation. Four hours of waiting, in which Doria and Sheela could do nothing while their newly trenched channels filled, all their work lost.

Meals and water were brought for the two women along with the dome workers' thanks and a personal visit by the director, Frank Herzig. Doria tried to be gracious. She may have succeeded.

The storm blocked most of Kellen's radio transmissions, except for snatches that sounded like reassurance. "... well ... all green ... okay ..." There was consolation there. At least her design was proving itself. Maybe someday, another strong woman with a vision would be able to start the work again, even if Doria was not around to see it.

At last, the technicians announced the concrete was set, and the two women spent the next two hours using the HVEs to back-fill around the pilings with large rocks and then progressively smaller fill material. At Sheela's suggestion, they supplemented this with mushroom-shaped pools of the remaining quick-setting concrete to ensure the increasing winds of the transition atmosphere wouldn't erode the area again. Since Doria's team would likely be living here soon, improving the installation was a good idea.

After the repair work was complete, the assistant director offered Doria and Sheela accommodations for the night, but the women declined. The storm carried on. Perhaps it was the thing most likely to endure on Mars as humans increased the atmospheric pressure. The thought of a planet-covering hurricane was ominous. But on the drive back to the Burren, they would at least be traveling downwind, so the noise and battering would not be as strong.

Kellen's transmissions grew stronger for a time and then seemed to fade, leaving only frustrating snatches of words and phrases. About halfway back to the Burren facility, Sheela signaled a stop and pulled her HVE to a halt.

"I'm concerned, Doria. Not sure if we're on the right path. What do you think?"

Doria checked her GPS readings for the tenth time, but they remained useless. She wished again that Mars held a real magnetic field, so they could at least guide by compass. It was like trying to navigate through a planet-sized bowl of runny tomato soup.

"We got nothin' to lose by goin' on, Sheela. Even if we drive wide by a mile or two, we should get a good signal from the base, and Kellen kin guide us. I'll lead and give you a break. We'll go slow so we can see a channel before we drive into it. Then we can follow it back to the base."

"Aye. Slow it is, Doria."

With no better option, they carried on slowly. Doria sat on the edge of her seat, peering out through the smudged windshield, her hands tensed up like a cat's paws on the controls. She could see only about twenty meters of featureless dirt, with lines of dust slithering over it like the very snakes Saint Patrick had driven from Ireland.

They'd gone about another half-hour in silence when the front of Doria's HVE lurched downward, and she was thrown back into her harness, bouncing her head off the backrest. She hit the brakes, and the HVE came to rest with its nose buried in a hole.

"Doria! What's goin' on? Doria!"

"I'm all right. Just a sinkhole."

There was a pause before her friend answered. "Can you back it out?"

"I don't know. I'll give it a go."

"Let me give you room."

Sheela's headlights receded a few meters. Doria shifted into reverse and eased on the power. The machine vibrated as the heavy tracks alternately spun and dug in the loose dirt. It didn't move. She felt her seat falling out from under her, and then she was sliding down at a sharp pitch, the lights bouncing over rugged rock and sand.

"Dor!"

The HVE bumped hard, shoving her chest-first into the harness.

She stopped breathing. The HVE didn't move. Seconds passed.

"Doria, talk to me."

"I'm all right, Sheela."

The HVE was tilted downward at a sixty-degree angle, and Doria was relieved it wasn't pointing straight down. They would have at least a decent chance of pulling it out.

"Don't follow me," she said. "I've just fallen into a cave. I bumped hard at the bottom on rock or something, so I don't think she's goin' any deeper."

"Praise the Lord. Don' move or even breathe. I'll turn around and reel down the emergency grapples."

At that angle, the headlights shone forward to reveal a deeper opening just ahead. It was wider and taller than the HVE and dust-free. Doria tilted the lights upward remotely and revealed a deeper cave. The lights struck a far wall, exposing black lines and splashes of green, blue, yellow, and the defining color of Mars, red.

"There's something down 'ere, Sheela. I'm going to climb out and take a look."

"Leave it, Dor. Whatever it is, it can wait. I'll pull you out."

"I think the HVE's nose is resting on solid rock. She's stable."

"Stay put. I'm going to set the grapples before you do anything."

Doria fought the urge to open the door immediately. Headlights flashed in her rear-facing camera. Sheela was turning her HVE around and backing up to the place where Doria's machine had fallen. She set the brakes and dug stabilizer rods into the ground.

There was a pause, then she saw Sheela staggering down the sandy incline.

Doria grabbed a hand light, popped her driver's door, and stepped out into a swirling wind. Most of the blowing dust was passing over the chasm. She could see Sheela's squinted eyes through her faceplate.

"You scared me to death," Sheela said. "Praise God you found a hard bottom."

"Thanks. But I found something. Come on. Let's take a look."

She waded down the slope of loose dirt to the front of her HVE and led the reluctant Sheela into the dark cave arch.

Beyond it was a large room that was mostly free of sand,

except for the spill that had flowed in when the HVE had breached the roof.

The headlights lit up the bottom half of the opposite wall, and the hints of colors and lines she saw captured her attention. And what they revealed sent an electric shock through her.

A drawing. No, a mural, a room-sized painting, the work of an intelligent mind.

She played her hand light over the mural, her heart beating harder. She fought to catch her breath. The pressure suit's tight faceplate seemed suddenly far too confining.

"Dearest God ..." said Sheela.

The mural was scratched and faded, marred by thin cracks and one rock tumble. Thousands of years old? Perhaps tens of thousands? The lights revealed oblong shapes colored pink and gray in the lower half, pale blue and yellow in the upper half. The shapes were separated by thin ribbons of faded green, forming a seemingly random network.

Doria stepped forward to examine the details, the subtle variations in the shapes and shades of green and yellow within the thin ribbons. Black scribbles—writing!—were scattered over the piece.

Sheela joined her. She brought her gloved hands to her facemask.

"Dor, it's ..." She swallowed loudly over the radio.

Doria finished her thought. "It's a map of our lands. There's the large area where we set the camp. These lines ..." She stepped forward to trace her finger along the ribbons of green. "These are Channels 5 and 6. And this large pool here—that's where you buried your HVE in a sinkhole last week."

"Dor, this is ... It's historic. The greatest discovery ever."

"Yes." Tears welled in her eyes. Was it luck that had brought them to this place, or providence?

"A bit of Irish luck, this. We'd never have found this if we hadn't gone to help the Domies. We don't have to fight, tryin' to trench through the hard rock. This map will tell us where to dig. The project's saved."

"Yes. We can follow the lines. We can dig where it shows us to."

Tears spilled over and ran down her cheeks. Tears of joy ... and of disappointment.

"But now we have to stop digging," Doria said.

"Whatever for?"

"Sheela, you said it. This is historic. We can't even think of moving another foot of dirt. We have to cordon this off and preserve it." She shook her head. "It belongs to everyone now, not just us."

Sheela stood silently, reflecting.

But it would be all right.

"We're now the discoverers and curators of the first Martian historic site," Doria said. "We'll have all the funding we need to preserve it and to excavate it at our leisure. And we won't have to ever worry about living in a dome. This can be our home to the end of our days."

But what pleased Doria most was that the ancient map proved her design was sound, that a place like this could endure on Mars, and could be built in other places.

The Burren had lived on Mars once before, and Doria and her friends had brought it back to life.

About the Author

CJ Erick stumbled into Dallas in search of love, great sushi, and access to big-box stores. Having found all three, he now inhabits the city with his wife, Cee, and their sweet black-and-tan hound, Saber-girl. Mostly retired from the reckless adventure of engineering, he now designs and builds space fantasy, gothic horror, cozy mysteries, and even a little romance, among other unbalanced visions from caffeine-deranged nightmares.

WHITE FEATHER

SHANNON FOX

Jae stared at the email on her screen and forced herself to keep her hands off the keyboard. She tried to focus on her breathing, counting out slow, even breaths, but her eyes kept reading and rereading the lines of the email.

Hi, Jae,

Thanks for sending back the logo revisions.

After careful consideration, I don't think your style and my vision are a match, and I don't want to take up any more of your time or mine. You can keep the deposit for the time you've already put into this.

Sorry it didn't work out.

—Kristina

Jae swore under her breath and pushed her chair back from the computer. Each fresh pass through the email was only serving to further rile her up, and she knew if she continued to stare at it, she might do something she'd regret.

In the kitchen, Jae put the teakettle on the stove and leaned against the sink to wait. The bright sunlight streaming through the window behind her reflected off the stainless steel fridge. It hurt her eyes to look at it, so Jae stared at the floor instead, rubbing her temples. She'd woken up with a headache, and the email had only exacerbated it.

Her doctor had warned her against consuming caffeine too soon after the accident, but Jae had shrugged it off. She needed to get back to work, and nothing focused her mind like a strong cup of black tea in the morning. Still, a small part of her wondered if the reason her headaches weren't going away was due in part to her refusal to heed that particular order.

As the kettle started to whistle, Jae took it off the heat and opened the cabinet next to the stove to grab a tea bag for her mug. But as her hand reached inside the cabinet, she froze.

A single white feather lay on top of the boxes of tea on the shelf.

Jae glanced around the kitchen in confusion, trying to work out how it had gotten there. She remembered her apartment complex's repairman had come the day before to fix the slow leak in the kitchen faucet. Jae had been running errands when he'd come by. Maybe he'd rifled through her things. Gone through the cabinets and left her this dirty feather as a calling card.

A fresh, hot wave of anger splashed through her. Jae snatched the feather from the shelf and dropped it in the trash. She turned the faucet as hot as it would go and scrubbed her hands with soap, the burning water eliciting an unconscious hiss of pain from her. But she didn't turn the water down. Who knew what germs that feather contained?

She thought about calling down to the front office to give them a piece of her mind. But as she dried her hands on a towel, she had a better idea.

Reaching into the pocket of her bathrobe, Jae pulled out her phone and dialed her mother.

Ever since Jae could remember, it'd just been the two of them. Jae and Leah. Her father had left when Jae was a baby, and though she was sure her mother must have had boyfriends over the years, none had made enough of an impression to make it as far as meeting her daughter.

Which was fine with Jae. As far as she was concerned, her mother was a warrior. A middle school teacher during much of the year, in the summer she'd always pick up a second—or even third—job doing seasonal work. Yet no matter how long and hard her mother worked to provide for Jae, she was always there with a listening ear and ready advice for whatever trouble her daughter was facing. That had remained true even after Jae had gone to college and moved out on her own.

Her mother picked up after two rings. After the exchange of pleasantries, Jae launched right into her story, explaining how she'd woken up to an email from her client firing her and then discovered someone had been rooting around in her personal belongings. She poured out all her anger and frustrations, holding nothing back. And when she was finally done, Jae paused, waiting for her mother to speak. She would know just what to say, how to fix it.

But when the silence stretched out between them, uncomfortably long and void of her mother's usually pat answers, Jae found herself speaking again. "Did you hear what I said?"

"Yes," her mother replied.

"And?"

"The client that fired you. Weren't there a few others you lost this month?"

Jae's stomach twisted. "Four. Kristina was the fourth one."

There was another long silence on the other end of the phone, which Jae again felt compelled to fill. "But it's fine, Mom. I have enough money to pay my bills if that's what you're worried about. I'll find more work."

"Maybe you should talk to someone, Jae."

"Talk to someone?" she echoed. "Like a business coach?"

"No. Like a grief counselor. About Felicity and the car accident."

Suddenly, Jae wasn't standing in her kitchen anymore. She was back in the car on that dark, rain-slicked road. Seeing Felicity reach for the volume control out of the corner of her eye, saying how much she loved the song that had just come on the radio. Hearing the screech of tires, feeling the jarring impact that slammed Jae's head against the side window. The sound of Felicity's scream. The glass breaking.

Jae was aware her mother was still speaking, though she hadn't been listening at all.

"I just think it would help, Jae," her mother was saying. "I saw someone after your father left. There's no weakness in asking for help."

"Just because I lost a few clients doesn't mean I need to go to therapy," Jae growled.

"I know you," her mother retorted. "You do good work. Fantastic work. People happily refer you all the time. So if you're losing clients in droves, is it them? Or is it you?"

Jae could feel her pulse pounding hotly in her ears. Her mouth opened, but she couldn't force any words through. Couldn't say the awful, terrible things slamming around in her head.

As she breathed through her anger, Jae felt her blood turn to ice as her mother's words fully registered in her brain.

After the car accident, the doctor told her to take some time off from work. Both to let her brain heal from the concussion and to allow herself to grieve for the loss of Felicity, her best friend. But a week later, Jae was back to work. She had projects and deadlines and bills. So many bills, magnified by an ambulance trip and an emergency room visit. It didn't matter what the doctor thought. He wasn't living Jae's life.

But the cold truth she'd been hiding from, that she'd been avoiding ever since Felicity had died, was that she was stuck. The sweet rush of ideas that had once flowed easily from her, the burst of excitement she felt at tackling a new project, the happy exhaustion she felt at the end of a long day of creatively stretching herself—all of it had completely stalled.

It now took every ounce of concentration and many, many cups of tea to drag even the most rudimentary designs from her fingertips. She found herself second-guessing font choices, wondering if those colors really looked good together, if her mind could actually be trusted to do this work anymore.

Because the fear that burned brightest of all was this: What if, when her skull had connected with the car window on that awful night, it had rattled all that was good and special and creative about her right out of her brain?

Jae swallowed. "Okay," she said softly. "I'll think about it, Mom."

The tiny old woman across the circle from Jae kept looking at her and smiling. It was beginning to creep Jae out, and she quickly looked toward the man who was speaking. He was older than Jae and, as she'd found out just a few minutes earlier, had lost his son after the boy had fallen in the pool and drowned at his ex-wife's house.

As she listened and tried to ignore the eyes of the old woman on her, Jae picked at her nails. It was an awful habit, she knew, but it was one of the ways in which her anxiety manifested itself. And if there was ever a time to be feeling anxious, it was sitting in this grief support group, listening to other people pour out their own feelings and tragedies.

It had been a mistake to come. She could see that now. Jae

could barely hold the space for her own feelings about Felicity's death, let alone listen to and be supportive of these strangers she'd met just half an hour ago, whose names she couldn't remember without a peek at their name tags.

Though she had discovered that sharing the details of the accident, explaining who Felicity had been to her and why her death mattered so much, had actually felt kind of good. Instead of bearing the loss all by herself, it felt like she'd broken off a few pieces of it and given it to the six strangers in the room to hold. Jae felt lighter somehow from having shared her experience.

She'd even explained what was happening with her work. How she felt creatively blocked. She'd shared what had happened last Saturday morning, when she'd woken up to Kristina's email, discovered that disgusting feather in her kitchen cabinet, and called her mother. That was when the old lady had started smiling at her, and whatever positive benefit Jae had gained from showing up tonight had abruptly cut and run.

When the group leader concluded the meeting, Jae quickly got to her feet and started for the door. But she wasn't fast enough to get around the guy in the wheelchair. Hoping her impatience wasn't showing on her face as she watched him maneuver around the furniture, Jae waited awkwardly in the center of the room. She kept her gaze firmly focused on the back of the guy's head to avoid making eye contact with anyone. The last thing she wanted to do was make small talk with one of these people. All she wanted was get home, take a hot shower, and go to bed. Her head was pounding something fierce.

Jae felt a light touch on her elbow and stiffened. She looked to her right and saw the old woman had come up beside her. She smiled up at Jae, apparently oblivious to her discomfort.

"It's a gift, you know," the old woman said.

Jae blinked as her brain scrambled to figure out what the woman was talking about. "I'm sorry, I didn't quite catch what you said."

"The feather. It's a gift from your friend."

"My friend?"

"What was her name, dear? The one who passed away. Felicia?"

"Felicity," Jae said, through clenched teeth.

The old woman nodded. Jae noticed her hair was so thin on the crown of her head, she could see through the wiry white strands to the spotted skin underneath.

"She's speaking to you. Just like my Marv does. Only he communicates with pennies, not feathers."

Jae almost said something unkind but bit her tongue at the last moment. She glanced at the guy in the wheelchair. He was lingering in the doorway, talking to the group leader. Jae looked back at the old woman and forced herself to smile. "What do you mean he communicates with pennies?"

"It started a few weeks after he died. I started finding bright, shiny pennies everywhere. On the sidewalk. In the bottom of my purse. On the edge of the bathroom sink. I thought it was coincidence at first. But the pennies kept coming, and I started finding them in even more impossible places. Until one morning I woke up and saw a penny lying on top of Marv's pillow. That's when I knew."

Jae noticed the wheelchair guy had finally made it out into the hall and the way was clear. She looked at the woman, who still had her hand on Jae's elbow, and glanced at her name tag.

"Thanks for sharing with me, Mary."

The woman patted Jae's arm. "Will I see you next week?"

"Sure," Jae said. She wondered if there was a special hell for people who lied to old ladies.

After her shower, Jae sat down at the computer in her office to check her email one last time before bed. A new email from one of her old college friends was sitting on top.

Hey, Jae,

Hope you're healing well after your accident. Not sure if you're back to work yet, but wanted to send over the name of someone I met who's just started a company and is looking for a great logo designer. I told her you were a fantastic graphic designer, and she asked me to put you two in touch. Her name's Robin. Her business card is attached. Hope you guys can connect.

Call me when you're feeling better and let's get coffee.

—Clint

Jae clicked open the attachment and drew in a sharp breath.

Underneath Robin's smiling photograph was a clip art image of a single white feather.

Jae remembered what Mary had said. That Felicity was speaking to her, somehow, with feathers. She stared at Robin's business card a moment longer, her eyes tracing the slightly blurred edges of the feather, before shaking the thought away.

Mary was an old woman and probably going senile. Jae grabbed the handle of her desk drawer and yanked it open to grab her planner. She needed to write a note to remind herself to call Robin tomorrow. And Clint.

As Jae lifted her planner, she felt something soft brush her fingers. She lifted the book all the way out and looked down in the drawer.

A white feather lay curled on the wood.

"What is going on?" Jae muttered. The feather definitely hadn't been there earlier. She'd cleaned up her desk before going to the support group. She would have seen it for sure.

With a trembling hand, Jae flipped opened her planner and wrote Robin's name and number on her list for tomorrow along with a reminder to schedule coffee with Clint. Then she dropped the book back in the drawer and slammed it shut.

She needed to go to bed. She was half-starting to believe there was some truth to what crazy Mary had said.

When Jae walked into group the next week, Mary was already there. She smiled and gave Jae a little wave.

"Did you hear from Felicia this week?" the old woman asked.

"Felicity," Jae responded. But she wasn't sure what to say next.

Just as Mary had described her experience with the pennies, Jae had started to find white feathers everywhere. Stuck to the screen door of her apartment. On the dashboard of her car. Between the pages of the book she'd bought the day of the car accident but never opened.

Jae hadn't told anyone about the feathers. Not even her mother. But she was freaked out, convinced that smacking her head against the car window had done more than slam a door shut on her creativity. Maybe it had also put a crack in her sanity.

But Mary seemed to know what Jae was thinking, without her having to say it. "The messages are important, Jae. She's trying to tell you something. You just have to figure it out what it means."

The sudden arrival of two other members of the group forestalled further conversation. But Jae kept turning Mary's words over in her mind all session long. And when it was done, she bolted out the door.

"I have a break between projects," Jae said. It was Sunday, and she was on the phone with her mother. She absently stirred a spoon through her lukewarm tea. "What would you think if I came home for a little bit?"

Her mother's response was careful. Guarded. "Did something happen?"

"No," Jae said. "I just thought it might be nice. To take a break. Rest."

There was a long pause. "You're sure you're okay? You didn't even want to take time off after the accident. Despite the doctor telling you to. And me."

"Yeah, and I'm starting to think that was a mistake," Jae said. "Maybe that's the reason I'm struggling with my work right now."

"Well, I'd love to have you home," her mother said. "I'm just surprised you came to this conclusion on your own."

What Jae didn't say, what she would never admit to her mother, was that she hadn't come to this decision on her own. Felicity had helped her. Felicity and the message written in the feathers.

After her last group session, Jae had woken up without a headache for the first time in a long while. She'd stayed in bed listening to the sound of the birds outside. Enjoying the feeling of being alive and not in pain. Then, she'd slowly realized the pattern of light the blinds were casting on her bedspread looked like a feather.

But instead of feeling angry and afraid, something inside her cracked open, and Jae found herself curled on her side, sobbing into her pillow. Or perhaps weeping was a better word to describe it. She'd cried at the hospital when she'd found out about Felicity. Cried at the funeral. And cried off and on during the days and weeks since the accident. But she'd never truly wept like this. Never felt the pain so viscerally. It completely overpowered her and seized her mind, paralyzing her, pinning her to the bed so she could do nothing but sob and mourn her friend.

She cried for what felt like hours, and when she finally felt her tears slowing, her breathing returning to normal, her thoughts went to Mary and the feathers. Too weak to get out of bed, Jae thought about all the feathers she seen over the last two weeks. Of the places she'd found them, what she'd been doing before, the things she'd been feeling.

Then, almost as if Felicity were standing in her room with her, she heard her friend repeat the words she'd said so many times since Jae had started her career as a freelance designer.

"You work so hard, Jae. You're going to burn yourself out if you don't stop to rest once in a while."

Later, when Jae finally pried herself out of bed and checked her computer, she discovered an email from Robin, the woman Clint had referred. Jae wrote back, introducing herself and outlining the details of the contract. Robin signed Jae's agreement and sent over the deposit. In her email, she expressed how excited she was to get started when she was back from her trip to Italy in two weeks.

And that was when Jae realized she finally had time to take the break she should have done after the accident. With no other projects on the calendar except Robin's, she had a whole window of time to herself. She knew she should probably use this time to look for more work, but as she looked at the feather on her windowsill, the one she'd originally found in her desk drawer, Jae again heard Felicity urging her to rest.

Jae was watching TV when her phone dinged with a new text. She grabbed it off the coffee table and opened a picture message from Robin. She was standing in front of a building, pointing at the sign overhead, and grinning. Jae lingered on the photo, feeling Robin's joy radiating through the photo, before dropping her eyes down to the accompanying text message.

They put up the new sign for the store today. It looks SO good!! I love my logo so much. I can't thank you enough! It's exactly what I wanted. I'm so glad Clint introduced us.

Jae smiled as she looked at the picture again. The logo had turned out really well. It was certainly the best thing she'd created since Felicity had died. Maybe even the best piece of work she'd done in the last year.

When she'd gone to stay with her mother, Jae hadn't really expected the two-week break to do much for her creatively. Sure, she recognized the rest was good for her, that she'd made a mistake in refusing to give herself space to heal after the car accident. But she was under no illusion that it was going to cure all of her problems.

So when she'd sat down to work on Robin's project, taking the first tentative steps into creating something new, she was surprised to find how little resistance she met. After two weeks off, her mind and her spirit seemed almost hungry to get back to work. As she sketched out new concepts on her drawing pad, she grew bolder and more sure of herself with each pencil stroke. Robin's enthusiasm about the preliminary sketches and ultimately the final project had only confirmed what she knew already: she was back.

Jae typed a quick reply to Robin and put her phone back on the table. Instead of going back to her show, her eyes went to the window behind the TV. She noticed that the stormy sky from earlier in the day had cleared and the sun was out. But more than that, she noticed something tangled in the bright spring leaves of the tree outside her window. A white feather.

About the Author

Shannon Fox is a San Diego-based writer of fiction spanning multiple genres. She grew up in the foothills of the Colorado Rockies before relocating to California to attend UC-San Diego, where she earned a BA in Literature-Writing.

Her short stories have appeared in the *Monsters, Movies &
Mayhem* anthology, the *Cursed Collectibles* anthology, *The Copperfield Review*, *The Plaid Horse Magazine*, and more. Besides writing,
Shannon has a passion for horses. She has competed at the
international level in the sport of dressage. Shannon also owns a
digital marketing company. For more stories from Shannon, visit
her at Shannon-Fox.com.

INTO THE VALLEY

WAYLAND SMITH

Back home, June meant warmer weather, baseball games, and spending time out in the woods, or at least it did to Tom Perkins.

In France, it meant a lot of running, hiding, shooting, and trying not to let the German bastards kill him. Most of his squad had managed to find each other after parachuting in, which was a minor miracle and apparently had used up all their luck for the foreseeable future. He ducked as another burst of rifle fire bounced off what was left of the wall in front of him.

"Are there any villages in this goddamn country that aren't ruins?" Henderson complained, seeking cover behind the same remnant of wall.

"See, that's what we do." Johnny Crater laughed. "We get through all this, come back here, and start a construction company. We'll be millionaires in a year." Crater always had some get-rich-quick scheme, and each one lasted maybe five minutes, until something new grabbed his attention. He popped up, fired a quick burst, and dove down when the enemy started returning fire.

Ryan, as usual, had nothing to say. His rifle barrel lay on top of a different piece of wall, and he was still as a statue. Finally, he fired a single shot. He nodded in satisfaction and murmured, "Two."

The enemy fire slackened slightly.

"Damn, Country can shoot!" Rosen was a skinny kid from Detroit who had never been outside the city until he'd been drafted. He was constantly amazed by everyone being so different from the people he'd grown up around.

Perkins leaned around the corner of the wall but pulled back before he even got to shoot as rifle fire kicked up dust and chipped the stone around him. "Damn!"

Sergeant Olson did an impressive baseball slide to end up behind Henderson and Perkins. "What's the story, boys?" the big man asked.

"Too many of them, and not enough of us," Henderson said.

"Country's doin' pretty good, though," Rosen piped up from his section of wall.

"Country always does pretty good," Olson agreed. "Can't stay here all day, though. We've got orders to push ahead. There's a company or two coming up behind us, and we're supposed to clear the way for 'em."

"What are we supposed to do, tell the Germans we gotta be someplace else?" Henderson asked.

"Something like that," Olson agreed. "We gonna let Country there have all the fun?"

"No, sir," Perkins answered. He leaned around the end and fired another short burst, immediately ducking back under cover.

As soon as the return fire started, Ryan squeezed his trigger and said a quiet, "Three."

"All right, enough of this shit. Let's take them," Olson said. "Perkins, Henderson, head for that wagon." He pointed to a wooden wreck a few yards closer to the enemy position. "Crater, Rosen, you're getting to that wall. Ryan, you know what to do. Everyone ready?"

There was a chorus of "Yes, Sergeant!" and Olson nodded and took a deep breath. He pulled a grenade out of his pack, wrapped his fingers around it, and then jumped up and threw. A shot passed through his upper arm, spraying blood over the ruined wall.

The others sprinted for their assigned positions as the explosion echoed behind the enemy wall. Spreading out their fire, the squad managed to force the Germans back, killing several of them, especially since Ryan took advantage every time the Germans broke from cover.

Rosen and Henderson went through the bodies of the fallen, taking some weapons as trophies. Crater grabbed a few enemy pistols and said something about selling them back home. Perkins patched up Olson's arm, and the squad took inventory of what they had left and what they had captured.

"Hey, Country, this more your speed?" Rosen held up a Mauser rifle.

A rare smile creased Ryan's face as he examined the weapon. He squinted through the scope, nodded, and slung it over his shoulder, filling his pockets and the space in his pack with extra ammo.

"You gonna fire a Kraut gun?" Henderson sounded appalled.

"Shoots better," was all Ryan said.

"Sarge, can he do that?" Henderson turned to Olson.

"Hell, son, he's the best shot we got. He says it shoots better, I'm not arguing with him. Are you?"

Henderson wilted under Olson's gaze. "No, sir."

"What I thought," Olson said. "Rosen, Perkins. See where that trail goes." He pointed to a beaten path leading away through the brush.

"You ever seen anyone shoot like Country?" Rosen asked Perkins as they scrambled up the path.

"Not so far," Perkins said. "I hope I never do, either. Especially not if it's coming from the other side."

They'd all gotten used to Rosen's perpetual excitement, but he wasn't anxious to have a conversation while they were scouting in German-held territory. They worked their way up a slope but stopped when the ground dropped away toward a river below.

"Holy shit," Rosen said.

"Holy shit," Perkins agreed.

"Go back and tell Sarge," Perkins said, staring at the river and the steep gorge below. As Rosen hurried back down, Perkins got as low as he could and peered over the edge.

"That's a hell of a lot of Germans," he muttered.

The squad regrouped near the top of the slope. Ryan moved up to observe while the others clustered together.

"What the hell do we do now, Sarge?" Henderson asked. "There's no way we're clearing out that many."

"You wanna just give up?" Rosen sounded shocked. "We can't do that."

"We can't take on a whole damn company by ourselves, either," Henderson shot back.

"It's probably not a full company," Crater said. "I mean, they gotta have lost some men besides the ones we just took out, right?"

Perkins reached under his shirt and rubbed a medallion he had on a chain, a nervous habit.

"It ain't gonna be easy, boys," Olson said. "But we've got a job to do." He held up a hand before Henderson could start complaining. "I'm not saying we take on that many—that's nuts. But they're down there, we're up here, and we can at least keep an eye on them."

"If they figure out there's only a few of us here, they're gonna run right over us," Henderson said, getting a few glares from the others. "And it's not like we can call for reinforcements."

Johnston, their radio operator, had been lost during the push inland from their drop zone in Normandy. The same grenade that had killed several of their squad-mates had destroyed the radio beyond repair.

"We can do this," Perkins said quietly. "We can."

Everyone turned to look at him.

"What the hell are you talking about?" Henderson asked.

Perkins pulled out his medallion. "My daddy carried this, and his daddy made it. He was a blacksmith." He took off the chain and passed it around. "Ever hear of the Spartans?"

The metal disc, worn smooth from years of handling, showed a profile of an ancient soldier with a huge metal helmet and an impressive plumed crest.

"Way back when the Greeks were a major power, they had these amazing soldiers, the Spartans. They were the best. In the battle of Thermopylae, just three hundred Spartans fought an entire army. They had a narrow pass the enemy couldn't get through or around." He pointed up the hill. "Kinda like that. The Spartans were heroes, warriors, and they fought an enemy who was trying to take over the world and end their way of life."

Olson's eyes narrowed, but he didn't say anything.

"You think we're like them?" Henderson asked.

"I think we've got better weapons than they did. We've got Ryan. We've got a company of our own coming behind us. Like Sarge said, all we have to do is watch where the Germans go. But if they start coming up here and taking the high ground?" Perkins looked at each of his fellow soldiers. "We can't let them dig in up here."

"You can't be serious. Tell him he's crazy, Sarge." Henderson looked around at the others. "You can't really be listening to this crap."

"Here's what we're going to do," Olson said. "Henderson, leave your rifle, your pack—anything that'll slow you down. You're going to find the battalion behind us and tell them what's going on. You find any stragglers along the way, send 'em here. We'll take the help. Everyone else, spread out on the ridge. Stay quiet. We're lucky, we just wait. We're not ... Well, it's gonna be a hell of a fight."

"Oh, you people are nuts," Henderson said. But he yanked his rifle off his shoulder, put down his pack, and stripped down to just his fatigues, belt, pistol, and canteen. "There's no way you're standing up to that." He jerked his head toward the enemy.

"Run fast," Olson ordered.

Henderson shook his head, looked around at them one last time, and took off down the slope.

"Man runs like a rabbit," Crater said.

"Let's hope that comes with the lucky feet. We're gonna need it," Olson said. "All right, boys, spread out, stay low, stay quiet, and don't do anything stupid." As the men started to move, he said, "Perkins, with me."

After the others were out of earshot, the sergeant lowered his voice. "Your daddy tell you how that story ended?"

Perkins nodded. "Spartans were wiped out to a man. Didn't figure that was a good part to share right now."

Olson shook his head. "You're something else, Perkins. Catch." He tossed the medallion back.

Perkins looped the chain over his head. "Thanks, Sarge."

Time ticked by slowly. Olson redistributed the remaining supplies. Henderson's rifle and all the extra ammo stayed with Ryan. Olson made sure everyone had one grenade; he took the extras, since he had the best throwing arm, even with the gunshot wound. The sergeant spent a lot of time with Ryan, who carefully kept under cover, out of the sunlight, and used the rifle scope to report on how many they were up against, where their officers were, and anything else that might be useful. Olson made careful notes in the battered notebook he'd carried since being given his stripes.

By the end of the second hour, the sun climbed higher, and everyone got thirstier. Three more men found their way to them, telling them about a crazy guy who was running like the devil was on his heels, west toward battalion headquarters. The newcomers looked a lot less happy about linking up with the squad when they saw the Germans at the bottom of the hill.

Perkins once again told his story of the Spartans, remembering how his father had spoken about the elite warriors, and they nodded, slowly.

A third hour slowly passed. The June sun was beating down on them, and the low brush wasn't offering a lot of shade. Crater was just starting to say something about how he hoped the day would end and the Germans would bed down for the night when a noise cut him short.

Looking down the slope, he signaled that two men were climbing up the hill. He shot a look at Perkins, and everyone tensed. One of the Germans carried field glasses.

Olson leaned close to Ryan and whispered, "Still got that captain picked out?"

Ryan nodded.

Olson said, "Him first."

They waited, hoping the men would turn back.

They didn't.

Finally, Olson flashed a hand signal at Perkins. Perkins and Crater shot at nearly point-blank range from their spot in the brush, and the two surprised men fell back down the hill. Almost at the same second, Ryan fired, and the German captain fell.

In the half-second of shocked silence that followed, Perkins yelled "Spartans!" and began firing at the group below them.

Olson lobbed all the grenades he could at different spots in the enemy formation, and Ryan coolly worked his way through the officers.

A murderous fire roared up the hill, shredding the bushes and adding blood to the stench of sweat, fear, and gunpowder that already filled the air.

Hours later, when Henderson returned with the lead element of a company that clearly doubted his story, they found a gorge full of dead Germans. Casings littered the rim of the small valley, and blood was everywhere. A few battered and bleeding men had bandaged themselves up the best they could. The bodies of the rest were laid out as neatly as possible.

Next to the big man with the sergeant's stripes was a younger private with a medallion in his hands.

Months later, the push to Berlin.

Sergeant Rosen looked at the new recruits. They all looked like kids to him. He wasn't actually much older than they were, but he'd seen so much. Too much.

"Are we really going to go after that whole group? Aren't they just going to surrender soon anyway?" Rosen thought the kid's name was Baker.

"Scared, kid?" he asked, not unkindly, and low enough the others couldn't hear.

"That's a hell of a lot of Germans over that hill," Baker answered.

Rosen smiled. "Let me tell you a story about a guy named Tom Perkins."

About the Author

Wayland Smith is a native Texan who has moved around a lot but is presently living in Northern Virginia. His rather unlikely list of jobs includes private investigator, comic book shop owner, ring crew for a circus (then he ran away from the circus and joined home), deputy sheriff, writer, and freelance stagehand. His novels include *In My Brother's Name* and the Wildside, Inc series about superhuman mercenaries. He has also been in numerous anthologies, including *HeroNet Files Volume 1*, and *SNAFU: An Anthology of Military Horror*. His hobbies include gaming, reading, and movies. (Of course I want popcorn!)

THE LAST WAKING PRINCESS

KAT KELLERMEYER

C lose your eyes. Clear your mind of all distractions."

Zeriah sat on a pile of cushions opposite Esdras, eyes shut and her fat, fluffy tabby who wouldn't still in her lap. The princess had lost track of how many times they'd sat like this, Esdras droning on in his low, easy tone telling her to close her eyes and clear her mind. Closing her eyes was the easy part, but it only helped her notice what she hadn't before: the birdsong coming from the eastern window; her cat, Renana, trying to wiggle herself loose; the soft chatter of the kitchen servants making the day's bread at the far end of the hall.

"My princess." Esdras's voice snapped her back to the present, and she mumbled an apology. He just closed his eyes and resumed his posture. "Clear your mind," he repeated. "Let it settle into a void, like a still pond on a moonless night."

Zeriah took a deep breath and tried to fish the distractions out of her mind pool. She was still searching for calm when he spoke again.

"And when you have done that, I want you to search for your happiest thoughts. The thoughts that make you feel most loved, most safe. Most *happy*. This is a happiness larger than a new toy or a fancy party. This is the largest happiness you can summon. Don't reach. Simply let the thoughts rise to the surface of your mind."

Zeriah's mind was still a cluttered puddle. Birdsong, cat, chatter—*happy*. The happiest thing she could remember.

There was the time Momma played hide-and-seek with her in the sand gardens. *No*, she'd tried that last week.

The time the kitchen surprised her with a batch of her favorite sweet rolls. *No*, she needed Big Happy.

Of course, her last birthday party! The one with the magician in the solarium who pulled miles of colored scarves out of his sleeves while he sang. She'd worn a brand-new purple gown with pink-chested bluebirds embroidered all along the hem. Just thinking about it made her feel warm. They'd had a tall cake with sea-glass colored frosting and shells adorning the top. She'd loved all of her gifts, and when it came time to blow out the candles, she did it all by herself—all eight of them! It was the first year she'd done it without needing Papa's help.

A shadow passed over the memory. *Papa*.

The thought slipped from her grip like a river stone and tumbled back into darkness. Renana made a low wail and kicked until Zeriah let her go. All the distractions came flooding back at once.

"My princess. Where are you now?"

Zeriah couldn't tell if she was imagining the disappointment in Esdras's voice. She wasn't sure she understood the question. "I'm ... here?"

Esdras let out a great sigh. "That's what I was afraid of. Open your eyes, my princess."

Zeriah winced as she did, but any worry was quickly snuffed out by Esdras's easy smile.

"It has been a long week, my princess. Perhaps we should take a break from your studies—"

"No!" The echo that came back to Zeriah sounded like the

whining of a baby. She squared her jaw and did her best to sound grown-up. "No. I want to try. I want to *help*—"

"It is not *helpful* to strain yourself like this," Esdras told her. "And it will not serve to draw your magic out—"

Zeriah shook her head. "I can try harder. I can be quieter! I can make my mind a pool—"

"These are not lessons one *beats* into oneself like punishment. The more you try to close your hand on your magic, the more it will elude you."

That didn't make *any* sense, and Zeriah said so in the loud, distinct tone of a princess.

Esdras laughed. "Sense only applies to what we understand, my princess. And there are none living who truly understand *magic*." He rose from the cushions, robes of ocher and violet shaking loose to his ankles. "Go. Keep yourself busy. And stay out of trouble." His eyes narrowed, but the smile didn't leave his face. "I've heard stories of how you pester the kitchen."

Zeriah shook her head again. "I didn't steal those oranges."

The corner of Esdras's mouth quirked. "Funny, my princess. I don't recall mentioning any oranges." He brushed her shoulder when she stayed staring up at him. "*Go.* And do try to think *happy* thoughts, my princess. *Big* happy thoughts."

Zeriah watched him vanish down a hall before she turned and trotted obediently out of the room. At least this time he'd given her an order she could follow. For the last four months, it felt like every day was the same lesson: think *bigger,* remember *happier* things.

Esdras once asked what she was thinking about, and she told him: Momma in the sand gardens, the day that other kingdom visited and they decorated the palace in brightly colored scarves and colored lanterns to greet them, the time Papa came home after being gone for two moons and brought her back a doll with blue stones for eyes. Esdras's smile went tight, and he asked if she couldn't think of anything *happier*. They sat for a full minute in silence until Esdras sighed and told her classes were over for the day.

Zeriah didn't understand how she could be any happier. Some days, with Momma sick and Papa sleeping, she didn't know how to be happy at all.

She traced her hand along the mosaic on the outer wall as she shuffled off in the direction she suspected Renana had gone. From this high up in the palace, she could see the top of the briar thicket, a wide gash of thorns and brambles and dense trunks. It stretched on like a spill of ink from the palace proper to the distant gates where the city began. She wondered if the city people knew the palace people were still alive. She wondered if any of the city people had tried to get through the brambles.

The grown-ups had all turned mean since the briar thicket had appeared—since Papa had fallen asleep. Zeriah was sad, but she hadn't turned mean. Not even when they ran out of strawberries. Not even after Emaron and the funeral fire.

Emaron had been her favorite of all the kitchen staff, and the only boy in the entire palace her age. He'd been out climbing, the same walls they'd always climbed together. She never thought he'd fall. Not ever. He'd struck his head so badly he didn't wake up. And with the newly grown brambles, there were no doctors to send for, no alchemists to come administer medicines.

For two days, Emaron lay in a bed. On the third day, he died. And on the fourth, the priests sang a chant and burned him on the funeral fire. Esdras had corrected her—a funeral *pyre*—and he'd tried to explain it was as much to honor Emaron as it was a necessity. Dead bodies carried disease. To keep them long was to invite ruin on one's house. Everyone who came to the funeral fire cried, but no one more than Zeriah.

It was the first death that was *hers*. She remembered her grandfather's funeral and the little memorial they had when their other cat, Theom, had died, but those had not prepared her for this. She'd grown up with Emaron. She always thought they'd grow tall together.

It had been months since the funeral fire. She hadn't noticed death before then; the way people talked or *didn't* talk about it, like it was a secret they needed to keep from her, or something children weren't allowed to know about. It was the same way they only talked about Momma and the baby when they didn't think she was around. The way they talked about the day the man cursed Father, like they knew best, like Zeriah hadn't been in the room, too.

To hear the servants tell it, Papa had been cursed by an evil magician with a great and terrible staff. They said Papa fought him in battle and he cursed him as he fell. But Zeriah had seen it all from her seat on Momma's lap. The man who had cursed Papa hadn't looked evil. He'd looked sad; he'd looked *hungry*. He'd come to the palace to talk to Papa about his problems. Zeriah hadn't followed his story—something about a fire long ago from when Grandfather was king?

She'd never really known Grandfather. But she knew Papa was a very nice Papa, the kind whose eyes got wet when you scratched your knee and cried, the kind who tried his very best to be good to everyone. Sometimes the servants whispered that Papa was so good because his papa was so *mean*. Grandfather started fires. Grandfather hurt people. But when Papa heard the man's story, he cried. He wanted to help, to fix things, but the man only cared about what had already been broken.

Zeriah didn't know anything about curses. She didn't know they could come in jars like the one the man held up over his head. She remembered Momma's arms closing over her and her belly like a shield. Zeriah watched the jar tumble out of the man's hand and shatter on the tile like a spark of flint. There was a great black wave that knocked the vision from her, and when she woke, the sad man was a smear of ash on the floor. There were brambles arching out from where he was *not* that wound up the canopies and walls and swarmed the outer gardens. By that night, they had filled the gap between the palace and the city beyond.

And worst of all, Papa wouldn't wake up.

That first week was the hardest. The briar thicket was too thick for the guards to cut through, and no one seemed to be coming to help them. The kitchen began rationing, and the meals since had been bland and gamey. Papa would not wake for all that his councilors and alchemists tried, and Momma was sick with the coming baby, and they made her stay in bed. She couldn't go to Papa's old meetings, or even play with Zeriah. But at least she wasn't asleep.

It was the second week when Esdras found the curse in one of his books. He explained to Zeriah that this was a very old curse, something made of hate and sorrow. He said the man must have been in great pain to have made it so *powerful*. Zeriah liked it when Esdras told her things. He never tried to make his words smaller for her.

The curse was a simple enough thing to break: a touch of magic would unsnare the briars and wake any sleepers. But there was the trouble. Papa was the only magician in the palace—in the city, in the land. All they required was the simple touch their king could not wake to give, and Esdras—for all his arcane knowledge—had no actual magical ability. There was only one person in the whole palace who might possess a *hint* of magical ability.

Zeriah was elated when Esdras told her. Magic had been her father's realm, a distant land she was allowed to view on occasion but never visit. If Esdras was right, she could travel to that land and end the curse—or at least wake Papa to help end it.

Her first lesson was that very evening. Papa had been sleeping for long enough the moon had turned dark and was returning in a milky sliver in the sky. The room was filled with people eager to see what might happen, nobles and servants alike who had been trapped with them in the palace. Some had long strands of brightly colored prayer beads wrapped around their hands. Others were crying and murmuring prayers. Momma was the only steady thing she could see, and even she looked like the softest breeze would scatter her.

Zeriah didn't like this room. Papa and Momma's room had always been bright and full of hanging planters that spilled over with ferns and vibrant buds. The room they'd moved Papa to was as dark as a tomb. Momma said the low-burning lanterns were meant to invoke *reverence*, but the only thing they made Zeriah feel was afraid. In the half-light Papa looked like something carved from wax. Not really alive. His lips looked dry and were flecked with dead skin. The only movement was the soft rise and fall of his chest and the flickering of his eyes under his lids. He barely looked like Papa anymore.

She didn't want to hold his hand, but she was good and did as Esdras asked her. They started the same exercise: *happy* thoughts.

"Happy enough to provide proper inspiration"—that's what he'd said the first time.

Zeriah's head started aching ten minutes in. She couldn't think any bigger. By the time thirty minutes had passed, she could hear people starting to whisper.

"What's wrong with her?"

"Why isn't it working?"

"Are we sure she's an arcane?"

A pair of servants near the door giggled, and the sound rattled around Zeriah's head until she was convinced they were laughing at *her*. Because she couldn't do it. Because it was silly to think she could do it. Because she could *never do it* and Papa would *stay asleep* and Momma would be *sick when the baby came*—

Zeriah braced a hand on the mosaic wall as she suddenly realized she was struggling to catch her breath. She hadn't even been running. She slumped on the floor, back pressed against the cool stone. Her head prickled for a bright, dizzy second as she fought to breathe. They still had time. Time for her to learn, time for them to fix all this. Esdras had told her so, and Esdras knew almost everything.

She was still sitting and breathing when a happy trill interrupted her thoughts. She looked up in time to see Renana's fluffy tail vanish around the corner of the next hallway down. And like that, the wave of sick passed by her. She pushed off the wall, ignoring the flood of gray at the corners of her vision as she raced off after the cat.

Renana gave a bright mew at Zeriah's footsteps before darting up the rack of dried beans and lentils stored in tall glass jars in the hall outside the kitchen. She climbed all the way to the top of the rack, to where the shelves ended and a long row of window gaps traced the wall just below the ceiling.

The cat gave one last flick of her tail before she vanished through one of them.

Zeriah set her jaw and scaled the rack, only bumping one glass jar, which she managed to steady before it could smash on the ground and alert the kitchen staff to her troublemaking. The gaps near the ceiling were narrow enough she had to flatten herself like a salamander to fit through. They were meant to let out the heat of the kitchen, not for princesses to sneak through, and she could feel the hot air blast on her face as she wiggled onto the row of cabinets that lined the kitchen's upper walls.

She was high enough up the staff working below would not notice her, high enough they'd never managed to catch her sneaking oranges and bits of candied ginger from their pantries.

She spotted her cat sitting on one of the cabinets at the far end of the room. Renana gave her a long, slow blink as she crawled in her direction, paying no mind to the glassware rattling in the cabinets below. Renana gave a mew of protest when Zeriah sat down beside her and pulled her into her lap, but she didn't make any move to resist beyond the noise. The moment Zeriah began scratching under her chin, Renana started to purr and went puddle-shaped in the girl's lap.

And for a few moments, it was just the pair of them and the sunbeam buried under Renana's wide purr. Zeriah didn't even realize she was listening to anyone speak until she heard someone mention the queen. She shook off the last of the daydream and peered over the edge of the cabinet to the kitchen below.

An older woman with her hair done up in a scarf snapped orders at the younger girls, who were all busy filling pots with water and stoking the open flames to boil them. Below her, a pair of girls folded fresh-laundered towels and placed them in large baskets.

One of them whispered to the other. "S'early, isn't it? Earlier than usual—"

"Not *so* early. My cousin Abidan was born this far out. He's a bit shorter than his brothers, but other than that, nothing odd about him."

"Yeah," the first girl said, dabbing sweat from her brow with her wrist, "but she's had such a rough go of it, with the bleeding and having to be in bed like that. And the doulas were supposed to be here, and we've missed the last three months' delivery from the alchemist, and we don't have enough, and it's just us—oh, sun and stars, Dalida, I don't think I can—"

The scarf-haired house matron clapped her hands loud enough to snap the room into silence. Her sharp gaze turned on the girl who had been speaking. "Helpha, I'm not going to repeat myself. I want less talking and more folding. That goes for *all* of you." Her eyes narrowed as she swept the room. To Zeriah, she seemed more a general than a house matron.

"Now, this isn't the first child I've seen brought into this world, and I suspect there are others here who can say the same. And if I am speaking of you, I need you to accompany me. Immediately.

Your queen needs competent hands who won't faint on the first push. Now, who will be coming with me?"

Two girls' hands shot up the moment she stopped speaking. A third in the corner only put her hand as high as her chest, looking much less certain than the first two. The house matron didn't seem to care and rounded them up and marched them out of the room, leaving the ongoing bustle to continue without her.

All at once Zeriah realized Renana was gone from her lap and nowhere to be found. The sun had disappeared behind a cloud, and the warmth she'd been sitting in had turned cold as stone.

Zeriah shimmied back through the window gap and took off running the moment her feet found the floor, past the fountained gardens, past the ballroom with the open ceiling and the canopies of fine sheer scarves, and up, up, up the stairs to the grand halls above.

Outside Momma's bedroom there were servants gathered in clusters. One of the girls tried to stop her, but Zeriah was too quick for her. But not for the one inside the room. That girl caught Zeriah while she was steps from Momma's bed.

"It's all right." Momma's soft voice calmed the scene. "Let her through."

Zeriah tugged her hand loose, glaring at the servant before hurrying to her mother's side. Momma was pale. There were drops of sweat collecting on her forehead, and her smile couldn't seem to stay in place.

"Hello, petal," she beamed, tugging Zeriah to sit on the bed beside her. "I'm very glad to see you. I have a surprise. Your sibling is going to be joining us a little earlier than we planned."

"But it's supposed to be another month," Zeriah said dimly. "W-we had another month. We had *time*." All at once her vision went glassy. "I've been trying, Momma, I've been trying so hard—"

Her mother pulled her into her arms. "I know, petal. And I'm so *proud* of you. I need you to be brave, all right? Just for a little while. You're going to be a sister soon. But until then, I need you to be *brave*."

Zeriah didn't feel like being brave at all, nose running and tears all down her cheeks. She nodded anyway. "I'll try. I'm *trying*. I-I'm trying to do magic, b-but I don't know how to *do* magic. I can't think of my Big Happy—"

"Oh, petal." Momma's shaky smile held steady a moment as she cupped her cheek. "Yes, you do. I know you do. You just need to find the right inspiration. The right *spark*—"

Zeriah sniffled and tried her best to stop crying. "D-do you have one?"

Momma smiled. "You, petal. It's always been you." She pulled her close enough to press her lips to her forehead and squeeze her tightly.

There was a rumble of sound, and Zeriah looked up to see one of the servants rise from Momma's bedding with a red towel. All at once the servants were pulling her away from Momma, pushing her out into the hall while others shouted and ran baskets of fresh towels into the room.

Zeriah stood still for a moment, not knowing what to do or where to go. Several servants nearly collided with her, until one finally shouted at her to go stand somewhere else. Zeriah moved like a dream to the next hall over, empty and closed up for the season, and stood there a very long while. She wanted to find Esdras. She wanted to make her magic work and fix everything so Momma didn't have to be sick when the baby arrived.

She shivered and turned to face the darkened wing before her. She knew where she needed to go. She took off at a run, sandals clattering in the empty hallway and folding back on her until she was enveloped in her own odd rhythm. She stopped outside the same dimly lit room from her nightmares. The door was closed up and it took her a long moment to convince herself to reach for it. Momma needed her to be brave. She'd *promised*.

Zeriah took a deep breath and stepped into Papa's room.

It was still strange to see him like this, shut up in a dark room with his arms folded across his chest. It reminded her of the way they'd folded Emaron's arms for the funeral fire.

Not dead, asleep. She repeated it over and over as she approached the man in bed who looked like her father. It couldn't be Papa. Papa's cheeks were never so gray. His hair was never so well-oiled and combed. This was a stranger. But perhaps the stranger could help her find Papa. Perhaps they could find help for Momma. But she had to wake him first. She could help Momma, but only if she could wake him first.

She pulled one of his hands off his chest to hold it between her own. She never realized he'd be so heavy. It was only as she stood there, hand in hand with a ghost, that she realized she was crying. That she'd been crying since she left Momma's room and she hadn't stopped and couldn't now.

She gasped for air as she tried to call any happiness to mind. Thoughts scattered like summer dragonflies, and she grabbed empty air as she reached to catch them.

Birthday. No.

The Solarium Fair. Nothing.

Holding Renana in the sun. Not so much as a single spark.

It should have been simple: a single spark of happiness. That was the only thing stopping Momma from being safe, stopping Papa from waking up. It was one happy thought and it was hers, and she couldn't do that one thing for them. And now Momma was going to die. They'd put her up on a funeral fire like Emaron, fold her hands over her chest like Papa. And all because Zeriah didn't know how to be happy right.

She sobbed so hard she began to cough.

And then someone was holding her, gently tugging her away from her father's ever-still bed. She didn't recognize Esdras until he set her down again on a couch in the hall. She cursed and shouted at him to take her back. He ignored the plea, pulling a long, blue handkerchief from the inner pocket of his robe. He dabbed at the tears on her cheeks.

She pushed him away. "Leave me alone! I can do it, let me do it—"

"My princess," he said gently, holding her by the shoulders until she relented and went still. "This is not the way. This is no way for you to access your magic."

"But I have to," she gasped. "Momma is sick. The baby is coming, and no one will tell me anything, and if I don't wake up Papa, she might ..." She rubbed a wrist across one cheek and sniffed hard. "I have to."

Esdras's smile was tired. "You have done everything you are able to, my princess. That is all anyone can ask. And what will be will be with your mother." When she looked confused, he gave a slow shake of his head. "Even if you were to wake your father and lower the brambles this moment, it is a day's ride to town, and another back. There is nothing you can do for your mother now but be still and be brave."

"I don't *want* to be brave," Zeriah shouted in a high-pitched rush. "I want to be sad. And angry."

Esdras considered her for a long, quiet moment, then drew her closer to his side and gave a small nod. "Then be sad. And be angry. And I will sit here with you, my princess."

Zeriah pressed both hands over her face and began to cry again. She slumped against Esdras with a defeated sound and didn't shrug off the hand he set upon her back. He rubbed small circles between her shoulders until she stopped crying. The dusk-orange hall had gone dark. She felt like a sun-dried bone: brittle, dry, and overbright. One of the maidservants found them sitting like that in the hall and bundled Zeriah into her arms.

The next morning, Zeriah woke in her own bed, wearing a pair of pajamas she didn't remember putting on.

Only one servant came to bathe her and braid her hair. It was the same girl who brought breakfast. Zeriah asked if it was because all the other servants were still with Momma. The girl tried to distract her by pointing at the vine that had started to flower outside her window.

The whole day was like that. She'd try to pry information out of the servants, and not one of them told her a thing. So it was on to distraction. She found Renana in the gardens, walking delicately along a high stone wall and joined her for the walk around. She tried not to think of Emaron or Papa or Momma or the baby.

She'd fallen asleep stretched out on the hot stones when she heard a servant shouting for her.

Zeriah's whole body went fuzzy with hot-cold again. She jumped down from the wall and ran like a streak of light. Her heart beat so loud she could hear it in her ears.

But then she saw that the servant calling for her was smiling.

It was another few days before they finally let Esdras take her to see Momma. It had been a very long birthing, and she was still sick, but everyone said she would be herself again soon enough. She was still ash-pale when they finally allowed Zeriah to visit, but her smile was easy and bright and doubled when she saw her daughter.

"Hello, petal," she said, shifting the bundle in her arms to let Zeriah see properly. "Say hello to your baby brother."

Zeriah bent to look. Inside the bundle, there was a tiny face, and one hand curled tight around one of Momma's fingers. His fingernails were smaller than the daintiest shells she'd ever seen, and when she touched the back of his hand, those tiny fingers wrapped around her own fingers. She drew a small, delighted breath.

"Hello," she told the bundle, marveling at how hard he held onto her. "I'm Zeriah, your big sister."

And the fingertip held tight in her brother's grasp began to glow, dimly at first, then a radiant blue light flickered along her finger like a flameless fire.

Her brother blinked and made a soft, wondering noise, the blue glow reflecting back at Zeriah in his eyes. She looked up from the baby to see her mother, tears streaming down her cheeks, and Esdras staring with his mouth agape.

Zeriah smiled back at them, hiccoughing with tears *and* laughter. "Look, Momma," she said, staring down at the tiny fist wrapped around her fingertip. "I found a Big Happy."

Esdras and Zeriah kept practicing in the days that followed, ensuring she had some measure of control over the power. At least enough to administer the touch.

Once again the dark room was crowded. This time Zeriah didn't mind. She knew what to do.

She walked to her father's bedside and took his hand in hers. She felt Esdras's hand on her back, steadying her, and she closed her eyes, drew a long, slow breath and imagined the still pool Esdras always told her to look for. When the waters were still, she whispered one request to them: *happiness*. Then she waited to see what came to the surface.

There were no birthday parties this time. Instead, there was the memory of falling asleep in Papa's lap while he read to her. There was the memory of picnics with Momma and long afternoons talking and laying in the tall grass. And there was the memory of the day she met her brother. She let bright, glittery happiness fill her from toe to brow. By the time she opened her eyes, both her hands were flickering like the southern aurora.

"All right, Papa," she whispered. "Time to wake up."

About the Author

Kat Kellermeyer is a loudmouthed punk from Salt Lake City who likes good gin, local music, and art in every medium they can get their hands on. When they're not writing (or consuming more art), you can find them drumming for Stop Karen, teaching young people music and life skills at Rock Camp SLC, or standing on a street corner shouting about social justice.

THE FIRST PROBLEM

ALICIA CAY

The tidy kitchen reeked of death. Detective Inspector Charles A. Dupin stepped across the threshold into the neatly kept but ramshackle house. He regarded the scene.

The victim lay on the plank-wood floor. Someone, the officer perhaps, had thrown a crisp linen sheet over her. One of the dining chairs had been knocked over, and a single letter lay unfolded on the table next to a stack of untouched post.

Mrs. Pearcey, the owner of the lodging house, stood in the doorway nearby, wringing her hands. Her abundant body blocked his view into the sitting room, where her lodgers would sit of an evening, smoking, playing cards, or doing their mending while bemoaning the luck that had brought them to this sad place.

Dupin had never been in this house, but he knew them well. Different folk came and went, and different wallpaper peeled from the walls, but they were at their hearts, all the same.

Dupin removed his bowler hat and kneeled next to the deceased woman. He pulled the sheet down to expose her face and upper body. Her face was puckered, swollen with death. She had pale skin and chestnut-brown hair. He removed his magnifying glass from a coat pocket, lifted the woman's eyelid, and observed the clouded iris; red pinpricks had blossomed on the whites of her eyes. He let the eyelid fall close.

The marks on her neck were fresh and pink—death having rushed in before they could turn to black and blue. He brushed a thumb gently across her cheek. What had this woman dreamed of when she had been a small girl? Surely not this end: a lost soul, attacked and demeaned in a lonely doss-house in Shoreditch.

Dupin slid his hand beneath the woman's and studied her fingers. The nail of her middle finger was cracked, a tiny fragment of wood slid beneath it. He returned her hand to her bosom. A sound, like the rustle of wings upon air, drew his attention to where Mrs. Pearcey hovered.

There, behind the landlady's wide hips, stood a young child of eight or nine. She had been hiding him. The boy's shock of dark curls stood distraught on his head, and his deep brown eyes, wide with animal panic, stared back at Dupin. The Inspector rocked back on his heels.

"Terrible sorry, Inspector," Mrs. Pearcey said. "He's what found her this way. Came and got me straightaway." She lowered her voice. "She's his mother."

Dupin replaced the sheet over the woman and stood. "This is no scene for a boy. Take him out—anywhere, but not here. Do it now."

Mrs. Pearcey turned, grabbed the boy, and tried to usher him up the stairs.

The child's face screwed up as he wailed in distress. His hands clutched at her apron, and he dug his heels into the rug. He was small, but the panic that shone in his eyes also gave him the strength of one far more grown.

Mrs. Pearcey struggled with him for a moment before the officer standing in the kitchen moved into the sitting room. He grabbed the boy's collar and began to drag him from the room.

"Here then!" Dupin said. He strode through and picked the

boy up into his arms. He could feel the child's heart jack hammering against his own chest. Dupin held him tight, trying to still that animal terror.

The boy's wails turned to screams, and tears ran freely down his face. He arched his back to pull away.

Emotion built in Dupin's chest, crying as the child did, to be let out. He held tighter. The child's hands, clutched into small red fists, beat down on Dupin's back. Dupin would not let him go.

He turned and walked out of the kitchen onto the narrow front porch. Clean air washed over them, the smell of London's East End's rank streets sweeter than the enclosed smell of death and sorrow that lingered in the kitchen—and would for days.

Dupin settled on the wooden bench perched on the porch and held the boy until his sobbing ceased. Then he sat the child next to him, sides touching, until the redness of the boy's face ebbed.

"I'm Detective Inspector Dupin. What's your name?"

The boy tried to answer, his chest hitching between syllables. "Sh ... She ..."

"She's your mother?" Dupin said.

The boy nodded, rubbing his eyes.

"You live here with her?" Dupin indicated the house.

Another nod.

"It's nice," Dupin said. "Very much like my house, red brick and with a porch."

The boy looked up at him, his eyes wet. "You live in a lodgings also?"

"More like a flat—with a kitchen to share. Comfortable enough for an old man." He winked at the boy. "I've got a room and a bed, and all my books are there. Do you like to read?"

The boy shifted his gaze to his hands, clutched together in his lap.

"What about your brothers or sisters—do they like to read?"

"Only got one brother. He's older than me." The boy sniffled and wiped his nose. "He likes books, always carrying them around. For school, you know."

"Is he at school now?"

The boy nodded. "At boarding school, in London. We visit him sometimes. Da' says I'll be off there soon, when I'm old enough to be away from ..." His eyes filled with tears again.

Dupin turned the conversation away. "Your Da', is he in London also?"

The boy shook his head.

"Have you seen him recently? Here, maybe?"

"They aren't together anymore."

"I see. Has your mum had any visitors lately?"

The boy stayed silent.

Dupin held his shoulders, letting the child work his way through it at his own pace, in his own time.

"She's a good mum then, eh?" Dupin said.

The boy's head sagged.

Dupin squeezed the boy's shoulder. "My mum was the best in all of London, further even, perhaps."

"Mine was the best in the whole world," the boy said.

"The whole world? That's impressive."

The boy started to sob again, his body hitching in spasmed breaths.

Dupin wrapped an arm around him. "I'm going to find the one who hurt your mum, and I will put them away for a very long time. You have my word."

The boy's voice was muffled by Dupin's jacket, but Dupin heard him all the same. "It won't bring her back."

Dupin nodded. This was the shame of his life's work. He showed up to help only *after* lives had been shattered.

🔥

Dupin left the boy on the porch with an officer and went back inside. He circled the small kitchen, then picked up the fallen chair and set it back against the table. Its legs squelched against the bare wood floor.

Mrs. Pearcey came through into the room. "Inspector." She looked at the table, then back at him. "Terrible sorry to cause such a scene. He's a dear boy—bereft, is all."

"Yes, of course." Dupin nodded. "Mrs. Pearcey, were you home at the time of the murder?"

"Aye, I was." She wiped her hands on her soiled apron. There were streaks of brown and black on it, soot or dirt from her cleaning.

"Did you hear anything?"

She swiped at a loose hair on her brow with a pinkie finger. "Not a pip. I was in another room, doing the tidying."

Dupin pulled the chair back from the table slightly. It made the grating sound again. "I see. Do you know of the boy's kin? They will need to be notified."

"May never spoke of none. Though"—Mrs. Pearcey lowered her voice—"not to speak ill of the dead, God rest her soul, but she acted like a single woman while here."

"She was sitting here when it happened?" Dupin pointed at the kitchen table.

"I suppose so," Mrs. Pearcey said. "As I said, I weren't in here. Didn't see nothin' nor hear nothin', if that's what you're askin'."

On the table next to the post was a mark in the wood. Dupin leaned over and, with his magnifying glass, inspected the table's wound. It was a single scratch several millimeters long, deeply dug and fresh. He picked up the open letter. It was addressed to the victim, Mrs. May Holmes. He read through it.

"This letter is from May's mother," he said. "It appears her uncle, a painter in Paris, has sent her a sum of money. She has asked for May and the boy to come home."

"Has she?" Mrs. Pearcey said. Her lower lids lined with tears.

"Can't say they wouldn't be missed. I've grown used to having the boy here." She dabbed at her eyes with the hem of her apron. "Never did have children of my own. Wadn't blessed as some are."

"I see." Dupin returned the letter to the table and continued around the kitchen. On the screen door to the porch, by the handle, was a reddish-brown smear. Dupin looked over at the woman on the floor. No blood had soaked through onto the sheet. So who, or what, had left the mark on the door?

"And you run this doss-house yourself? Is that safe?"

"Aye, it is." Mrs. Pearcey squinted at him. "I only take in ladies at my lodging house. This ain't one of them filthy doss-houses, as you said, that take in all sorts, like them in Spitalfields. I run a clean house, safe for women. The door is bolted at ten o'clock sharp every evening, an' I serve 'em breakfast too, sose you know. My ladies get at least one meal a day." She stood with her hands on her hips and her legs apart, as though defying him to move her.

On the counter by the woodstove lay a brown parcel. Dupin used the handle of his magnifying glass to carefully pull open the wrapping. Inside was a fresh cut of beef. "Steak for breakfast. That *is* something."

"That ain't mine," Mrs. Pearcey said. "I can afford to keep the house, but not hardly a cut of beef that fine. Times being what they are an' all."

Dupin inspected the meat with his glass. There were black flecks smeared on it, fine as coffee grounds. He rubbed some onto his fingertip and moved it between his thumb and forefinger.

Mrs. Pearcey continued, "May brought it back with her from the day's shopping, is all."

He sniffed the material, then lightly tapped his finger to his tongue. Not coffee, but garden dirt.

"Gets her meat from that butcher at the market, the one in the corner stall. I won't go to him."

"*That* butcher?" Dupin asked.

Mrs. Pearcey frowned. Her hands, big for a woman, curled, and she hid them in her apron pockets. "Whatever you call *those* people. No good foreigns."

"I see," Dupin said. "Mrs. Holmes could afford steak, yet she stayed here?"

"The butcher was sweet on her," Mrs. Pearcey said. "Tried to woo her in with that meat. Up to no good, if'n you ask me."

Dupin cocked an eyebrow and perused the crockery on the shelves, which included an unsightly mismatched bunch of copper pots and chipped serving dishes. "Was she close to anyone in the household, one of the other—"

"She 'n the boy share a room with Violet—Mrs. Watson, that is. Loves on May's son like he was her own."

"Where is she now?"

"At work, I'd say. Came to the city to earn money while her husband is away fighting for the Crown. He's a soldier, though it ain't no excuse to up and leave your family if'n you ask me."

"And your husband? He lives here with you and the women?"

Mrs. Pearcey's lips yanked down at the corners, deepening her frown. "*Mister* Pearcey, if you must know, up and ran off like the coward he is, near six years ago. Ain't seen nor heard from him since, thank the good Lord."

"Yes, I see," Dupin said. He retrieved the letter, folded it, and placed it in his inner jacket pocket. "There's an officer just outside. He will remain here until someone comes to retrieve ..." He nodded down at May Holmes. "And, Mrs. Pearcey?"

She stared down at the body, hands on her hips, scowling like the devil had just asked her for a cup of tea.

"Do let me know if anything else turns up, an address perhaps, for the boy's father. He needs his family now."

Her face softened slightly. "Aye, I do say. Here is where he calls home now. You let him come back, you hear me? He'll be safe with me an' my ladies."

The screen door swung open, and an officer rushed in. The boy stood outside, eyes locked on Dupin.

"Sir," the officer said. "There's a riot near started at the Mid-Field Market. Come quick."

Detective Inspector Dupin hurried into the waiting hansom cab, and the driver reined the horse into action. They shot past the people walking through London's East End—the poor, the gamblers, the drinkers, and the workers. They were Dupin's people, his charges, and he held a soft spot in his heart for them all.

At the market, the stench of unwashed bodies and freshly butchered meat hit Dupin as he leapt from the cab. He shouldered his way through the jeering crowd, behind an officer swinging his baton at the backs of the onlookers.

At the center of the commotion stood a man of considerable size, tall and broad-shouldered, his black hair slicked back with sweat, and his lips hidden beneath a thick, oiled mustache. He held a butcher's blade in his right hand. "Get back, you bastards!" the man yelled.

Dupin squeezed his bulk through the middle of the mob. The crowd yelled back and stamped their feet. Someone threw a rotten apple at Dupin's head.

"Here then," Dupin roared. "Break up this madness. Go home! All of you, get back!"

He ushered the butcher into the corner stall, and let the other officers break up the crowd. They handled the angry people with violence—a few broken teeth and more than a few black eyes—before getting the riot under control.

Dupin turned to the butcher. "I'm Detective Inspector Dupin with the London Police. How do you do, sir?"

"How do I do?" The butcher twirled the knife in his hand.

"You see how I'm doing. These English bastards, come on me for no reason."

Dupin detected the slight tang of an accent beneath the man's words. "What is your name, sir?"

The butcher took a deep breath. "Joseph Metzger."

Dupin scratched at his chin. "Jewish, then, although I detect a bit of an accent. German, perhaps?"

Joseph swung the heavy cleaver into the slain pig on his chopping block. "Unless you've come for pork, leave me be."

"Unfortunately, Mr. Metzger, that I cannot do. I am investigating a murder. And it seems these people, neighbors of Mrs. Pearcey if I am correct in my deduction, believe you culpable."

"Someone's gone and offed the old bitch then, and you think I've something to do with it?"

Dupin glanced around the workspace. The knives gleamed in their rack, polished and sharpened to cut bone with a single swipe. The man's appearance was pristine, his apron crisp and white. Only the old flannel he used for wiping his hands was tainted in any way. The place was impeccably clean. The butcher, who dealt in literal blood and guts, was the tidiest gentleman this side of the Thames.

Dupin frowned. "No, the day finds Mrs. Pearcey alive and well. I've come on account of Mrs. May Holmes."

Joseph froze. "May? What's this got to do with her?"

"You sold her a very fine steak this morning, one that, as my understanding has it, she could not afford to purchase."

"Not that it's any of your business, nor anyone else's, but it's possible, from time to time, I supplied her with a nicer cut of meat than she had means for. She's a fine woman, and kind to me. Which isn't always the case with the locals."

Dupin tapped the buttons on his coat. "I see, and were you involved with her, romantically?"

The butcher went as pink as the pork before him. "Went

'round to her lodgings once to ask. Got run off by that Mrs. Pearcey."

"Yes?" Dupin prompted.

"That was it," Joseph said. "Mrs. Pearcey said she wouldn't have a man the likes of me coming 'round her establishment getting all the neighbors talking."

"So, May wouldn't agree to see you."

"That's not what I said. Saw her once is all, went for a walk in the Hyde, talked a little." The butcher went a darker shade of pink. "She is the kindest woman."

"I see," Dupin said again.

"But why would that be of interest to a detective? It's no crime to be sweet on a lady."

"No crime at all," Dupin agreed. "Murder is, however."

"Murder? You said Mrs. Pearcey was fine." The butcher paled visibly. "May?"

Dupin's chin sagged. "It is my unfortunate duty, Mr. Metzger, to inform you that I was called to her lodging house today ..." He cleared his throat. "After Mrs. Holmes was found murdered."

The butcher turned away. There was a basin of fresh water, and Metzger took to scrubbing his hands aggressively with soap and water. When he spoke again, his voice was rough, clotted with emotion. "And Mrs. Pearcey, she sent that mob here, did she? Thinks I had something to do with it?" He turned back to Dupin. His hands were scrubbed clean, his fingernails shone. The pink of his cheeks had blotched, and he fought against the tears gathered in his eyes.

Dupin's brow creased. "She may think that, and your neighbors, too, perhaps. For that, I am sorry. You should go home until their anger abates. I will keep an officer here to watch over your business."

All the pieces were there, lined out in a tidy row of evidence. One only had to look to see the obviousness of them. This man had not killed May, but Dupin knew who had.

Mrs. Pearcey and the boy followed the officer into the station. She looked furious. Her cheeks and forehead were red, and wisps of her gray hair had come loose in the London wind, lending her the appearance of one who strayed too close to madness.

Dupin stood to meet them.

Mrs. Pearcey spotted Mrs. Watson behind one of the polished wooden desks and glared. "She ain't his kin. I was told you'd found his family. What's this all about then?"

"Yes," Dupin said. "Mrs. Watson has kindly agreed to look after the boy for the time being, as his grandmother is too ill for travel."

"I've spoken on the matter, Detective," Mrs. Pearcey said. "He can stay with me, where he belongs." She held the boy's hand. He whimpered slightly.

Dupin went to her and placed his hand on Mrs. Pearcey's white-knuckled grasp. "Here now, Mrs. Pearcey. It's okay. Everything will be okay." He pried her tightened claw off the boy's hand, then ushered the child over to his desk. "Stay here, son."

The boy sat, grabbed Dupin's smoking pipe, and began to tap his fingers against the wood.

"Mrs. Pearcey," Dupin said. "The reason I've brought you here today is to place you under arrest for—"

"Arrest!" Mrs. Pearcey hollered.

The scratching of pencils stopped as the secretaries' attentions lifted from their paperwork. The officer who had brought Mrs. Pearcey in placed a hand on his baton.

Dupin waved a hand at the officer. "Yes, Mrs. Pearcey, you are under arrest for the murder of—"

"Murder!" Mrs. Pearcey cried.

The boy dropped the pipe onto Dupin's desk with a clatter, his wail the desperate cry of a broken-winged bird. Mrs. Watson reached to comfort him.

Dupin could hear her soothing sounds and the boy's muffled sobs. He clutched the sides of his coat.

Mrs. Pearcey planted her feet apart. Her fists dug into her hips, defiance written in the lines of her face. "The devil's in you, *Detective*, accusin' me like this. I'm a humble woman, I fear God, an' I run a clean home. You want to keep the boy? Fine by me. I'll offer you a good day and be on my way."

"You will do no such thing, Mrs. Pearcey, not today. You see, there is proof of your crime. Your first telltale was the lie you told me."

"The devil to you!" Mrs. Pearcey yelled.

"The devil, madam, has no part in this play. *You* told me you did not hear a sound this morning, yet when I picked up the dining chair, it made enough noise to bring you into the kitchen. Then there is the matter of the steak. You were aware of the fineness of its cut, yet it was still wrapped when I got there."

Mrs. Pearcey's jaw clenched.

"You saw it this morning when May arrived home from the market because you were in the kitchen with her. And her letter—were you there when she read it? Or perhaps you came in after? Either way, she would have been eager to share her good news with you. Good for her, bad for you. May was leaving and taking her son. You have always wanted children, told me so yourself, and you have not hidden your fondness for the boy."

"Ain't nothing wrong with that, as I see it," Mrs. Pearcey said.

Dupin went on. "But there *was* something wrong with her relationship with the butcher, *as you see it*. You made your feelings on that matter quite clear. In fact, he told me about the time he came to call on May. The time you chased him from your home."

"What of it! Them people got no business in our country, an' she ain't got no business raisin' a child to see as such."

"Raised how?" Dupin asked. "To be tolerant of others? To be

caring and kind? Those ways must seem foreign indeed to a mind such as yours."

Mrs. Pearcey grunted beneath the scowl inked in red anger across her face.

"Upon further inspection, I noticed a smudge of blood on the screen door." Dupin glanced at Mrs. Watson and the boy, his tear-stained eyes wide as he watched Dupin in action. "It was a blood-less murder, so one could believe that Mr. Metzger left the mark, a smear of dried blood. Certainly there *is* blood in a butcher's trade. But what of the dirt, I asked myself. How did plain garden soil come to be on that steak?"

Dupin scratched his chin. "I spoke with Mr. Metzger this afternoon. He is as fastidiously well-kept a man as I have ever met, far too tidy in his shop and appearance to call on a lady with the mess of work still on his person. Nor do I believe he would have returned to your home after his first encounter with you. So you see, he doesn't fit. Doesn't fit at all."

Dupin tapped at the buttons on his jacket. "What does fit, Mrs. Pearcey, is that after May confided in you the contents of her letter, an argument ensued between the two of you. What sordid things did you accuse her of in your anger? That she would show interest in a Jewish butcher, or that she was interested in a man at all? By your own admission, you are not a fan of foreigners *or* men. Not after being abandoned by your husband. Did Mr. Pearcey till the hatred in your heart, I wonder, or is it all your own?"

Mrs. Pearcey spat on the floor.

Dupin nodded. "Keep your secrets if you like. I already know the biggest of them all. I suspect that, in a fit of rage, you threw that fine cut of meat onto the porch. You later retrieved it and attempted to wipe it clean, where it left its mark on your apron. I admit at first I believed those marks to be simple soot and house-hold dust, but it wasn't. It was ordinary dirt, trailed onto your porch from the front garden. You tried to put the kitchen back together, didn't you? After you crept up behind her and strangled May Holmes to death."

The hard lines of Mrs. Pearcey's face fell. Her shoulders slumped. She tugged up the hem of her housecoat and covered her eyes. "I wadn't blessed with children," she wailed. "Bad enough some women leave their own behind." She glared at Mrs. Watson. "But worse when they bring one along, make you care for 'em an' open your heart to 'em. Then in comes one bad post and off they go."

True tears leaked from her eyes—her only real sorrow. Her color paled from red to gray, and the volume of her voice fell until her words were whispers.

"They all leave in the end, an' I just couldn't ..." Her head shook. "Couldn't take another one leaving me, is all."

The boy buried his face in Mrs. Watson's coat.

"I'm sorry, child," Mrs. Pearcey said. She took a step toward Mrs. Watson and the boy, holding out her hand. "I didn't mean to hurt her. She wouldn't listen, is all. Wouldn't listen to reason!"

"Reason?" Dupin said. "Reason does not live in your mind. It does, however, live in mine." He nodded at the officer. "Mrs. Pearcey, under order of the Crown, I hereby place you under arrest for the murder of Mrs. May Holmes."

The officer pulled out his irons and snapped them around Mrs. Pearcey's wrists—a final statement on reason. The old woman winced under their weight.

As the officer took hold of her arms, moving her toward the cells at the back of the station, she yelled, "Ain't no way to raise a child, I tell you. Ain't right to take him from a loving place. It was her fault!"

The officer marched her from the room.

Dupin kneeled and placed a hand on the boy's shoulder. He turned from Mrs. Watson's coat to face the detective. His face was puckered and wet.

"I'm sorry, son, for what happened to your mum, and to you."

Dupin's face twisted as the emotion in his chest beat at his ribs. The boy's chin sunk. Dupin lifted it up to look him in the eye. "Your mum is not here in body, but she is in here." He tapped the boy's chest, directly over his heart. "She will always be with you."

"Nanna," the boy said. "She really can't come?"

"Not now, but I have spoken with Mrs. Watson. She's told me all about you, and has offered to take you with her for a time."

"That's right," Mrs. Watson said. "The detective and I worked it all out. We're going to my house in Cornwall. My husband will be home soon, and I've earned enough to keep us fed until then."

"Would that be all right with you?" Dupin asked the boy.

The boy looked up at him, his eyes still leaking, and nodded.

Dupin smiled. "Have I kept my word to you, then? I found who done it, yes? Now I'll see to it she's put away for good."

The boy stayed still, his eyes on Dupin's. The detective waited, letting the boy work his way through it at his own pace, in his own time.

"Detective?" Mrs. Watson said. "The train will be along soon. We must be going." She took the child's hand in her own.

"Yes, of course," Dupin said. He made to stand.

The boy thrust the detective's pipe, still clutched in his small fist, into Dupin's hand.

Dupin chuckled. He ran a thumb across the worn wood of his favorite Calabash pipe. "You know, my landlady has been on me for some time to give this up. Doesn't like the smell of it, I presume. How about you keep it for me?" He handed the pipe back to the boy.

Fresh emotion fell from the boy's eyes. He placed the pipe carefully into his trouser pocket, then pulled his hand from Mrs. Watson's and wrapped both arms around Dupin.

"When I grow up, I want to be a detective, just like you," he whispered against Dupin's neck.

Detective Inspector Dupin, afraid his voice would betray him, hugged the boy back, tight enough to feel the child's heart beating against his own chest. It was calmer now, inspired perhaps.

When the boy pulled away, Dupin took his hand. "Here's a secret, just for you. Keep your eyes open, Sherlock Holmes. That's how you will see the things no one else wants to see. Keep them open and see the world."

Sherlock offered a shy smile to the detective, then took Mrs. Watson's hand again.

The woman led him away, chattering all the while. "I've got a boy at home, you know. He's about your age."

"Neat," Sherlock said. "What's his name?"

"John," she said. "John Watson, after his father. Oh, I think you two will get along just famously. You'll see."

About the Author

Alicia Cay grew up on her dad's collection of classic sci-fi, fantasy, and horror. She has a BFA in Interior Architecture and worked as a 911 dispatcher for twelve years.

Her short fiction has appeared in WhimsyCon's *Wit & Whimsy—Volume 2* and MileHiCon's *Adventures in Zookeeping.*

She's had a loyal love affair with books since she could read, collects quotes, and suffers from wanderlust. She currently lives in Denver with a corgi, a kitty, and a lot of fur.

Visit her at aliciacay.com.

MI JACULPO

OCTOBER K SANTERELLI

Jaculpo sat up with the fluid grace of a peacock, all sinuous bends and golden skin beneath tumbling curls the color of sunlight. Leonardo couldn't help but reach out and run his fingers down the other's back, tracing the goldsmith's spine. It made Jaculpo shiver. The artist liked to watch him shiver, liked the delightful twitch of muscles and the faint wrinkle of his nose.

The goldsmith turned, annoyance fading as his brown eyes traced the lines of Leonardo's body until the blanket hid him from view. "You are tempting, as always," he said, voice warm as amber honey.

"Come back to bed," Leonardo entreated, fingers tangling in the other's.

"Haven't you got work to do today, Leonardo, son of Piero? You can't avoid it by hiding up here with me," Jaculpo said, a sharp edge to his words. Despite that, he did lean over to drape himself over the painter. His weight was comforting. "What was it your father said when he sent you here? 'You are a bastard child. You will never amount to anything unless you impress Ser Verrocchio!'"

Leonardo sighed, curling his arm around the goldsmith's

shoulders. "And today is my best chance, I know. I know." He leaned in, nose tracing the smooth line of Jaculpo's jaw.

"Then tell me, Leonardo di ser Piero da Vinci. What has you so afraid?" The low words rumbled between their chests like a roll of thunder in the distance.

Leonardo took a deep breath, pushing a hand through long hair the color of nutmeg, dark eyes fixing on Jaculpo's. Of course he knew. He always knew. "What if I am not good enough?" he answered, voice barely above a whisper. It would carry no further than the confines of the wooden bed frame with its feather-packed mattress and tangled bedclothes.

"What if you *are*? What if you are to become the greatest painter in the entire history of the world? The greatest sculptor? The greatest tinker?" Jaculpo asked, heat in his voice.

Leonardo laughed. "*Inventor*, my bird. The word is inventor."

Jaculpo rolled over and pushed himself upright, stooping to grab his shirt off the floor and pull the plain white linen over his head.

The artist propped himself up on his elbows, drinking in the sight. "It is a shame to hide away such beauty. Will you be back in my bed tonight?" he asked.

"No, another calls for me, and *you* have to focus. If I were to come back tonight, you would not try as hard," Jaculpo said airily, hunting for his trews upon the worn wooden floor.

Leonardo let his gaze drift. The room above Verrochio's work-shop was small, but a window set below the slope of the hipped roof let in a stream of warm golden light that pooled on the floor. Morning sun haloed the blond as he sat at the foot of the bed, tossing his curls with a frustrated huff.

"Have you seen my pants?" he asked.

"Yes, last night," Leonardo answered lightly, an impish note to his words. The goldsmith tossed his hair and huffed, the way he always did when irritated, his features painted in shadows and his hair aglow like a flame.

"What exactly did Verrocchio want from you? Remind me," he said. A soft "Aha" followed, and he rose triumphantly with his trews in hand.

Leonardo sighed in defeat, sitting up at last. "He said he was going to have me work on one of his projects today. I don't know which one. We'll be collaborating—for the first time." He swung his legs to the floor, watching the goldsmith as he hopped before him, trying to free his left foot from the confines of a pant leg.

It would be bittersweet to return to the narrow wooden bed when it did not hold the warm promise of Jaculpo, but that was the way of things. The time he spent with others was a way for the blond to supplement his meager commission and let him afford his silk doublets and fine wines.

Leonardo rose to help Jaculpo tighten the laces of his burnished orange doublet, their foreheads a scant hair's breadth away. They toyed with one another's fingers. The artist reveled in the smile that played around Jaculpo's lips. He couldn't resist leaning in to kiss him. It lingered on, sweet with milk and honey from the night before. In the end, Jaculpo pulled away to find his boots and pull them on.

"You ought to get dressed," the blond said, fussing with his curls in the small polished metal mirror above the washbasin. "Hurry now. You can't avoid him forever."

"Help me?" Leonardo pleaded.

"You are not so helpless, are you?" Jaculpo chided. Despite his words, he bent to find the artist's tunic, which had gotten kicked partway beneath the bed in their haste to undress last night.

The sight of the young man kneeling at his feet stirred a hunger in Leonardo's heart and kindled a heat beneath his skin. Jaculpo sat up on his knees, and the artist traced a finger along his jaw.

The goldsmith leaned into the touch, expression softening. Even still, he rose and dumped the tunic into Leonardo's arms. "You cannot tempt me. Off to work with you, Leonardo da Vinci,"

Jaculpo scolded, swatting at a hip as he passed. "I will see you in a few days."

"Jaculpo."

The young man stopped at the top of the stairs. He turned, a brow arched expectantly.

"I am the poorest of those you spend time with, the least of them in status, and yet you come to me most often," Leonardo began, heart pounding in his chest like a bird desperate to take wing. "Dare I hope ..." He could not say the words out loud.

A smile curved Jaculpo's lips. "A few days, Leonardo," he said, descending out of sight.

He stared at the door long after the goldsmith had disappeared before rising to dress. His mind wandered. He had come to Florence nine years past, when he'd been fourteen, to learn to paint and draw and sculpt by the grace of his father and the kindness of Master Verrocchio. Until the past year, he had thrown himself into that work with all the dedication he could muster.

Then, he had met Jaculpo.

It had been a delightful sort of madness, falling for him. Leonardo had made trips to the goldsmith's jewelry stand when he'd had no need for trinkets, lying about needing a reference for this or that drawing. Long afternoons had been spent in the sunny marketplace, drawing and trading witticisms and stealing glances at one another.

It turned out that the beautiful blond lined his pockets with extra gold from men who fell for and slept with him, something he admitted to Leonardo with challenge in his gaze. Leonardo decided it didn't matter to him nearly as much as Jaculpo did.

The first time they had kissed had been the night they had stolen apples from a lady's garden. Jaculpo had been invited to a party by one of the rich men who called upon him, and Leonardo had snuck in over the garden wall to meet him. It had been thrilling to do something that felt so dangerous. The kiss had been born of elation and success and tasted of the stolen fruit.

Beneath the tree's rustling boughs and the moonlight, their relationship had begun.

Months passed spent in pleasant company. They had picnics in the sunlit gardens of Verrocchio's workshop. They napped in the hayloft above the inn's stable. They attended masquerades and snuck away to dance with one another in abandoned corridors. Every stolen moment was treasured, for both knew that should the wrong eyes see them their story would end in tragedy. Once they had tried to stay away from one another. They could not. Together, they had more adventures in a single year than the artist had ever dreamed of having.

Yet in all that time, Jaculpo had never taken a single lira from Leonardo.

He draped his paint-spattered smock over his clothing and pulled on his short boots. The artist descended into the workshop proper, the steps creaking softly beneath him.

Stones in various states of sculpting rested on wooden pedestals, the dust and detritus they shed littered across the floor. Easels stood where the light would catch them *just so* through the broad open windows. The smell of paint and plaster filled the air in a way that reminded Leonardo of home more than his mother's house ever had.

"Aha! The young gallant finds his way down to us before the sun begins to fall. I am impressed," Verrocchio boomed in a voice like an ox.

Despite his age, the white-haired Master of the Arts stood straight and tall. The only sign of his heavy years was carried in the swollen knuckles of his hands and an ache in his wrists that he complained of often.

"I saw your Jaculpo leaving. Early for him, isn't it?" His jest was good-natured. He had long ago accepted Leonardo's fondness for the goldsmith, aided by Jaculpo's charm and charisma.

"Is it not yet noon? Excuse me, Master, I find a sudden

longing for my bed," Leonardo teased in return, turning on a heel as if to return upstairs.

"As you wish, as you wish!" Verrocchio waved a hand dismissively. "*The Baptism of Christ* can be completed without your hand, worry not." His voice was light.

Leonardo stopped short, wasting no more time playing. *The Baptism of Christ* was going to be a masterpiece. The brushwork was already beautiful, and something in the composition made the eye linger. He turned toward the wooden plank in the corner. "Do not be so hasty, Master. I am here."

"Come, then, and look upon it. Tell me what you see."

Rough charcoal lines covered the wood, and three figures had already been painted. Jesus stood in the center, garbed only in a brightly striped cloth while John the Baptist poured water over His head. A dove flew down from God's own hands to bless His Son. A young angel knelt in the corner, looking skyward in fervent adoration. The background was composed of a river dotted with stones, its curved bank, and a broad swath of sky—all unpainted.

It wasn't quite right, but Leonardo couldn't put his finger on why. The background was balanced, the expressions were poignant, but he still could not help but feel the painting was ... hollow. Empty.

"I see ..." Leonardo began, only to stop. Would his Master accept such criticism on his work? Verrocchio rarely painted in the first place, preferring stone to tempera.

"Speak, Leonardo. I know your eye is well suited to this. I have watched it grow. Say what is on your mind," the old man said. If he had not sounded genuinely interested, the apprentice may not have said a word—but he did.

"It is missing something, Master—beyond the unfinished background. There is something about the composition, in the way all of the figures interact." He paced before the painting, brow furrowed.

Verrocchio remained silent for a few minutes as Leonardo tried to find the key to solving the puzzle. When the Master rose, it was with a creak like a gnarled tree in a breeze, crackling and popping as he stretched. He halted Leonardo's pacing by clasping the artist's shoulders in his hands and guiding him to stand in front of the wooden plank.

"Your task, my boy, is to fix it." He put a clean brush between his apprentice's fingers and pushed him to sit upon the stool. "Call for me when you have it!" he boomed as he walked away.

Such trust was a measure of great respect. Leonardo had not anticipated being asked to fix his Master's greatest work to date. He had suspected he would be chiseling at stone, despite it being his weakest field of study. An overwhelming sense of panic descended as he stared at the unfinished work.

The breeze tickled at the nape of his neck and the ends of his short beard. A bee droned lazily, bumbling from painted flower to painted flower in the hopes that one held nectar. A bird trilled brightly somewhere outside.

Nothing. Nothing was coming to mind. Years of study culminating in this one task, this chance to prove himself, and now he could not even begin.

Dust danced in the air in a swirling *sarabande*. Somewhere in the distance, he heard the scrape of a *garzone* boy sweeping the floor. Sunlight warmed Leonardo's back, sinking beneath his clothes and into his body like Jaculpo's warmth did when they curled up together in bed.

That was it!

He pulled over his palette and hastily began mixing oil paints upon its surface, admiring the colors as he made them. A vibrant blue to match the robes of the other angel and John the Baptist, regal and elegant. A red to match Jesus's striped loincloth, and a pink for flushed cheeks. Gold like a sunbeam, captured and encased in paint. Pale olive for the skin.

Charcoal coated his fingers as he sketched a figure roughly

into the corner of the painting, just beside the previously painted young angel. The face he drew was as familiar to him as his own. More so. He had drawn it a hundred times already. The charcoal dropped onto the table with a clatter, and the brush rose once more.

He loved the way a paintbrush looked just after it had been dipped into the paint. The way color clung to the bristles, easily discarded and just as easily soaked up within the hairs. He dragged his stool across the floor with a scrape and bent to the task at hand.

Golden curls came first, tumbling over a shoulder. Jaculpo's fell just like that when he laughed, when he turned his head to see if Leonardo had caught his clever little jest, when he wanted to see if the artist was watching him, or sometimes, even, when he was cross.

An earnest face, eyes turned upwards toward the figure of Jesus. The goldsmith who had filled Leonardo's heart to the brim wore the same look when they imagined the world together, huddled close. When they spoke of the futures they dreamed of, surrounded by sweet summer hay. When they whispered in the ephemeral flicker of candlelight before bed of how they wished things could be.

A robe, draped over the angel's arms and pooling upon the stones beneath him, was cradled close to his chest the same way Jaculpo had held Leonardo's tunic just that morning.

The angel's own robe came next, falling over his legs and feet, hiding them from sight and yet clinging to them in the same way the blankets often tangled around his suitor.

He wished he could convey in the paint the way Jaculpo smelled. The sharp tang of metal and the crisp sweetness of apples. The way he always tasted of sweets, any and all sorts. Sweet fruits, sweet honey, sweet pastries. It didn't matter what kind, the goldsmith would filch as many as he could and pay for what he couldn't.

Leonardo poured his heart and soul into capturing the face of the blond, the bearing of him. It was easy to capture the innocence and kindness of him, that side of him that emerged only when the two of them were alone. It was harder to capture the passion in his eyes and the curve of his lips, or his devotion in the careful cradling of Jesus's robe. Adding the halo to the angel's head completed the look to perfection, and he wondered why he had never noticed it above Jaculpo's head before.

He lost himself to the paint, to the colors and the folds of fabric and the gleam of sunlight in the strands of golden hair.

Eventually, he turned to the unfinished world of the painting. The stones beneath the two angels were pale and white, like the stones of the piazza where he and Jaculpo had first met. The water around Jesus's feet was crystalline clear, like the fountain in the courtyard of the lady's palazzo, where he and Jaculpo had danced beneath an apple tree after their first kiss. The broad swath of sky turned blue, the same bright color of the awning above Jaculpo's stall in the marketplace.

He hardly noticed the time, or the way the light in the studio had begun to fade.

At last, he sat back. His eyes roved over the work. His heart warmed. "I found it," he whispered.

The sunset had summoned Verrocchio from the depths of the workshop, covered in a layer of dust that made him look like one of his sculptures brought to life. His boots on the worn stone floor of the studio were as familiar a sound as the villa doors closing each night.

"Well!" he boomed. "Let me see what you have done, yes?" The Master picked up a brush as he came around the edge of the wooden plank.

Brilliant light from the sunset painted the new angel in burnished gold, bringing life to his eyes at last. Leonardo swore he could see the figure inhale and hold it fast. Even as the light faded, he held it, as if that final moment of glory had finished the tableau.

Verrocchio stood beside his apprentice in stunned silence, head tipped back and eyes drifting slowly over the drying paint. "You fixed it," he said at last. "You found what it was missing."

"Love," Leonardo said softly. "It was missing love."

His Master set the paintbrush down on the edge of the table, tucking his hands behind his back. Leonardo remained on the stool, fingers loose around his brush. In silence, the two watched the day's last light go from gilding the painting to barely touching it with its light. The *garzone* boy came out to light the lanterns around them, then vanished.

"Have you told him?" Verrocchio asked as the sun finally sank out of sight behind the hills.

"No," Leonardo answered, "but do you know, I think I will."

About the Author

October K Santerelli is an author from Denver, Colorado. He writes primarily epic fantasy and spends his free time gardening and gaming. He lives with his two dogs and his best friend, and writes full-time. "Mi Jaculpo" is his first published short story. He is the cowriter and art director for the graphic novel, *The Chrestomathy*.

ONE FOR HUNGER, TWO FOR JOY

TANYA HALES

Because I needed the day to go perfectly, I made sure to wear my best pair of fake glasses. Square. Thick-rimmed. Very nerdy, which was the whole point.

After all, muses only visited those who took things seriously.

Our car pulled into the high school parking lot, and my mom gave me her classic reassuring smile. "You've studied so hard. You've got this."

I grinned. "Those exams are going down!"

She tried to reach into the back seat to grab my backpack for me, but I beat her to it, saying, "It's fine! I've got it!" I didn't want her to notice the bulges from my unusual cargo.

It wasn't textbooks that I was bringing to school today.

I reached for the door handle, then paused. Trying to keep my voice natural, I said, "Did you hear about the winner of the statewide art contest?"

Apprehension replaced my mother's former look of pride. "Yes, I heard you and Dad arguing about it."

"We weren't arguing. Well, maybe a little, but only because he didn't believe me at first that the competition's winner was only fifteen." I paused. "And muse-touched."

My mother didn't even breathe for a moment. Then she leaned forward and told me softly, "Dilly, you don't need a muse to succeed."

"I know, I know," I said, trying to sound carefree. "All I'm saying is that muses do choose teens sometimes."

My mother began twirling a lock of her dark hair, and I almost reached out to still her hand. I only refrained because I had that particular nervous tic as well. "You're smart enough on your own," she said. "You've got talent and work ethic. Why wish for a muse when you can make your own inspiration?"

My eyes flicked toward the car speaker, which was playing one of Stella Hashimoto's newest songs. She'd been visited by a muse four years ago and had since been the rising star in any musical genre she tried. She was only twenty-two, but no one else could measure up to the sheer amount of talent her muse had given her. No one but other muse-touched musicians.

In fact, since 2000, *all* the people making significant contributions to the creative and scientific world had been muse-touched. And my parents knew it. The only reason they argued that I didn't need a muse was because they didn't think I could get one.

I'd prove them wrong.

As if sensing my skepticism, Mom put a hand on my knee. "You, Diella Magnolia Whitfield, are good enough to succeed, even if a muse never graces your presence. Got it?"

I gave her a placating smile. She was wrong, of course, but I had to convince her that I believed her. My plans today depended on it. "You're right. It's about elbow grease ... study ... all that good stuff."

Her face lit up with relief. "Exactly. Now go crush those final exams. You'll do great."

We said goodbye, and she drove off, leaving me on the high school curb alone. She was right. I would do great. But I wasn't going to be taking my exams.

Nervous excitement zinged through my stomach like electricity through tangled wires. I stepped away down the sidewalk, refusing to look back at what I was leaving behind. I had a muse's attention to attract.

I ended up outside a tiny café downtown called the Sated Owl. It looked like the sort of place a starving artist might go if they wanted to brood over their creations and drink inappropriate amounts of coffee.

Before stepping inside, I glanced around. No one could see or hear muses except for those who were muse-touched, but in interviews I'd heard muse-touched people describe how their muses looked like ordinary humans. How many muses were running around, invisible to anyone but those they blessed with their inspiration? Were there any here now?

Just in case, I murmured, "Muses, you'll want to see this." Then I stepped into the café.

I claimed a table and laid out all my pages of drawings. I had notebooks full of detailed plans for the graphic novel I'd been dreaming of making for years. I had character drawings, reference images, and dozens of sketched pages. Yet, even after years of practice, I knew my art wasn't nearly good enough. I lacked experience and training. I couldn't make my brilliant vision a reality on my own. But if I had a muse ...

I'd been sketching for about fifteen minutes when someone slid into the chair across from me. I looked up to see my sister, Eddy—short for Edwina—out of breath with her black hair disheveled like she'd run all the way here.

"I got your text. I can't believe you're really doing this."

I gaped at her. "And I can't believe you're here! You weren't supposed to ditch school, too."

She shrugged like missing a day of final exams was no big deal. "You're going to need backup. So what's the plan?"

I let out a breath. Eddy was fourteen, two years younger than I was, but she was my stalwart rock. I felt stronger knowing she'd be with me. The nervous currents in my belly settled.

I tapped my pencil on the page before me. "Attract a muse. Be so awesome they can't ignore me anymore." My research had taught me that every muse was looking for something a little different. But, every time, they chose people who were talented, driven, and a bit quirky.

"Well, duh," Eddy said, "but why like this? I still don't get it, Dilly. Why aren't you finishing your exams to attract muses with all your straight A's?"

I snorted. "If only they were interested in smart kids acing tests. That must be too mainstream for them. I think muses want to see something a little more ... edgy."

"Edgy. So you chose a"—she lowered her voice—"run-down little coffee shop filled exclusively with old people having pancakes, toast, and milk ... because it's edgy?"

I looked around. There *were* a lot of elderly people inside the small, dim café, but still.

"Hey, just look at the situation at large!" I insisted. "This is edgy! By ditching my final exams, I'm proving to my muse how serious I am about my art. A lot of people will never forgive me after this. Mom and Dad will feel betrayed, my teachers will be disappointed, and my grades may suffer permanently. There's no going back. But I'm doing it anyway."

I had to.

I'd been taught in school that muses had once been a metaphor for inspiration. But at the turn of the millennium, that changed. Literal muses, often the ghosts of creative individuals, began visiting and granting people insane amounts of talent and drive. Many speculated that the muses had always been there, doing this throughout history, just invisibly. Now, though, people could see them. Some people anyway. Those the muses deemed worthy.

I was going to be one of those people.

I needed a muse. I was desperate for one the way a starving man feels hunger. No matter how hard I worked, most of my art was worthless to anyone but me. I knew I could never be happy until I'd created something with real value, something amazing.

I pulled out a stack of pre-sketched comic page layouts. All the details were in light pencil so I could glide through the inking without pause.

"It's go time," I said. "Time to make this look easy."

As Eddy sat beside me, foot tapping to the rhythm of the old jazz song playing on the café radio, I got to work. Using my lucky pen, I drew crisp, smooth, beautiful lines over my sketches, making them gleam in the dim light. I worked fast, my pen sliding across the paper like an Olympic skater on ice. I finished one page, then another and another.

I smiled to myself. I had to look like a professional.

"You've gotten a lot better," Eddy said grudgingly as she admired my work.

I grinned, passing the inked pages to her. "Erase the pencil lines for me, will you?"

She rolled her eyes, but complied. That was good. Looking like I had an assistant would lend me credibility.

We worked together for hours. I didn't even realize it was almost 3:00 until I heard my stomach rumble.

I got up to buy us some sandwiches. When I came back to the table, I noticed someone had settled at the table next to ours. The dark-haired young man was eyeing my drawings with interest. That would be distracting. If he kept ogling my art from across the tables, there was no way I'd be able to focus. I took a seat next to Eddy so that my back was to the boy.

Eddy took her sandwich as she poked through one of my binders. She pulled out an old paper covered in video game level designs. She grinned. "You should work on this. It's bound to bring all the muses to the yard."

I snatched the paper so fast that I tore the corner. "No! Absolutely not! I can't let them know about my secret love." I threw the paper onto one of the seats and out of sight.

"I was kidding. You always take things so seriously." Eddy flicked my fake glasses. "Nerd." Her voice held a forced casualness, and I knew what she was thinking. She was remembering the days when we had once designed video games and maps together. It had been our greatest shared passion. But it was a carefree fun I'd left behind eons ago.

I didn't work on things for fun anymore. Now I worked with purpose. I had to create something that mattered, something that people would remember. And a passion for video game design was not that, even if it had been my first love.

"Well," I said, "now that we've made some solid progress, I think it's time for my props."

First, I put on a trench coat and fedora. It felt like something an angsty 1920s artist might wear as he wandered around the city at night, seeking inspiration. Next came an extra-long blue pencil and a large toy peacock.

Eddy stared at the stuffed animal like it was a true symbol of my insanity.

"What?" I demanded. "I like peacocks. Flannery O'Connor liked peacocks. They're obviously inspiring."

I looked to see if the boy was still watching. He was. Even worse, one of the café employees walked by and chuckled.

I pressed my lips together. I was beyond the point of embarrassment.

I surveyed my props and murmured, "If only I'd been able to find a typewriter ..."

Eddy flipped through my comic pages skeptically. "What in the world would you do with a typewriter?"

"I'd look creative, that's what!" I took the papers and sorted them with an important air. The hat made me feel important. "There have only been a handful of muse-touched comic creators, and I bet it's because all muses are stuffy and old-fashioned. They probably all have mustaches and top hats, or dresses covered in cat hair. Looking young and hip will only scare them away."

My phone lit up. Mom was calling. She must have realized I was missing.

I took a deep breath and continued inking my pages. Eddy's phone went off next. She ignored it too.

Several hours and a million missed calls later, Eddy said, "Mom is texting. She thinks I'm with friends, but she's freaking out about you. She says if they can't find you soon, they're going to call the police."

"The police?" I demanded. "Isn't that a bit extreme?"

Eddy gave me a look. "Not when it's about you. You're their goody-two-shoes who's never broken a family rule. If it's me missing, life goes on, but ... you know." Her fingers danced across her phone screen. "I'm telling Mom you're fine and that you just need some space right now."

I began twirling my hair around my finger and had to force myself to stop. "But now they know you're involved."

She nodded. "You'd better pull this off, or we're both dead. What else do you have in that bag?"

By the time night fell, we had every prop of mine out and in use. I was doodling new comic book layouts in my thickest, most artsy looking leather-bound notebook. I used a feather quill pen dipped in a bottle of expensive ink. I even held the end of a fake wooden pipe between my teeth. Muses often appeared during moments of people's great performances, or when they were in the throes of creating something amazing. Would this work?

My parents had called us a dozen times each and sent us increasingly pointed messages about how they were going to confiscate our favorite belongings and ground us for eternity. My desperation was mounting. Good thing the café stayed open all night. We might need it.

The dark-haired boy was still sitting behind me at his table. He was reading a battered paperback novel, but he kept throwing me amused glances. Well, who cared if he thought my efforts were hilarious.

I put my quill down and began twirling my hair again. This time, I didn't stop myself.

"This is it," I whispered to Eddy. "I'm desperate enough now. My final phase of the plan is to show the muses how serious I am. I'm going to delete all of my social media accounts."

Eddy's mouth fell open. "No way."

I pulled out my phone, heart hammering. Would this finally be dramatic enough to matter?

Behind me, the boy chuckled. I turned to glower at him. Did he mind? I was about to lose years' worth of records of my life and adventures, and he thought it was funny? My eyes locked with his. He grinned.

"What do you keep looking at?" Eddy asked me, not bothering to keep her voice down.

I turned back to her, embarrassed that she couldn't read the social cues. "Not so loud!" I whispered. "That boy over there. He keeps watching us."

Eddy strained her neck, looking around. "What boy? Are you talking about the barista? Because he's, like, sixty."

I wanted to smack my forehead. "No, the guy one table down from us."

Eddy stared at me with a mixture of concern and alarm in her eyes. "You've finally lost it, haven't you?"

I gaped at her, then turned to stare at the teenage boy who was back to reading his book.

"You can't see him, can you?" I stood from my chair so fast that it fell over.

The boy looked up as my chair crashed to the ground, then flashed me a charming smile.

I marched over to his table. Eddy followed, looking ready to restrain me in case my madness took over and I leapt on the table to do an insane jig.

"Do we know each other?" I demanded of the boy.

Panicked, Eddy asked, "Dilly, who are you talking to?"

The boy's smile widened. He had a very nice smile. His eyes were so dark brown they looked black in the low café lighting. I felt myself sinking into his gaze for a moment until I gave my head a little shake to snap myself out of it.

"We don't know each other yet," he said, "but we could get acquainted if you're interested."

I stared, then grinned, heart bursting with elation, and whirled toward my sister. "Eddy, we did it! You can't see him, but there's a guy sitting here. Right here! I can see and hear him. Do you know what this means?" I grabbed her shoulders, squeezing them tightly. "It worked!"

Her face was awed. "You're muse-touched?"

The boy cleared his throat. "Not quite yet."

I turned back to him eagerly. "Why? Do we actually have to touch?" I considered leaping across the table so as to get it over with, but then he stood.

"Please, let's take a look at what you've got."

Eager to obey, I pulled Eddy back to our table as the boy came over to examine my comic pages. He looked at my open sketchbook with interest, but made no attempt to flip its pages.

"You can't interact with anything, can you?" I asked. "To move things around or look through my papers?"

He shook his head. "Muses are spirits. The only thing I'll be able to interact with will be you. If I choose you."

Eddy glanced back and forth between me and the empty, silent air I was talking to. She looked distinctly unnerved. "This is going to be hard to get used to."

I ignored her, asking the muse, "What do you mean, if you choose me?"

He relaxed into his chair, folding his arms behind his head. I noticed a large tattoo on his arm. It was a beautiful depiction of a bird tangled in thorny vines, its beak open, its eyes hollow. "Well, we've only just met. I need to decide if you're worth it, don't I?"

My heart sank. "I thought that's why you showed up." What more would I have to do?

"Let's start with introductions," the boy said, unmoved. "You can call me Chance. And you are ...?"

"Diella Magnolia Whitfield," I said, trying to sound confident, like I was at a job interview. "But you can call me Dilly."

"Well, Dilly, you should know that this"—he gestured to all my props on the table—"was the most hilarious thing I've ever seen anyone try in order to attract a muse."

"Hilarious?" I huffed, mouth falling open. I turned to Eddy. "He thinks my techniques to attract a muse are hilarious!"

Eddy blinked slowly at me. "I would have found it hilarious too if you hadn't been so serious about it."

Chance snapped his fingers. "That's it exactly. You took your quest so seriously I couldn't help but come and find out more. So, tell me. You make comics. Is that your end goal?" He suddenly ducked his head to look under the table. I peeked down and saw the page of video game maps had fallen to the floor, face up.

"Ignore that!" I insisted, sweeping the page away with my foot. "That's just something I used to do for fun. But not anymore. I make serious art."

His raised his eyes to meet mine. "Like comics?"

I pressed my palms against my jeans to wipe away my sweat. What if he didn't like my answer?

Noting my hesitation, Chance said, "Muses are drawn to whatever appealed to them in their former life. Which is why you're in luck." He gave me a dazzling, yet somehow devious smile. "Because I personally like comics. I even went through a video game phase before I got serious."

I blinked. If he'd enjoyed video games while alive, he couldn't be a very old muse.

Chance stretched his fingers to pop his knuckles. "Shall we get started?"

My stomach jolted. "You mean you're going to help me?" My heart hammered so hard that I wanted to leap up and run circles around the table in excitement. "So what can you do for me?"

Chance leaned forward, and I found myself sinking into his gaze again. "Would you like to find out?" He reached his hand out, then paused. "Just one more question." His eyes narrowed calculatingly. "What are you willing to do in order to create something that matters?"

"What am I willing to do?" I whispered. "Anything."

Eddy was staring at me, wide-eyed. "I hope you're not selling your soul—"

The outside world melted into a blur as Chance's hand touched mine. He moved to stand behind my chair, leaning over my shoulder as he guided my hand. The room around me faded away. Even my sense of my own body dissolved. All I could feel was his guiding touch as he moved my fingers to grab my lucky pen. Together, we picked up one of the unfinished comic layouts and put pen to page.

It began like a burst of fireworks. My hand moved impossibly fast across the page, yet it felt like the most natural thing in the world. Perfect lines of ink flowed from my hand at what seemed like the speed of light. Full character drawings appeared like blossoming flowers. Panel lines and speech bubbles and sound effects. Page after page—all full of ink and art.

I became vaguely aware of Eddy at my side, laying down more sheets of paper in front of me as I filled the ones I already had. She seemed to be moving in fast-motion, like she, too, was unbound from the tether of time.

In what felt like a few minutes, I finished inking every comic page I'd previously sketched out. I considered switching back to a pencil to finish some more layouts, but with Chance's hand guiding mine, I chose to flip to a blank page and begin drawing in ink with no sketches to guide me. What once seemed impossible was now the obvious solution. Why sketch first when I could go straight to the finished product?

And the illustrations pouring out of my fingers were perfect.

I was vaguely aware of night passing and daylight reappearing through the windows. People began to gather around the table. Eddy explained something distantly to them as I worked. Someone touched my shoulder, trying to shake me out of my trance, but I shrugged them off. I had work to do.

People were taking photos and videos. I ignored them.

Eddy tried to push a cup of water to my lips. I shoved it away. How dare she get water near my art!

I heard my mother's concerned voice as she tried to press food into my hands. Oh, so she was finally here to witness my brilliance? I pushed the food away. Didn't they understand how important this was? Was Chance the only person who understood? I could still feel his solid presence at my back, his firm, insistent guidance on my hand. He and the pen were the only things that were real.

Night fell again. I could feel a dull ache behind my eyes, but my work was not done. I drew even faster. I knew I could finish my entire graphic novel in one sitting if I kept this up. And yet, something was changing. Even though the art still poured from my fingers, it felt distant now. Everything was growing darker. I was fading.

I saw myself drawing as if from a distance. The empowered, artistic Dilly sat glowing in a spotlight, while the ghostly apparition that was my current awareness sat cold and tired in the dark.

Chance walked toward me out of the darkness. He stood next to me, arms folded, and watched the muse-touched version of me continue to draw flawlessly.

"You're holding up well. Many artists collapse or give up after just a few hours. They don't have enough resolve. You obviously don't have that problem."

I remained sitting on the black, empty floor, staring numbly. "Is it supposed to be this way? This whole experience has felt so ... rushed. And now ... so distant."

"Every muse is different. This is just how I work."

"So working with you will always make me feel this ... empty? There won't ever be peace?"

Chance snorted. "Did you get into this business for peace? I thought you got into it so you could make something amazing."

More time passed, and an aching coldness closed in on me. I was being crushed by a weight I knew I couldn't bear much longer.

I whispered, "I'm dying, aren't I?"

Chance laughed. "Of course not. I didn't take you for the type who'd die so easily."

My shoulders slumped under the unknown pressure, even as my other self continued to draw. "When will I get to rest? When will this be done?"

Chance crouched beside me, giving me a pitying smile like I was a whining child. "It's never done. Sure, you can eat and sleep sometimes, but you only win by never truly stopping. If you stop, you lose."

"So I'll never be satisfied?"

"It's not about being satisfied. It's about being remembered. It's about accomplishing something that makes your life matter."

I shook my head, wishing I could break this numbness. "That sounds like a great way to never be happy."

"Listen," Chance said, finally sounding angry, "someday you will die. Someday, everyone will forget you. Unless you do something worth remembering. You need to make something they can't possibly ignore, something they can't possibly forget."

I sensed in him a wild hunger, a yawning, craving emptiness. All those things he was describing ... those were things he had never had. He'd failed to make something lasting while alive. He'd been forgotten.

I suddenly noticed that Chance wasn't crouching casually anymore. He was kneeling, his shoulders bowing just like mine were. The same weight that was upon me was crushing him as well. I looked at his tattoo of the bird entangled in thorns and shivered.

I struggled to breathe. "We can't go on like this."

It wasn't just about me anymore. We were in this as a united whole. We were intertwined, our creative journeys coming together as one.

Chance looked at me, and I could see the dark desperation in his eyes. "We have to. We have to create something that matters."

I gazed at the version of me drawing flawless pages of art. She was brilliant. A genius. But also ... empty. She had once created things because it brought her joy. Now she'd decided she would never be happy until she made something that people would love, praise, revere ...

But would it ever be enough?

"I know you said it's not about being satisfied," I told Chance, "but if you died right now—for real this time—would this have been enough? With the crowd around us and the spotlight on our creations, do you feel like you could finally rest easy, knowing that your life mattered?"

I thought about the pages of video game designs I'd joyfully created with Eddy. I thought of how I'd abandoned them once I'd decided that having fun wasn't a good enough reason to do anything. Chance seemed to have gone through something similar.

Tears filled my eyes. How I wanted to sit down with Eddy now and create simply for the sake of creating. No expectations. Just joy.

Asking myself just as much as Chance, I said, "If your soul died now, would you feel like something was still missing?"

Our gazes locked, intertwined.

"Happiness," I whispered. "Don't you want it?"

Chance closed his eyes.

I closed mine as well.

Once again, I could feel myself at the café table, feverishly putting ink to the paper. I could feel Chance's hand on mine, pushing me onward and onward.

"Let me go," I told him.

"No. We're not done."

"Let go of me and listen!" I took a shuddering breath, struggling to focus past the crushing pressure. "I want you to have a turn. A chance to create the things you never did while you were alive."

Chance said nothing.

"What is it that you love?"

I felt his grip slackening, his guidance waning. My hand slowed. Everything slowed.

"Let me help you," I whispered.

This time, I took his hand. I pressed my pen into his trembling fingers and helped hold it steady. He couldn't truly touch the pen, but he could touch me. Together, we could do this.

For a moment, we were completely still. Painfully so. Then, Chance's hand moved. My hand moved along with it, carefully, slowly moving the pen in beautifully delicate strokes. Before, his guidance had been all fierce, brilliant efficiency, but now his touch was gentle, almost loving, like he didn't want to miss a single moment of how it felt to create his own art again.

He finished the last lines, and I finally opened my eyes.

On the paper before us was a bird with outstretched wings. Unlike the tattoo on his arm, this bird did not have hollow eyes. Its eyes were bright, its mouth open in wondrous, glorious song.

I breathed deep, feeling the weight lift.

The raw, empty hunger in both of us was gone.

And finally ... there was joy.

I slumped in my chair and looked at Chance. "I think I need a nap."

Finally able to see clearly, I looked at the crowd of people around me. Most were strangers. I even saw several news reporters. But sitting beside me was my faithful sister. Her expression was both expectant and relieved. Behind her, I could see my parents approaching, food and water in hand like they'd just been waiting for me to snap out of my trance.

I had a lot to explain.

But I had time.

"After the nap," I said to Chance, "I know what we should work on."

He squeezed my hand. "What do you have in mind?"

I ducked under the table to pull out the sheet of video game level designs. Setting it before us, I smiled. "Let's work on something fun."

About the Author

When Tanya Hales was a baby, she enjoyed books by chewing them to pieces before eventually moving on to the higher art of reading. Tanya splits her time between her work as a writer, an illustrator, and a mother, all of which she loves intensely. She now lives in the Utah Valley with her family, constantly daydreaming about imaginary worlds.

THE HUNTER AND THE HUNTED

RAPHYEL M. JORDAN

I t was another beautiful summer day in the country of Dahomey, Africa, as Oseye climbed a lone tree set upon a hill. The young woman gazed across the terrain of a valley below, evaluating the layout of the land. The area was lush and green, complimented by a riverbed that was fueled by a nearby waterfall she had just taken a drink from.

"I've finally found it," the huntress said to herself, relieved.

Venturing to the river below wouldn't be easy, given that wild game would be present upon arrival. Lions wouldn't trail too far behind. However, Oseye was more concerned about another predator, one far more exotic and treacherous, perhaps even supernatural. She was hunting the Grootslang.

Legend said the creature lived in a faraway cave located in the south, though it often journeyed to this specific riverbed in her region since it offered the freshest water. The beast—part elephant, part snake—was an accidental abomination made by the deities when the world was new and they were unaware of the consequences in making such a powerful creature. While most hunters avoided the land because of the creature, Oseye had no choice but to risk an encounter if she wanted to pass her trial and become a Mino warrior, one of the all-female elite soldiers chosen to defend her country. Besides, she'd have a little help as soon as *he* arrived.

"Most mortals stay clear of this land," a voice below her proclaimed. "Was I that bad of a teacher?"

"There you are, Agé." Oseye hopped down from the tree. "Thanks for meeting me here."

"My dear Little Oseye, as Fon of the Hunt, you know it's my duty to guide you. Besides, you're a favorite."

Oseye smiled as she leapt into his greeting arms. His face had remained unchanged ever since she was little. Her friend's skin still looked as fresh as umber, perfectly molded on his refined physique, and his hazel eyes glistened in the sun. Clean-shaven, he boasted a prominent jawline. Many would describe Agé as being the most handsome specimen of a man they had ever seen, if he were but a man. Fons like him were deities credited for creating and bringing order to the world, each gifted in a specific role.

Agé pulled away and examined Oseye, a proud smile on his face.

"I always look forward to this day," he said. "No matter how many times I've witnessed it. And to think you now face the trial to become a Mino ... I must be getting old."

"Very funny."

"You human creatures grow too quickly for my liking. I won't know what to do with myself when I hear that you are to be married."

"Can we make sure that I survive all nine days of the trial first?" Oseye led her friend down the hill toward a ledge. She pointed at the riverbed.

Agé examined the terrain, then groaned. "Please don't tell me you intend on hunting *it*."

"Only with your blessing, of course," the huntress was quick to say.

"Did you bring diamonds in case it needs to be bargained with? The Grootslang's cruelty can only be quenched by jewelry."

"You know candidates can't bring anything during the trial, otherwise I would've brought my spear." Oseye spread her arms wide. "See? No shoes. No water. Not even a machete. Just as instructed."

"Was your common sense left behind, as well?"

Oseye punched him in the arm. "Fon Agé, surviving the wilderness alone will not be enough for me to pass the trials. Everyone back home thinks I have it easy since one of the great Fons is always at my side to help me directly. I have to risk it—no options, no bargains."

Agé placed his hands on his hips, a stern grimace etched over his face. "Oseye—"

"Don't look so worried, silly. With you here, I'm certain we'll manage, and then everyone will know I am truly worthy of becoming a Mino."

Agé shook his head and chuckled. "You know I'll never be one to say you're incapable of anything, Oseye."

"Great! Then let's go!"

The Fon grabbed the huntress by the hand before she hurried off. "But first, we need to talk."

In all her years, Oseye had never heard Agé sound so serious. Something was wrong, or at least something was about to be wrong. Given the sternness in his eyes, Agé was about to give her the most dreaded news imaginable.

She released the Fon's hand, backing away from him as if he was plagued by an illness. "You're not going to help me."

When Agé didn't deny it, Oseye's stomach twisted and churned. Her skin turned cold as ice, and her heartbeat raced. She had always drawn comfort in knowing Agé would protect her. He had to. He was the deity of hunters. It was his responsibility. *She* was his responsibility!

"Little Oseye, let me explain—"

"You can't leave me, Agé! Not now. Am I being punished? What wrong have I caused you?"

"No, dear child," Agé said, cupping Oseye's face. "Throughout your young life, never have you done me wrong. You are the purest of souls. Such is why you can see me in the flesh."

Oseye shut her eyes as tears ran down her face. "Then why are you abandoning me? I need you."

"And that's exactly why I can't do this task with you. I've spoken to my kin, and we all agree that my favoring you has diminished your potential. Oseye, you must learn to manage on your own just as any other would, even more since you want to become a defender of your state."

He sat on the grass, bringing Oseye down with him. "You and I have had a unique bond. Because you can see me, I've been able to train you, travel with you, make you the hunter any soul would dream of being. You've had quite the advantage your entire life because of it."

Oseye wiped her eyes. "Advantage? Fon Agé, I've worked twice as hard to prove my worth to my people because everyone looks upon me with jealousy and disdain. And yet, I don't care because I have you. Don't you see? Without you, I have nothing. I *am* nothing."

Agé shook his head. "You speak your own truth, yet you still don't understand why I shouldn't help you." The Fon stood up. "I will still watch you from afar, and you will even hear my voice in the wind if your heart is willing. Beyond that, you're on your own. If you truly want to prove you're worthy of becoming a Mino to your people, then you'll manage without me, just as everyone else does."

Oseye grumbled as she curled her fingers into fists. "That does sound fair, but what about the Grootslang? I can't fight it alone."

"Then you best leave this place and stay clear of it. No one told you to fight the beast."

The huntress stomped the ground, annoyed. She hated it when he was right. Then she took a deep breath, calming herself.

"If this is what it takes, Agé. The least I can do is try, as you've always taught me."

The Fon winked at her. "Then be careful. I believe in you."

A breeze from the west swooshed by, as it always did before Oseye and Agé parted ways. Leaves swept around the Fon, and he disappeared, leaving the huntress, alone. She backed away from the ledge, her spirit shaken.

"Agé?" she called out. "Are you there? You said I could hear you in the wind."

No response. Apparently, his absence had already broken her heart beyond repair.

The huntress examined the riverbed again, which now appeared farther away with more treacherous terrain. Something bristled in the grass from behind, and she spun around. Any other day, she would've shrugged it off, accounting it for a small rodent. Today, however, it could've been a wild dog, a lion, maybe even a warthog. It was a dreadful summer day in the country of Dahomey. Maybe her becoming a Mino was a foolish dream, after all.

Then the huntress laughed at herself. "Enough. I can do this. *They're* wrong."

A sudden howl in the distance shook the ground like thunder, numbing Oseye's thoughts. Flocks of birds in the trees below flew away as the game approaching the riverbank scattered. She narrowed her eyes as the Grootslang—a hundred meters away—strolled toward the water.

Seeing the beast in the flesh, Oseye realized the legends had gotten it wrong. The Grootslang's head was shaped like an elephant—its trunk curled in so it wouldn't drag across the ground, and two giant tusks arched toward its mouth—and its scaled tail was the size of a python. But the legends had neglected to mention its four strong legs and its body reminiscent of a wildebeest. Given its physique, it had to be as strong as it was fast. Chasing down a human would require little effort.

"Agé?" she heard her timid voice call out.

The Grootslang stopped, forcing Oseye to cover her mouth. Surely it couldn't have heard her! The creature turned its large head from left to right, as if searching for what had interrupted its drink. The monster sniffed the air, then locked eyes on her.

"It's okay," she assured herself, backing away carefully. "At least *he* believes in me."

The monster howled again, and Oseye scanned the ledge in search of something—anything—she could use to defend herself. Her options were limited.

Stories warned that people died within a minute of the Grootslang spotting them. The only way to survive an encounter was to lay all valuables at its feet, but since Oseye had nothing, she would have to use the environment to her advantage. Crawl into a cave. Go through the woods. Leap into the river and hope it would diminish the creature's scent of human flesh. Since the waterfall was too high for a safe dive, the only option Oseye had was that stupid tree back on the hill she had climbed.

The Grootslang roared, giving away its position. It was now only fifty meters away. Impossible! No creature could be that fast.

Oseye ran for the hill, the wind cutting at her eyes. When she reached the tree. Instead of grabbing the nearest branch and climbing, however, she tugged with all her might trying to break it. She wouldn't back down. Mino warriors were meant to fight. *Conquer or die.* That was their motto.

The branch refused to give way, despite her efforts. The monster snarled like a wild dog as it neared. Oseye gritted her teeth, pulling at the tree again. The branch gave a timid creak, but nothing more.

"Break, damn you!" she cried. "Please!"

The ground quaked with each stride the monster made toward Oseye. She was going to be ripped to pieces and eaten alive like an antelope. Death wouldn't be instant, but slow, agonizing, and mortifying.

"Agé, help!"

The branch snapped off into her hands, and she spun around to swing with all her might. She was greeted with rows of teeth slicing into her right shoulder. The pain was so great that her screams were lost in gasps. The Grootslang lifted her body off the ground with its mouth, shaking her with such ferociousness, she thought her shoulder would dislocate.

She clawed at its nose with her free arm, and in return, the monster smacked her in the face with one of its paws, using its trunk to pin her down.

Though in a daze, Oseye saw splatters of red on the once-green grass—blood that had once belonged to her. But nothing was hers anymore. Since she had no jewels to exchange, the Grootslang would claim her life, and she couldn't do anything about it.

"Stop," she heard herself plead.

How cruel, to be killed so horribly on the first day. If any remains were left to be found, her family would not even have the peace of knowing she had put up a fight. They would forever conclude she had suffered dearly, too weak to defend herself, just as they had always told her. That she died because she was useless.

The huntress tried to squirm free, enraged at the thought. She still had so much to prove, and no creature—whether it be normal or mystical—would dare take that dream from her. She'd show the Grootslang. She'd show them all.

Oseye screamed at the top of her lungs and grabbed the nearby broken branch with her free arm. She rammed the jagged end into the monster's face. The creature yipped like a hyena as it swatted her away. Seizing the opportunity, the huntress scurried off, holding her wounded right shoulder, knowing the monster would be quick to recover and punish her dearly.

She reached the waterfall's ledge. If the Grootslang didn't kill her, the impending drop would. On the other hand, the fall could kill the monster, as well. The creature rubbed its blinded eye before turning its attention back to her, and Oseye eased her heels to the ledge, smirking.

"Face me, monster!" the huntress demanded. "I'm right here."

The Grootslang charged, and just when Oseye was about to dive away, it stopped and, without warning, smacked the huntress off the ledge with its tail and into the stream below.

Oseye awoke to the clamor of wildlife amid a dense and dark oasis. It was nighttime, the full moon offering little light beyond the few pokes it made through the lush leaves overhead. She must've been out for hours. How fortunate for her that the legend about the Grootslang losing a person's scent in water was true. Regardless, she had more troubles to deal with beyond being eaten.

Oseye rubbed her left cheek, feeling around the edges of three deep gashes slashed across it as she trudged out of the stream. She examined her right arm, the water having numbed it along with the blood loss. Upon reaching the tiny shore, she curled into a ball. She sneezed; she'd catch pneumonia if she didn't warm herself soon, her wounds hastening the process.

Her first day of the trial had seen her being mauled by a supernatural predator, tossed into a river, and her clothes drenched. Oseye rolled onto her back, swallowing the cry building in her chest. She had failed. Thinking she could fight the Grootslang was beyond foolish. Now it'd be on the hunt for what she had done to its eye, and she was in no shape to fend for herself once it found her. Perhaps she was better off hurrying back home to safety.

No. She'd rather die than prove the naysayers right. Oseye

eyed the stream. Maybe it was *deep* enough. Maybe she should just end it all now.

"My poor Oseye. Look what it did to you."

Agé towered over her, and she turned away, ashamed. She didn't want to see him peering down like she was a pathetic specimen that would eventually die like any other mortal.

Instead, the Fon rolled Oseye onto her side, and she bit her lip as the movement pulled at her injuries. "That horrid thing. Your wounds run almost to the bone."

He stood up to sniff the air, then chuckled. "And you made quite the friend in it, didn't you? It's a good ways from here since losing your scent, though it clearly hunts for you. You need to get up, quickly."

The huntress, however, refused to budge. "I'm finished, Agé."

"You most certainly will be if you don't clean those wounds and dry yourself. You'll die of fever."

"Look at me, Fon Agé!" Oseye cried. "I'm left alone for a mere moment and look what happened. Who cares about a fever when I obviously can't survive a single day in your absence, let alone nine?" She covered her face. "What the others think of me is true. I *am* useless."

The Fon crossed his arms. "Don't you ever speak such foolishness again. In all the ages, I've rarely seen a soul endure a physical encounter with that monster. And yet here you are, not only surviving an attack but wounding it in return. Trust me when I say that those who shed blood from the Grootslang don't have much time to brag about their wounds."

Oseye laid her head on the ground, still transfixed on the deep end of the stream. "Those poor lot were probably just smart enough to give in to their fate."

"No, my Little Oseye," Agé said. "Those poor lot were weak enough to give up on living. You, however, still have something to prove. And it's not to your people. It's not even to me." He directed Oseye's face to his, then pointed at her heart.

"So, is this what this is?" Oseye asked. "Surely the deities do not send monstrosities into our lives just to prove your points."

Agé rubbed the young woman's scratched cheek. "Never. We do not toss hardships on you out of mere amusement, though it's not our place to stand in the way of them. It's called life. It's joy and pain. It's laughter and tears. It's just. And yes, it's even cruel." The Fon grabbed Oseye's hand, squeezing it. "And that's what makes it beautiful. Not ugly. Just beautiful."

"I don't see how that's even possible."

"Of course, you can't," Agé said, laughing. "Why, it's a notion that even your elders struggle with. But that, Oseye, is the value in discovering such a truth."

Oseye looked away from the stream and into her friend's piercing eyes. "But that sounds impossible. I don't know if I can do it. I don't even know if I can do *this*."

"There's only one way to find out." Agé helped the huntress sit up. "Treasure this brief failure you had today and grow from it. Sunrise brings a new day, meaning you'll have another chance. Now, can you stand?"

Oseye examined the Fon's extended hand. He was always quick to catch her when she fell. Hold her when she cried. Now he wanted to help her up, only to leave her upon doing so.

"Will you still not help me, just this once?" she begged.

Agé smiled. "No."

She held his gaze, tears streaming down her face. "Then you can't even promise I'll survive this ordeal, can you?"

Her friend shook his head, hand still extended. "No. Are you scared?"

A sudden howl from afar silenced the entire jungle. The Grootslang had caught her scent again.

"Am I scared?" Oseye repeated. "More than you know."

And then the huntress grabbed Agé by the hand.

"Dear Little Oseye, I knew I could always believe in you." The Fon pulled her up, and with a gust of the west wind, he was gone.

The distant howl from the monster rang again, though Oseye no longer quivered at the rumble it made. Bruised and battered, she went deeper into the jungle, prepared to make what would be her final stand.

Oseye had traveled the entire night through the jungle, only stopping to tend to her wounds with whatever herbs she had found in the brushes. She was beyond exhausted, her injured body drained of energy. Even so, she pressed on, knowing her pursuer was nearby.

At noon, she took a brief rest and sharpened what had to be her tenth wooden spear. She had created a half-kilometer square perimeter around the oasis, learning the layout of the land so she could prepare evasive routes. Her plan was to attack the monster with her agility and a barrage of spears, hoping to tire out the beast. But she knew this creature of legend took pleasure in hunting down and toying with humans, and one that had caused it bodily harm would only entice its craving.

Had she not been injured, Oseye could've made more weapons, but she forced herself not to lose heart at her small stockpile of spears. She was hurt, but so was the monster. She had to believe in herself just as much as Agé did, if not more.

Another flock of birds scattered in flight as a deep growl shook the ground once more. The creature was close. Oseye grabbed a spear and crawled into a narrow passage made of tree roots. From there, she spotted the Grootslang lurking ahead, sniffing the ground, following her scent.

"That's right," she whispered. "Come and get me."

The creature paused and hissed as if hearing her words.

Oseye clutched her spear, the monster close enough for her to see its wounded eye.

Don't panic, she told herself. *Wait until it's in range.*

The Grootslang approached the opening Oseye had crawled through, and she pulled her feet closer to her body. She had chosen this spot because the narrow passage was too small for the beast to fit into. It would have to find another way in. But the only opening large enough would place it right over Oseye's hiding place.

The monster eased over to the opening.

Closer.

It lowered its head.

Closer.

It locked eyes with its prey.

Now!

Oseye thrust her spear, aiming for the throat. The monster quickly shifted to the right, and the spear stabbed its shoulder instead. The huntress crawled deeper into the pathway as the Grootslang cried out, roaring as it ripped apart the roots that protected Oseye. It slashed her left thigh with a tusk before grabbing and pulling her out of the passageway with its trunk.

Oseye hollered, unleashing a barrage of jabs into the creature's face and paws, refusing to let up.

The monster pulled away, dropping her. It tried to recapture her with its tail, but Oseye had already shimmied out of reach. The fall had broken her spear, so she left it behind.

She slid down to a lower level of the oasis, aiming for another spear she had propped against a tree.

The monster leapt and landed in front of her, blocking her from the weapon. Instead of lunging at her, it began circling her, looking for an opening to strike. The creature had learned not to underestimate her.

Good.

Oseye flung her arms into the air and roared at the Grootslang as she charged after it. Startled, the monster's back arched up like a cat. It swatted at Oseye, but the huntress slid underneath the creature, grabbed her second spear, and scurried up the tree.

She climbed with the grace of a dancer, despite her wounded arm and leg.

The Grootslang leapt, swiping at her, but it couldn't reach her. The wound she'd inflicted on its shoulder had split wider.

This was far from Oseye's original plan, but at least she was still alive. For now. Though the monster was hurt, a wounded four-legged creature could still outrun a wounded two-legged person like her. Her only hope now was to outclimb it.

Oseye could see the entire extent of the canopy upon reaching the top of the tree. She tried to catch her breath, but the trunk suddenly wobbled as the Grootslang dug its claws into the wood. She clamped onto the tree with both hands, her spear falling to the jungle floor.

As it neared, the creature seemed to grin at the trapped Oseye, as if knowing it had won the game.

Oseye closed her eyes and took steady breaths, refusing to panic. "Dearest Agé," she said aloud. "What would he do?"

A sudden breeze whooshed by the huntress, leaving what sounded like a gentle tune in its wake. Then it brushed by her again, as if an unknown presence was behind it.

"Strike," she heard the wind whisper.

Oseye tightened her grip on the tree. "What?"

"Little Oseye, strike now!"

She looked around at the emptiness surrounding her. "Agé? Is that you?"

When the tree shook again, the huntress glared at the monster, angry that it had the audacity to toy with her existence. She wouldn't give in. She couldn't. Maybe it just wasn't in her nature to do so. How interesting.

Oseye balanced her weight against the tree trunk, readying herself.

"I'll always believe in you," the voice in the wind declared.

"And I will not become the hunted," she shouted to the Grootslang. "Conquer or die!"

Oseye, taking faith in the whispers of the wind, leapt from the top of tree and toward the monster, arms extended, knocking it off its perch. Branches exploded as the huntress and the monster plummeted through what felt like a bottomless pit until the creature crashed into the ground with Oseye atop of it. She tumbled and rolled across the ground until her body came to a halt.

Lying on her side, her heart pounded against her chest. Was she alive, or had her spirit crossed over too quickly to notice? The sudden ache in her ribs suggested it was the former. Oseye tried to stand but fell over as soon as she put weight on her right leg. A simple ankle sprain, and perhaps a few broken ribs. Fair enough, all things considered. She stood again and shuffled to the motionless creature, grabbing her dropped spear along the way.

"Don't worry," Agé said, appearing next to the Grootslang. "It's dead."

Oseye dropped her spear and fell to her knees, exhausted. "That could've gone better."

"And it could've gone worse." Agé sat in front of Oseye, crossing his legs. "I knew you could do it."

"But I had to see it for myself," the huntress concluded. "This lesson would've been much more pleasant had you just said it."

"I believe I did, though the most valuable lessons are often born from experience not words, my Little Oseye. I'm glad this was to be the final lesson I could teach you. I would call this a fitting end between the two of us."

Oseye's jaw dropped. "A fitting end?"

Agé's smile seemed forced as he blinked tears away, and the huntress grew light-headed, knowing what he meant.

"You mean you will leave me this time ... forever. But I thought your absence was just for a brief period!"

Agé crossed his arms, somehow appearing more human than Fon; he was shaken, disheartened, and filled with sorrow.

"It's for the best," he said, his voice cracking. "You've taken the first steps in becoming a Mino who can defend her people. Since

I have nothing more to teach you, it is only fair that I put my eye on one who truly needs me."

"You mean another child," the huntress said.

Oseye wanted to tell Agé how she couldn't journey through the passage called life without him, how she was too weak, too afraid. Then she glanced at the Grootslang—the creature she had managed to defeat on her own—and sighed.

"I hate it when you're right," she joked instead.

Agé chuckled and grabbed her by the hands, kissing them both. "Though you may no longer see me in the flesh, my spirit will always be with you in every path you take."

"And I can hear your voice in the winds if my heart is willing, right?" Oseye wrapped her arms around him, holding him tight. "Thank you, my dearest Fon Agé, and know that you will forever be my most beloved friend to the end of my days."

Agé laughed. "To the end of your days. Now, that's the spirit."

The two embraced for another few moments, as if Agé was just as scared to let go of Oseye as she was to let go of him. She knew that walking in the presence of gods was one thing, but to be in the company of a true friend was a gift few had the privilege of experiencing. Yet somehow, Oseye of the Dahomey Kingdom had been blessed to have had both, if only for a brief chapter of her life.

The huntress tensed when a lovely breeze from the west passed by. She shut her eyes, feeling the fabric of Agé's robe fade away beneath her fingers.

"*Goodbye, my Little Oseye. And remember, I'll always believe in you.*"

The Mino warrior picked up her spear and hobbled deeper into the jungle. It was a glorious summer afternoon in the country of Dahomey. Day one of the trial was complete with eight more to go. She figured she'd manage. The wind, after all, had told her so.

About the Author

When drawing fanfic graphic novels was no longer fulfilling enough as a teen, Jordan ventured to greater adventures in story-telling. Now, when he isn't busy saving the world through the trusty arsenal called "video games," the author fancies creating new worlds and adventures for others to enjoy.

He's expanded these adventures through his podcast Stories for Nerds, where he collaborates in writing sci-fi and fantasy adventures with authors Abby Goldsmith and Scott Parkin.

To stay up to date with Jordan's latest projects,

visit StoriesForNerds.com or RaphyelMJordan.com.

TAKE ME FOR A RIDE

MIKE JACK STOUMBOS

It was the brightest light I'd ever seen, and it stung tears in the corners of my eyes.

Then again, it might have been the sweet sounds of Leslie on the brass. Trust me, the way he played could have convinced anyone that French horn is indeed the language of love.

Yes, sir, the High-Dive stage might not have been the most glamorous venue, but when those lights warmed your face and that music reached your ears, you wouldn't trade it for the world. And tonight, the walk onto this stage would be a massive step in my career.

To paraphrase good old Neil, it was a small step for this man but one giant leap for his music.

I was just finishing the number that had first put me on stage: "Not a One-Trick Pony, I'm a One-Man Band." Of course, there were cheers and hollers from the crowd. I grinned at them. Wasn't hard to put on the grin. Didn't have to fake anything for this group. They gave the kind of energy that would have had me pure pickled if I'd had more than a thimbleful to drink that evening.

Letting my guitar hang comfortably from my shoulder, I took

the microphone in both hands and said, "This one goes way out there. To the stars."

Of course, the cheers grew louder. They knew what was coming next.

Now, "One-Man Band" might have gotten me front and center on the High-Dive stage, but it was "Take Me for a Ride" that would take me right to the top.

I knew it. The rest of the band knew it. My soon-to-be-agent knew it, and I was getting pretty practiced at saying the A-word.

It's easy to lose yourself in a fantasy while on stage, but I had a job to do. So I closed my eyes, breathed in, and sang out the opening, as if I was trying to reach the flying saucers themselves ...

I wanna kick that dust right off my heels
And go to a place where I can feel
Lighter! Lighter than air.

My fingers started working the strings without my having to tell them to, accompanying me as I went on,

I wanna clear my head and set my mind
To leaving this whole world behind
Away! Oh, way out there.

I could hear the hi-hat behind me, that shimmering tinsel sound marking time, then speeding up. Having switched his timbre to tenor, Leslie joined me on the sax, just as I slid into the chorus.

Yes, I plan on flying far
And my aim is to the stars
I don't know how I'd get there if I tried
They say you can't get there by car
So pick me up, and take me for a ride!

I liked that folks sang along. I do love that spotlight, but I have never minded sharing it, even in the days when I truly was a one-man band or playing backup. But tonight, I got to front with a loyal brass-and-winds boy, a lovely lady on the keyboard, and an ever-ready, super-steady drummer. Not to mention a chorus of people on their feet, crowding the dance floor in front of the stage. I could barely make out their faces through glare and the dust, but every expression I caught was smiling, and every voice I could hear was singing, especially on the refrains.

Just one day on the radio and a few more online, and I had more than a handful of strangers who knew my lyrics, whether or not they'd ever seen my show in person. My informal manager had said it would help sell me to the real-deal agent. Tonight, I was determined to give them something new, something they couldn't get from a radio performance.

So as soon as I finished the second chorus, I slipped away from the microphone and jetted backstage at a lightning pace. I knew I had a full sixteen measures of Leslie going to town while dear Miss Garcia-Grey vamped the chords that kept him in line. It was more than enough time for me to effect my quick-change.

Take off the guitar strap, pop on the helmet and cape. Then wait for the gentleman with the cymbals to start the crescendo— by now, we called it "the takeoff."

At the cue of the big crash, I ran out on stage again, fists forward like Superman, an open-faced space helmet on my shoulders, and an attached American flag flapping behind me.

The crowd squealed and laughed and hooted with delight.

Taking the mic again, I said, "Thank you, ladies and gentlemen! Give it up for my man, Leslie, on the saxophone." I gestured to Leslie, who gave a flourish, his Edgar-Winter-white mane tossing as he worked the tenor. "And of course, Miss Garcia-Grey on the keys." G.G. did a sweeping glissando and led me right into, "Who could forget big Tony on the drums?"

In about two seconds, Tony slammed out something I can't describe and dropped right back into the hi-hat beat.

"A very special thanks to our lightboard designer and all-around tech gal, the unmatchable Jerrilee." Though I couldn't see her, I suspected Jerrilee gave the loudest *whoop* of appreciation at her own mention.

"Had a great time playing for you all this evening. Remember to tip your bartenders and head on home safely. With my head above the clouds, I am Spaceman Mort. Now, one more time, ladies and gentlemen. Sing along if you know the words."

We went through the refrain again, a little slower this time, and as far as I was concerned, the whole club joined in. A bass drum hit, and I dug into the coda, that signature end and my favorite part of the song:

I wanna be the guy that sings
For intergalactic queens and kings
So pick me up ...
Leslie blared on the sax.
Yeah, pick me up!
G.G. swept the keyboard.
Well, pick me up, and take me for a ride!

I was out among the crowd within minutes of the finish. Folks of all ages were paying me compliments, and some of the younger snapped selfies, which were easy to tag and link now that my songs were online. I grinned and laughed through the whole procession as I made my way toward one of the VIP booths and the collective brains that had already launched my song through the stratosphere.

"Hey, Mort! Mort!" called Jerrilee, as if I hadn't already seen her and might be in danger of going deaf. Jerrilee was the kind of natural redhead who dyed her hair redder so no one would forget it, and who wore her denim like she was showing on a Milan catwalk. She waved me over with both arms and pulled up a chair for me on the edge of the booth.

Her wild enthusiasm couldn't have been in greater contrast to

Dale Bishop, who sat with both forearms on the table, his sharp nose practically carving lines in his scotch tumbler. He wore glasses and a sport coat, even on a warm night, and had styled his dark hair like something you only see in magazines and movies. But Dale also wore a pleasant smile, his eyes glinting behind his glasses.

"Mortimer," he said with a nasally New York accent. He half stood and shook my hand. Felt like a practice handshake instead of the real thing. "It was a great set. I'm pleased to have heard it."

"Thank you, that means a lot." And I meant it too.

Jerrilee sat back down and, leaning perhaps a little too close to Dale, said, "He gets that kind of reaction every night he performs here." I almost expected her to punch him in the arm, like she would have done for me. But, exuberant as she was, my good friend and personal promoter was determined not to get in the way of this deal.

Dale played it cool. "You don't have to keep selling me. Mortimer, I think you've got a great style and sound. Feels a little like Frank Sinatra meets John Wayne."

"Well, Dale, I believe Frank Sinatra *did* meet John Wayne."

They both laughed at that, then Dale sidled into business. "I've checked off everything on my list. Do you have any questions for me?"

I shook my head. "No, sir."

"Then let's hit the paperwork." Dale opened his briefcase and took out the relevant folders and pens.

Jerrilee squeezed my shoulder before donning her own reading glasses to give the contract a final pass.

They talked through the laundry list one last time as a kind of formality. Now, I'm not going to claim I'm particularly schooled nor that I'm particularly dumb. I did my due diligence by talking it over with Jerrilee, my interim manager and the one solely responsible for YouTubing the demos that first caught Dale Bishop's ear. For the contract, she had enlisted one of the bartenders, who'd just wrapped up an online accounting degree. After a fine-tooth-combing hit no snags, we all decided the contract was on the up-and-up. Plus, according to the professional, it was in his best interest to keep me happy and making good music.

The fellow was about as sharp of mind as he was of nose. He'd already proved his salt, beyond what Google could tell Jerrilee about him, by getting me on the radio before I was even signed. It was a no-money deal, so no need to handle a percentage, but he wanted to show me he was bona fide.

I think he also wanted to see how I'd play on the morning drive time. I played so well, the morning folks requested me clear into the evening.

According to Jerrilee, my social media standing soared more in that one day than it had in weeks under her management, so she completely stood behind the decision to work with Dale.

Tonight, he had a couple more orders of business to address, which we took care of right there while the staff closed down the bar. I let the agent do the talking and tried not to show my nervousness.

"This one is a 'Protection Clause,'" he said, handing me another sheet of paper. "Essentially, you acknowledge that you are not intentionally misleading or offending anyone with your lyrics. There's a note to say that views you express online are your own and do not reflect the firm that represents you."

Jerrilee nodded. "Like for social media."

"So it's a CYA clause," I observed, hopefully demonstrating that I wasn't totally out of my depth.

"It's to cover *all* of our assets, Mortimer," he amended, with a slight chuckle on his own joke.

Jerrilee chimed in, "Well, you don't have to worry about anything from Mort here. He doesn't have a controversial bone in that big, lovable body. His only vice is his science fiction obsession."

"Well, hang on now, I wouldn't call it a *vice*." I wondered if I should have objected to the words *fiction* or *obsession* instead.

But Dale Bishop took it well and agreed. "Neither would I. Now," he went on, smoothly transitioning, "as of today, we're doing a bit of a write-in for a travel clause, to be renegotiated at a later date. This says it's to be handled on a case-by-case basis, but the general agreement is that, barring emergency or late notice, you will do your best to meet booked appearances, and that expenses, including time away from other scheduled work, would be covered. Pretty standard."

I looked to Jerrilee, who gave me a not-at-all-covert thumbs-up.

"As long as you're not gonna 'take me for a ride,' Dale." We shared another laugh.

With everything in order, I licked my finger, turned the page, and clicked that pen to life. I initialed and dated each of the highlighted sections with a fair degree of giddiness. Finally, on the pivotal dotted line, I put down my John Hancock, which had the good fortune of including "John" right in the middle of it.

"Mortimer Johnston" stared right back at me in black ink.

We shook hands, and that, as they say, was that. I was an agented musician.

G.G. set the tone as soon as I entered the greenroom. Longtime piano player, Miss Garcia-Grey wrapped her arms around me and squeezed harder than I'd imagined she could. "Oh, we're going to miss you so much, Mort!"

I tried to laugh it off. "What are you talking about? I'm not going anywhere anytime soon."

"Oh, you're going places," Tony assured me. Other than the bouncers, Tony was one of the few people around here who was intimidatingly larger than me. But despite the Danny Trejo mustache, he was secretly a softie. "It's been fun playing with you."

Sitting askew on the dusty leather couch, Leslie remarked, "At least now we'll be able to clean all of the space stuff out of the greenroom."

He wasn't wrong. Over the years, I'd been strumming, then singing backup, and finally fronting my own songs here at the High-Dive, and I had quite a solid corner marked off. I didn't even need a strip of tape with my name on it. People could tell Spaceman Mort's area by the model shuttles, the hanging solar system, and pictures of the great American heroes from John Glenn to Elvis. And if that didn't tip them off, there was the box of assorted costumes and props I'd collected, stashed under one of the tables and a few more backstage. Probably the craziest was the time I'd rigged an "astronaut chair" to hang from the ceiling grid—I'd had to sign a few "protection clauses" for that one too.

Grinning, I took Leslie's hint and went to put away my props and my space helmet.

Cool to the point of sounding cold, Leslie asked, "How's your new agent feel, *Spaceman* Mort?"

It was true that until "Take Me for a Ride," I hadn't really let my sci-fi passion fly publicly, but then it was "Take Me for a Ride" that was really moving my career. I had not only been making more headway with fans, but I was playing happier and writing more lyrics than I ever had. Dale Bishop saw that too.

"He thinks it's part of my brand. He says he doesn't mind the space cowboy motif, as long as I keep writing songs and show up to gigs on time. I mean, it's not like I'm going around claiming I've been abducted by aliens." I snapped my guitar case closed and did one last check of my area.

Big Tony wondered aloud, "What would you do if they took you up on your request and actually came to get you?"

"Count my lucky stars," I said quickly, keen to hit the road.

G.G. spoke next, one of her slender, pianist fingers tapping her temple. "You know, I've never understood. What is it with you and the little green men?"

I put up both hands in a telling *whoa-there* gesture. "Oh, hey, don't pigeonhole me. I don't care if they're green, blue, silver, or polka-dotted. Don't have to be men either. Hands, claws, tentacles —as long as they have a spaceship, I'm in."

Big Tony laughed. "Oughta put that in your next song, Mort."

"Oh, I got a million floating around, ready to hit paper. But that's another day. Gotta get some sleep before work tomorrow."

Guitar in hand, I started toward the outer door, but I noticed that all three of them seemed to half-heartedly block my path. G.G. fidgeted, and Tony had trouble meeting my eye.

Trying to lighten the mood, I told them, "Hey, it's not like I'm leaving tonight. We've got more shows on the schedule—hell, I'm still playing backup for other headliners. Only difference is now I've got someone to argue for better pay and more bookings."

They answered in murmurs and nods. I suppose I could have stuck around and analyzed it, but I didn't see much good I could do to tend to hurt feelings, insecurity, or jealousy. Maybe they weren't feeling any of that and were just being awkward. Or maybe I was miffed because none of them had said "Congratulations."

I exited into the alley. I didn't need to check out at the bar, seeing as my single-pour was more than covered by my performance, so I enjoyed the night air stroll as a solo tour.

As a performer, even when I was just playing basic blues backup for someone else, I usually had the luxury of arriving early and staying late. Not wanting to find scratches or vomit on my car, I always parked it at the far, far end of the lot. It wasn't the prettiest vehicle, but it had a glorious moonroof, and it was in my day job's budget, so I took good care of it and didn't complain.

I wasn't even halfway there when a howl overhead nearly knocked me off my feet.

It was a warbling, shrieking sound, like an underwater

bumblebee on a megaphone, and some kind of force pushed against me, scattering dirt in all directions. A brief blue light slashed by. I closed my eyes and covered my face. I braced for I-didn't-know-what.

But as soon as it had arrived, it was gone, leaving no trace.

I inspected my own shoes, saw that they were still on gravel. The only lights came from the High-Dive itself and the street-lamps. And, of course, the stars.

"What in the hell?" I wondered, slowly turning to look around me. "Now, either that was a sort of stealth helicopter, or—"

Then a truly blinding light interrupted me.

I found myself strapped to a chair, blinking against a peculiar, pulsing sun, while strange sounds piped in from all sides. Clicks and swells, like some sort of synthesized violins. And movement —the shadow of a hand or an arm. I barely dared to breathe.

My skin tingled, my arms completely covered in goosebumps. The hair on the back of my neck wanted to poke straight out, but I was pressing into the seat. Instinct told me to get away from whatever was in front of me, but this little voice in the back of my head urged me to lean forward and say something.

My throat seemed to take charge before I told it to, and I heard my trained stage voice cut through the various noises.

"Hello!"

Then, "Who's there?"

And finally, "Where am I?"

A disjointed tone, like an out-of-tune electric guitar on high gain, blasted then gradually faded. A shining outline of a head and shoulders cut off part of the main light. Sparkling reflections glimmered where the eyes ought to be.

An otherworldly voice informed me, "You are Spaceman Mort."

I only got as far as opening my mouth when another voice, this one higher pitched and less metallic, came from my left. "You are coming with us."

"I—"

And then a third figure appeared from the right. I could see a silvery suit and long fingers. This one said nothing as it approached.

I started to recoil, but stopped myself as something caught my eye.

Between the flashing lights and bizarre sound effects, I could see the seams of polyester and the edge of knobby rubber gloves.

"You will sing for us!" announced the first voice again, with a telltale echo effect.

I took my time. Hung my head, counted to my cue without tapping my foot. "Okay. I'll tell you what you want to know. But the truth is, I can't take you to my leader, because"—I squeezed my eyes shut and grimaced—"I'm the President."

They tried to keep quiet, but I could have sworn I heard one stifled snort of laughter.

"And, tell you truly," I went on, "if you're looking to make a deal, you'll be disappointed. Everything on Earth has already been claimed by some alien race or other. Elvis weaponized the big isle of Hawaii a long time ago, the Coneheads claimed the pyramids, the Cardassians assumed human form—I can't even keep up with it all."

A guffaw sputtered from farther away, somewhere behind the light fixtures, which were flashing in a pattern similar to the one we used on stage.

The alien directly in front of me reached up a hand to its own throat and turned off the voice synthesizer. "All right, that's enough, Mort," she said. "Guys, hit the lights."

The bright spots and strobes shut off with a telltale, breathy thud, and the house lights came up in their place.

The foremost alien took off her head, and—lo and behold!—Jerrilee was underneath. Behind her over the bar hung a large banner, reading "Congratulations!"

"Nicely done, Jerrilee," I told her. "Who was on the high voice?"

I looked to my left, and big Tony, still wearing my own Spaceman Mort helmet, took in another breath of helium before he said, "Surprise!"

"Finally," said Leslie, shaking his head from the light booth, but I knew his annoyance was only for show.

G.G. had been the third alien, and, looking around the bar, it seemed as if every server and bouncer had been in on the gag.

Jerrilee approached to unstrap me from the chair, the same one that I'd hung from the ceiling just a few weeks before. "So, when did you figure it out?" she asked me.

"Rubber masks and Star Trek suits can only get you so far." I indicated G.G., who was struggling to take off the tightest of the alien faces. "But you got me good."

I could see a couple of them chuckling, giving me a "Yeah, sure" look.

"No, truly," I insisted. "For a minute there, I thought I was being abducted by the real thing."

"You just wanted to believe," replied G.G., her hair more than a little mussed and matted following its confinement.

I had to laugh. "Yes, sir. Even when I was wetting my pants and sweating bullets, it was one of the most exciting things that's ever happened to me."

"It was all Jerrilee's idea," said Tony, which didn't surprise me one bit.

"You didn't actually mess yourself, did you?" asked Leslie, also unsurprising.

Jerrilee practically spat at him when she said, "Jeez, Leslie, *that's* what you pick up on?"

While I made my way off the stage and toward the cold beer waiting for me at the bar, I could hear Leslie continue behind me.

"Look, I was against the kidnapping from the start. What if he'd hurt someone?"

"No one got their fingers broken!"

"Yeah, and I never actually wet my pants," I assured him. "Just an expression, Les."

Leslie's worries assuaged, I turned to the group as a whole. "But, truly—thank you. I can't think of a better way to celebrate getting signed."

I don't know who started the applause, but soon all the complaints and concerns had washed away with some genuine well-wishing among friends.

It felt more like a birthday than a goodbye party. Still, as the bar staff and my fellow musicians headed out one by one into the night, I had that feeling in my gut that nothing would be the same. Maybe my days here would come to an end faster than I'd predicted. I truly did not know where my new agent would take me, and it could be a one-way ticket.

Jerrilee and I left arm-in-arm, still buzzing with excitement. When we reached her red Chevy, she said, "You know, you're gonna make it really big."

"Yeah, but I'll still be the same old Mort to you."

"I don't know." She opened the driver's side door and stepped inside. "I was pretty starstruck when I saw you up on stage tonight."

"Starstruck," I mused, gently closing the door behind her while she got situated at the wheel. "Wonder what I could do with that as a title."

She put one elbow out the open window. "Hey, in all serious-ness. Wherever you go, whatever you do, know that I'm gonna be here to support you. First and number-one fan, Mort. I mean it."

Not one to shy away from my emotions, I felt my eyes mist up. "Jerrilee, I could search the universe and never find a friend like you."

"Mmhmm." She turned the key, and her Chevy sparked to life. "I like it. Write that song first."

I waved Jerrilee off.

I was the last to leave, guitar in hand on a warm summer night, perfect for stargazing. I knew I had to get back to the real world and my day job after a short sleep, but the thought of just staring up into space was mighty tempting.

I was crunching across the gravel lot and had taken out my keys, when a funny little thought tickled the back of my brain. I'd never asked the crew how they'd made the crazy helicopter effect right before they'd fake-abducted me. Maybe they'd had a drone with an industrial fan and some kind of electronic sound-mixer? Setting up the High-Dive's lighting grid had been pretty cool, but that low flyer was something else.

Resolving that I'd ask Jerrilee about it tomorrow, I unlocked my car, and went to lift the handle—

And everything went white.

My head pounded, my ears plugged and popped. I felt a certain kind of dizziness and nausea. I was about to holler that no joke is funny the second time, when my vision started coming into focus.

There was indeed a lot of white, but the lights were not blinding or incessantly blinking. The ceiling was a low dome, and the floor around me was a little golden ring that buzzed with a strange kind of electricity. But most importantly, there was a spaceman standing just outside of the ring, facing me.

The head was dark, with round eyes above a pointy beak, all

of which appeared smooth and sleek. Totally unlike a cheap rubber mask, and with no visible seams.

The spaceman pointed a device at me, some kind of tablet I'd never seen before, whose screen and display seemed to hover about an inch above the metal, as if projected. And it was being operated by a hand with three fingers and a thumb.

"Excellent," said an electronic voice, whose mouth did not match the movements. "All vitals accounted for. Transportee, Mortimer Johnston, and instrument, acoustic guitar —undamaged."

I looked down at the guitar case, still gripped in my white-knuckled hand. This time, I couldn't even make a sound, let alone ask a question.

"How are you feeling?" the spaceman asked, putting on something that almost would pass for a smile. "Oh, don't worry. The first transport is always a bit disorienting. You'll have plenty of time to adjust. I'm looking forward to hearing you in person—I've been told the radio doesn't do you justice."

The alien gave me a thumbs-up, then turned to tell someone else, "We're ready to launch." He went to a panel on the wall, activated it with a gesture, then started to manipulate a bunch of symbols I didn't recognize and could hardly describe.

Truth be told, I couldn't even tell if I was moving or not, but I was damned sure that they had me on a ship. I didn't know whether to scream in terror or call out a hallelujah. For some reason, I wondered how I would tell them that I already had an agent.

Then, something I'd thought was a wall hissed open, and in walked a short man in a sport coat with a sharp nose. He was about the same height and shape as the alien at the wall console.

"Ah, Mortimer!" said Dale Bishop. "Can I say again how glad I am that you signed on? We were worried someone would snatch you up before we did. Weren't we?"

The alien at the wall console agreed. "We made that mistake

with Elvis. Waited until he got too big, and by then it was a mountain of paperwork. Luckily, you gave us express invitation."

Dale Bishop, my agent, reached a hand up to his face and smoothly peeled off the skin, revealing a beaked face with round eyes. When he spoke, the movements matched perfectly, and the well-practiced voice with the New York accent sounded the same as ever. "Well, Mortimer, are you ready to play 'for intergalactic queens and kings'? We've got you bookings you won't believe!"

The room started swimming before I noticed I was swaying. My fingers went cold, and the guitar slipped my grip right before I fell backward. I heard Dale saying something, but I couldn't make out his words. My head felt fuzzy, my ears rang, and—my friends—I saw stars.

About the Author

Mike Jack Stoumbos is an emerging fiction writer, disguised as a believably normal high school teacher, living in Seattle with his wife and their parrot. Like Spaceman Mort, Mike Jack writes lyrics and performs his own songs; many of his creative projects can be found at MikeJackStoumbos.com and @MJStoumbos on Twitter. His previous ventures into the funny side of sci-fi and fantasy have appeared in the anthologies *Galactic Stew* and *Cursed Collectibles*. He is particularly excited to be published alongside Kevin J. Anderson, who has been a huge source of inspiration throughout Mike Jack's literary journey.

HYDE PARK

SHANNON FOX

Cassian drummed his fingers against the steering wheel of his car as he waited for the gate that blocked his long, private driveway to fully slide back. When the way was clear, he pressed his foot against the accelerator, and the Ferrari F430 shot forward with a growl.

Dusk was falling, and as he crested the top of the driveway, the sun had already slipped below the horizon, its light painting the ocean below in a wash of red and pink hues.

After parking his car in the garage, Cassian hurried up the short flight of steps to the house's main level. His footsteps echoed through the front hall as he strode toward the kitchen. When he had first toured this house with his mother, she had described it as "cold." Even the jaw-dropping ocean views hadn't been enough to soften her distaste for all the concrete and glass. But to Cassian, it was perfect. The sterile surfaces and hard edges lent a particularly masculine energy to a house that had been specifically crafted to take advantage of the incredible panoramic views.

In the kitchen, Cassian poured himself a finger of whiskey

and took a sip before walking down the hall to his bedroom. His guest would be arriving soon.

The sun had fully set by the time Cassian entered the master suite. He stood at the floor-to-ceiling glass windows, drinking whiskey and watching the last of the light drain away as night descended.

"Cassian," a voice rasped.

He didn't turn. He knew who was in the room with him and didn't care to look upon his face.

"The new film premieres tomorrow night," Cassian said, swirling his glass. "At the El Capitan. They're already calling it the blockbuster of the summer. I think the studio will green-light the next film by week's end."

"You should be proud," the visitor said.

"I am." And he was. The miniseries he'd pitched and produced just six years ago, *Hyde Park*, had initially attracted a small but mighty following that soon exploded as more and more people began tuning in. Now it had become a cultural phenomenon spawning two feature-length films, the second of which debuted tomorrow night.

"You don't sound like it."

"You still haven't told me what you want in exchange for your help on the next film. I assume that's why you're here."

His guest chuckled, a sound that never failed to make Cassian's stomach twist in fear.

"The woman," the visitor said.

Ice entered Cassian's veins. "What woman?" he asked, though he had a feeling he already knew.

"The blonde. Veronica."

The room tilted, and for a moment Cassian wondered if the big earthquake they'd all feared had finally struck Los Angeles. But when he placed a hand against the window to steady himself and took a deep breath, the room snapped back to normal. Cassian closed his eyes.

"No," he said. "Not her."

"You asked me what I want."

"You can't have her," Cassian said, putting as much force as he could muster into the words. "She's not like the other ones. She'll be missed. Someone will come looking for her, and when they discover what you've done ... No, it can't be her."

"The price is the price," the visitor said.

Cassian opened his eyes and stared out into the inky darkness. "She's the star of my new film. Not an addict or a streetwalker. If I bring her here, or anywhere, someone will remember seeing her leave with me. And when her body is found ... It just can't be done. I won't be able to get away with it."

"We have an agreement, and the agreement must be fulfilled. What happens to you after that is not my concern. This city is full of thousands of young men just like you, who would do anything for success, to have what you have. I can find another." The visitor chuckled. "I don't think you can say the same. Unless you've found a way to create your films without my help?"

Cassian swallowed hard. He'd tried with this last film. He really had. But without the inspiration the visitor provided him, without watching him hunt and kill ... Cassian's writing felt hollow. Stilted. Unremarkable. He doubted anything had changed in the intervening time.

"Bring her here after the premiere," the visitor commanded.

"Tomorrow?" Cassian's voice sounded strangled to his own ears. "It hardly gives me time to plan."

"That is not my concern. If you wish to have my help in the future, you will bring her here tomorrow night. If you want to return to the man you were when I found you, you need only say so."

Having witnessed the viciousness with which the visitor killed, Cassian doubted he would let him walk away from their agreement so easily.

Cassian brought the glass to his lips and drained the last of the whiskey, allowing the taste of it to flood his senses as his thoughts spun out into the abyss of his future. Even if the visitor somehow let him live, his life as he knew it was over. He was utterly incapable of creating at the same level without the source material the visitor provided. He could try, he supposed, but he knew he'd gone too far down this road, dug himself in too deep. The studio, his crew, the actors—they would notice something was amiss. They would wonder where Cassian Charles, the genius writer-director, the wunderkind of Hollywood, had disappeared. Would wonder who this hack was who had taken his place.

He lowered the glass and leaned his forehead against the window. If he wanted his career, his life, to continue, then he only had the one choice.

"I've never been up this way before," Veronica Zeismer said from the passenger seat of his car.

Cassian tightened his hands on the steering wheel and stole a quick glance across the car at her. Veronica's gaze was focused on the landscape outside as the Ferrari hurtled past towering gates and dense foliage cloaked in darkness. She was no doubt trying to catch a glimpse of the homes that lined one of the most exclusive streets in Pacific Palisades.

"Not many people live up here," Cassian said. "It's what attracted me to this area."

Out of the corner of his eye, he saw Veronica smooth the fabric of her dress. He reached across the car to place a hand on her knee. He could barely bring himself to touch her, knowing what was going to happen as soon as they got to the house.

But Veronica was smart, at least as far as beautiful young actresses went. When he'd asked her to come back to his house after the premiere, he was sure she'd formed an idea of what was really behind the invitation. Indeed, she didn't stiffen or pull away from his touch, but placed her hand over the top of his and gave it a soft squeeze.

Her skin felt warm, the flesh of her palm smooth and pliable like a ripe peach. He had a sudden vision of it splitting open under the light pressure of a knife and tried to shove the thought away.

"Are you all right?" she asked.

He realized, to his embarrassment, that he must have made a sound.

"I'm fine," he said, shooting her a quick smile. "Just had something in my throat."

Silence hung heavy over the car as they continued to climb toward his house.

"Can I ask you a question?" Veronica asked.

Cassian felt his stomach twist. "Sure."

"I've always been curious how you came up with the idea for *Hyde Park*. I mean serial killers are nothing new. There are plenty of TV shows and movies about them. But the killings are so ... inventive. So detailed. It almost seems like you witnessed it for yourself."

He licked his lips, allowing himself a moment to collect his thoughts, to step fully into the practiced lie he'd constructed for just this purpose. "History is full of stories of serial killers and their crimes. It wasn't hard to repurpose some of the details. But to answer your question, I've always been fascinated with the story of Jack the Ripper. I've read lots of different theories about the murders and who was behind them. So one day I started to wonder what it would be like if modern-day Los Angeles had its own Ripper. And the story kind of evolved from there."

"That's why the Hyde Park killer's victims are all prostitutes and drug addicts," Veronica said. She nodded as if suddenly connecting the dots. But Cassian knew she was only flattering him. He'd told her nothing that he hadn't already repeated on every late-night talk show over the past six years. "You were copying the profile of the Ripper's victims."

"Exactly," he said. That, and it was the kind of prey he'd been told to go after.

"How fascinating," she replied. "So who do you think the Ripper really was?"

Cassian glanced at her. "You really want to talk about this?"

"I told you in my audition that I have a healthy interest in the macabre." Her tone was light, teasing. "I wasn't kidding about that."

The car shot around a bend in the road, and suddenly they were at the foot of Cassian's long driveway. He hit the brakes too hard, and Veronica let out a yelp as the seat belt no doubt contracted tightly across her chest, as his own had done.

"Sorry about that," he said. "The entrance still kind of sneaks up on me."

Veronica let out a weak laugh as they waited for the gate to roll back. The car's headlights illuminated part of the driveway beyond but were no match for the thick tangle of bushes and trees that lined the road up to the house. Cassian might have found it unsettling if he didn't already know what the night had in store for them.

Veronica cleared her throat as Cassian steered the car up the driveway. "You didn't answer my question," she said. "About who you thought was behind the Ripper killings."

"There was a man who drowned in the Thames. His body was found not too long after the last murder. Even though there was little to connect him to the killings while he was alive, it always made sense to me. That as monstrous as the murders were, there was still just a man behind them. It doesn't seem that far of a stretch to imagine that perhaps he grew remorseful and decided to end it."

By Veronica's silence, he wondered if she was disappointed in his answer. After all, that wasn't the kind of killer who was behind the murders in *Hyde Park*. That man was utterly evil. Devoid of every last shred of humanity. Perhaps that was the sort of response Veronica had been hoping to hear.

As he pulled up to the house, Veronica let out a gasp.

"This is your house?" she asked.

"Yes," he said, his hand already on the handle of the door. Though he, too, felt awed at the sight of it; he'd forgotten how impressive the house looked when it was all lit up. He usually didn't leave the lights on while he was out. But tonight, he'd hoped that in doing so the house would appear welcoming. Inviting. That if Veronica had felt ill at ease at all on the drive over, the lights would help settle her—and cloak his true purpose in bringing her back to the house.

Cassian darted around the front of the car to open the door for her. He watched as she unfolded her lithe body from the car. Veronica had dressed in a figure-hugging red dress for the premiere. Though he was sure the gossip columns might call it plain, he thought she looked stunning.

She lingered, staring up at the house until Cassian gently pressed a hand to the small of her back.

"Shall we go inside?" he asked.

Lacing her fingers through his, Veronica allowed him to lead her through the front doors and across the foyer. Her heels echoed in the cavernous space.

In the kitchen, he took down two wine glasses from the cabinet and set them on the oversized island. "Red or white?"

She fastened her incredible blue-gray eyes on him as she replied, "White. Red wine gives me a headache."

"Me too," he said. "I was only going to drink it to be polite."

Her lips curled mischievously. "Trust me, you don't have to worry about being polite with me."

Cassian forced himself to chuckle, to give her his most flirtatious smile. "I'll be right back," he said.

He strode down the hallway, past the temperature-controlled wine room, to his bedroom at the end of the hall. He kept his stride even, unhurried, though his heart was hammering in his chest. Only once he was safely inside the bathroom did he allow himself a shaky breath as he sagged against the closed door.

The visitor would be here soon. Somehow Cassian always knew when he was on his way. Which meant he only had to entertain Veronica a little while longer. To pretend that everything was normal.

He caught a glimpse of his reflection in the bathroom mirror. Though he was not yet thirty, dark shadows had taken up permanent residence beneath his eyes. His normally pale skin looked bloodless, even for him. He smiled at his reflection and wondered how he'd convinced Veronica to get in a car with him. He looked as unstable as he felt.

Cassian staggered toward the sink and turned the faucet on. He splashed some cold water on his face, the shock of it jarring his brain to action.

Was he really going to do this again? Was he actually going to allow another woman to die in service to his art? And in his own home no less?

He grabbed a towel off the sink and rubbed his face with it. The answer, he knew, was yes. Because, as the visitor had clearly spelled out for him the night before, he really had no choice.

Cassian gripped the edge of the sink with both hands and forced himself to take deep breaths. It would all be over soon. Very soon.

On his way back to the kitchen, he stopped and selected a bottle of his favorite white wine. He doubted Veronica would get to drink very much of it, so he might as well choose something he enjoyed.

As he stepped back into the hallway, he heard the sounds of the piano drifting from the great room. A tune he recognized but couldn't quite place. He listened for a moment as the notes tumbled out from beneath Veronica's skilled fingers. He hadn't realized she played.

The wine glasses were on the counter where he'd left them. But Veronica had helped herself to the block of Havarti cheese he kept in the fridge. It, too, was on the counter beside a long, serrated knife.

"I'll pour you a glass," he said, popping the cork on the wine bottle.

"Not too much," she called from the piano.

Cassian ignored her, filling her glass nearly to the top.

The sound of the piano died away, and he heard the scrape of the bench against the concrete as she stood up. Her heels clicked across the floor as she approached.

He looked up and flashed her his most charming smile as he handed over her glass.

She pretended to pout. "I told you not to pour me too much. Now I'll fall asleep on your couch for sure."

He forced himself to chuckle. "Trust me, you falling asleep on my couch was never the plan."

The lights of the kitchen picked up the golden tones of her honey-blonde hair as she tilted her head to the side. Her eyes drifted to his lips and then back up again, settling on his eyes.

And despite the sick feeling in his stomach, the sense of dread that had been his constant companion all night, Cassian found himself wanting to kiss her, too.

He took a step toward her and slipped a finger under her chin, lifting her face up toward his. Veronica set her wine glass back on the counter and closed her eyes, surely waiting to feel his lips brush hers.

But all at once, Cassian became aware that they were not alone and dropped his hand. He stepped back from Veronica and looked to the left, already knowing what he would find there.

"I knew you wouldn't be able to walk away from it," the visitor said. "Just like all the others before you."

"Cassian?" Veronica asked. "What's happening?"

He forced himself to look back at her, his cheeks burning with shame.

"I'm sorry," he said.

Her brows knitted together in confusion. "Sorry for what?"

Cassian shook his head, unable to get the words out. It had been easier with the other women. He hadn't known them, so it'd been easy to tell himself that they didn't matter, that the world was better off without them. That their deaths were no great loss.

"Cassian," Veronica said. "Look at me."

Tears pricked his eyes as he stared at the window over her shoulder. He knew he couldn't look at her face. If he did, he wouldn't be able to give her up.

He could hear the visitor already moving toward them. All Cassian had to do was hang on for a few moments more and it would all be over.

Warm fingers suddenly gripped his jaw as Veronica grabbed his face and forced him to look at her.

"Tell me what's happening," she said, her eyes scanning his features, seeking answers that he was unwilling to give.

But as he stared back at her, he felt the last bit of his resolve crumble. He couldn't do this to her. Couldn't stand by and watch her die.

Before he could talk himself out of it, he broke free of her grasp and reached for the knife on the counter.

As he turned to face the visitor, Cassian was gratified to see that he seemed taken aback by the turn of events.

"Think of what you're doing, Cassian," the visitor said. "Think of what you're giving up."

"I have," said Cassian. His voice shook as he answered. "And it was never really mine to begin with. The success, the house, the car ... all of it. I should never have walked down this monstrous path with you. But tonight, it ends."

His hand trembled as he raised the knife above his head. But as he brought it down toward the visitor's heart, the fear fell away, and his grip tightened on the weapon. Cassian let out a cry as he drove the blade in as deep as he could. He was dimly aware of Veronica screaming in the background.

Suddenly exhausted by the effort, Cassian's knees buckled, and he collapsed to the floor. Pain bloomed through his body as he hit the concrete.

Staring up at the lights of the kitchen, he heard Veronica talking to someone. She sounded as if she were deep underwater.

"Hello, yes, I'm at the home of Cassian Charles in Pacific Palisades, and there's been a stabbing ... He stabbed himself, I mean. Please hurry, we need help. There's so much blood ..."

About the Author

Shannon Fox is a San Diego-based writer of fiction spanning multiple genres. She grew up in the foothills of the Colorado Rockies before relocating to California to attend UC-San Diego, where she earned a BA in Literature-Writing.

Her short stories have appeared in the *Monsters, Movies & Mayhem* anthology, the *Cursed Collectibles* anthology, *The Copperfield Review*, *The Plaid Horse Magazine*, and more. Besides writing, Shannon has a passion for horses. She has competed at the international level in the sport of dressage. Shannon also owns a digital marketing company. For more stories from Shannon, visit her at Shannon-Fox.com.

BOW DRILL

JACE KILLAN

Micah steadied the carbine repeater and pointed it at the shadow approaching his barn. His eyes weren't what they used to be, especially an hour before dawn when all the shadows seemed to move, but he was certain this shadow belonged to somebody. It was too small to be a bear, even a black bear. Those wouldn't be in the valley this time of year anyway.

Over the decades, ranchers like Micah had run most of the wolves out of the valley, and this shadow moved quickly, then stilled, waiting. Not as tactful as a wolf. And only one. Not a pack or a tribe. This somebody was all alone.

His finger found the trigger, and Micah nearly popped one off to end the mystery, part of it anyway. He wouldn't know why someone had come here to the base of Mount Graham, in the night, miles from town.

He'd wonder until he got answers, so he stayed his finger and waited.

Half an hour passed, the cool breeze stirring up his sour musk. He'd need to bathe soon. It was either the smell or the mosquitos, and he'd put off the mosquitos long enough. The shadow hadn't moved in a bit, and Micah nearly thought he'd imagined it. Or he'd lost track of it. Either way, he figured that with dawn coming, he ought to check it out.

He tiptoed like his mentor, the Apache he called Grandfather, had shown him, rolling toe to heel. He stepped, careful not to stir any brush that might make a sound. Only feet from the shadow, he saw it was a human, curled up on her side. An Apache girl, given the dark, coarse hair and leather gown.

She wasn't moving.

He poked her with his rifle. When she didn't respond, he poked her harder. Her bare feet were torn from the desert rock and sagebrush. He withdrew a knife, ready to use it if this were a trap. Crouching low, Micah rolled the teenage girl onto her back and drew close, listening for breath.

It was there, but faint.

He slapped her across the face. "Hey."

Her eyelids lifted, but she didn't speak, and they quickly fluttered closed. Her face was soiled, lips chapped. He searched for blood but didn't find any wounds.

She needed water.

Certain there weren't any others about, Micah picked up the girl and draped her across his shoulder like a bushel of cotton, ready with the rifle in his free hand if he needed to use it.

By the time he reached the porch steps, the sky had turned a dark purple. Any moment now it would change to light blue and the sun would break out over the eastern hills.

Micah figured the girl had died when he couldn't get her to drink. He took to washing her scraped feet, but when he disinfected her soles with brandy, the pain brought the girl to consciousness. Awake, she downed several ladles of water, vomited half of it, then took to drinking more.

"Careful," Micah said in Apache.

"Your water is salty," she replied in English, with barely a trace of a native accent. "I've had better tasting sweat."

"It's what I got." Micah sniffed the water. He barely noticed the smell after twenty years. He shrugged and dropped the ladle in the wooden bucket. "You're welcome."

"For what?"

"For saving your life." Micah rose from the table where he sat. The Apache girl didn't respond. "Ain't very talkative, are you? You got a name?"

"Rebecca," she said. "Foster."

"Foster? You Yani's kin?"

"Granddaughter." Her words were soft, weak.

"Granddaughter? Your grandma blind?"

"I don't have a grandmother," she said. "Least not that I remember."

"Everyone's got a grandma, Becky. It just surprises me that Foster found someone who thought he was good-looking enough to mate with."

"He's not my real grandfather."

"Ah, well, that makes sense." Foster was known to take in strays. He'd taken in Micah, orphaned at the age of six, after other Apaches had killed Micah's parents. Micah had called him Grandfather, too. But that was another lifetime ago.

Micah found a bowl and looked in it—clean enough. He wiped out the crumbs with his hand and spooned in some cold beans from a pot on the floor. "How is that old bastard anyway?"

"Dead."

Micah sat the bowl down in front of the girl, trying not to react to the news. He didn't care for Foster none, not since the old Apache had shot him and left him for dead. It took everything Micah had to not go string up that sonofabitch after learning to walk again. But that was twenty years ago. Time had healed Micah's wounds, though the scars remained. They hadn't spoken since.

And now, he'd learned that his once-friend and mentor, the man who had raised him, had died. He couldn't help but feel regret for not having had that reconciling moment. Foster had never offered an apology. And Micah had never sought one out.

Like a rifle blast to his gut, Micah recalled their last encounter with perfect clarity. The two had bumped into each other outside the courthouse. Micah would have drawn his sidearm if he'd had it on him. Instead, he raised a finger and pointed at Foster. "I ever see you again, I'll kill ya."

He hadn't killed Foster, though Micah had seen him exactly three times after that. Each time, Foster had been in town, going about his business. They avoided each other. Too much regret. Too much shame there. Hard feelings that only grew harder, like scars.

Micah cleared his throat. "How'd he die?"

"Murdered."

"Murdered? By who?"

"Some fellas from the Chacon Gang—Burt Dodee and Willy Gomez."

"How long ago?"

"A day's past. Grandfather told me that if anything were to ever happen to him, I should find you. That you were a Foster too."

Micah wasn't listening. Despite their past, Micah owed it to Foster to track down his killers. Deep down, under the resentment, beneath the hurt and anger, sprouted a seedling of guilt. Maybe it stemmed from not dealing with Foster himself. Or maybe it was because Micah had always believed that their story would have an ending. Foster's murder left too many things unresolved.

Micah called up what he knew about the Chacon Gang. Chacon had been arrested for murder a year or so ago but broke out of the Graham county jail. Most believed he'd escaped to Mexico. Burt Dodee and Willy Gomez, however, had been spotted outside of Morenci a few weeks back. Word went out that folks travelling should be wary of doing so alone, as those bastards were known for thieving.

With a murder hanging over their heads, they'd be doing one of two things. Looking for the girl before she talked to authorities or heading for Mexico.

"Did they see you?" Micah asked.

"They think I'm dead. They torched his place and thought I was inside."

They'd be heading to Mexico then. "Were they on horses?"

"Yes."

He could guess that they'd come down from Foster's place at the base of Mount Graham and wrap around either east toward Wilcox or west through the Apache lands. Prudence would say head to Wilcox and from there take a straight shot to Bisbee or Benson. But maybe they wrapped around west to avoid traffic. Micah wouldn't know until he got there and looked, followed the tracks, but that would take time. More time than he had if he wanted to catch up and head them off before the Mexico border.

But Micah knew he'd spend weeks wondering, searching, waiting. The tracks would show him.

"I'm going after them. You can stay here. There's hardtack and flour under the bed. Water from the well out back."

"I'm going with you," she said around a mouthful of beans.

"You'll just slow me down."

"I'm going with you. I'm not drinking this piss you call water."

"You don't even have shoes."

"I bet you have an old pair of boots under that bed too."

Micah considered her. Her face was flush with life, not like the corpse he'd pulled from the field. If it came to it, two would be better than one. If she could keep up.

"Can you shoot?" he asked.

"Foster taught me. And you know how good of a shot—Sorry. I didn't think …" Her face flushed with embarrassment.

"He tell you what happened?"

She nodded. "Said he was drunk and thought you were someone else."

Micah shrugged off the bad memories. The ones he'd hidden away under his bed of anger. He stuffed them back down; he wasn't ready to digest them yet.

"We gotta go." After finding her an old pair of boots three sizes too big, he directed Rebecca to saddle the two quarter horses in the barn. He prepped several bags with food and ammo. He hung two bedrolls over his shoulders and several leather canteens. This time of year was nice enough, but cooled down at night. He also took his small stash of six-shooters, four of them, and two rifles.

Rebecca had the horses saddled by the time he arrived, and she helped him load the saddlebags and gear. She looked funny in the boots that nearly rose to her knees, but she hopped onto the stallion no smaller than fifteen hands. Even in her dress and too-big boots, it was like she'd done it a thousand times.

She did well keeping up with him. By midday, they'd gone up the belly of Mount Graham and were nearing Foster's place. The streams trickled down and converged into the Frye Creek that fed out toward Safford. Up above the streams, smoke lifted from the smoldering remains of the barn and ranch house. Several apple trees dotted the windy path that led down toward the creek, and the smoke.

Without direction, Rebecca unsaddled, snatched a rifle and a box of ammo, and climbed the hillside that overlooked the once-standing ranch house. Smart.

Micah continued on with caution. He scanned the area. Red-tailed squirrels dashed up and down trees, unaware of the violent remains nearby.

It had been years since Micah had been here, but it was still familiar to him. He'd grown up here. Swam in that creek. Planted those apple trees. Swung from the porch swing, now ash. He'd caught and skinned a black Mojave rattler under that massive tree up the way. It'd made for some good stew.

What remained of Foster lay at the foot of a charred brass bed frame near the cast-iron stove.

Anger seeped from under Micah's bed though he tried to contain it. It came from many places. It came from Foster, the drunken Indian who'd shot him, the loving mentor who had never apologized. That hurt more than the bullets. It came from Dodee and Gomez, the bastards who had killed his onetime friend. And, if he were being honest, it came from himself, too, his pride, his refusal to forgive Foster.

Foster had taught Micah how to track, so it didn't take long for him to get his bearings and recognize the outlaws' imprints in the clay and surrounding brush. To his surprise, the tracks didn't head back down the mountain, but continued up. He motioned for Rebecca to follow with her horse along the ridgeline above as he kept to the tracks flanking the creek.

A mile later, Micah and Rebecca's paths converged at the falls, which were as beautiful as Micah remembered.

"That them?" Rebecca pointed at the scrub oak with a disturbed section beside it.

"Yep. Good eye." The outlaws had peeled away from the creek and headed toward a trail that lead further into the mountain. They weren't going around it, but over it.

Micah and Rebecca hurried their pursuit. With two of Foster's tracking students on the search, they went much quicker than Micah could have on his own. When they reached the trail leading up to Granite Point, they found a small wagon and a dying mule. It had been shot four or five times in the side and lay, in agony, bleeding out, with vultures circling above. The cart's owner was found several yards away in a gulley. Looked as though they'd used him as target practice after pushing him in. Rebecca put the mule out of its misery.

By the time dusk fell, they were climbing the switchbacks

near Turkey Flats, a beautiful view of the valley outstretched below them.

Dodee and Gomez weren't moving fast but were still miles ahead of them. Micah had spotted a campsite a couple hours back where the outlaws had stayed last night and, by the look of things, hadn't started out again until midday. Seems they'd found a stash of whiskey in that wagon and went to drinking.

The air chilled quickly in the mountains. Micah asked Rebecca to tend to the horses while he prepared the fire. Frowning, he realized he'd run off without his sack of matches and flask of whiskey. Must've left them on the bed.

"Foster ever show you how to make a bow drill?" Micah asked.

"No. But I saw him do it a couple times."

Micah thought about forgoing the fire, but they'd need it to keep warm at night. It was straight up chilly now. Also, out across the night sky, dark clouds formed. He'd been in these mountains enough as a boy to know it didn't take much prodding for them to turn into a nasty storm.

"Best I get on with it then." Micah went down to the creek. In the light of the half moon, he saw what he needed, but he could have found what he was looking for even in complete darkness. He bent over and combed his fingers through clumps of grass on the creek side. He did this several times to several clumps. With each pass, he got a little more dead grass that he used to form a bird's nest, wrapping it around, intertwining it just like a robin might.

Cottonwoods flanked both sides of the creek. They'd been following the green canvas all day up the mountain. He should have thought on it earlier; he could have found a dozen dry pieces to use, but he'd assumed he had his matches. After several passes, he located a dead branch, about three inches wide, that he broke from the towering cottonwood.

Back at camp he split the branch longways using his knife

and a rock, then split it again. It offered a nice plank that he broke down to the length of his arm.

"Help me with this, Becky." Micah handed her the plank and his knife. He showed her how to hollow out an inch-wide bowl and notch it, like removing a small slice of pie from the hollowed-out bowl. "The notch is most important," he said, repeating the exact lesson he'd received from Foster. "It lets the embers fall out. Otherwise you're just drilling on top of yourself and making a mess."

Rebecca got to work carving. Micah went searching for a dead yucca. They'd seen thousands of yuccas that day, but after looking for twenty minutes, Micah worried they were too high up the mountain to find one now. He moved away from the creek, keeping his bearings so he could find camp again. After walking about a mile, he found a pod of yucca and breathed a sigh of relief. He took one of their shoots for the spindle, and he broke off several arms of the yucca for the fibers he'd fashion into a rope.

Back at camp he snapped off a ten-inch piece of the yucca shoot with his boot and gave it to Rebecca. "Carve this down. It needs to be round like a spindle, straight and smooth. But don't take off too much. It's got to be thick enough to sit in your hole there." He pointed at the plank where she'd hollowed out several inch-sized bowls. He hadn't asked her to do more than one, but she must not have been lying when she said she'd seen Foster do this before. He'd use the same plank for months making fires from his bow drill.

Almost there.

Micah broke the rest of the yucca into a section as long as his arm. This would serve as the bow. Then he took the tip of the yucca arms and peeled back the needle until it gave way, tearing down the length of the arm and removing several strands of plant fiber. He did the same to the others, removing the needle tips and starting to weave the fibers into a quarter-inch-thick rope about four feet long. He pulled on both sides of the rope and felt it hold.

One more piece.

He returned to the creek where he found a smooth rock that fit nicely in the palm of his hand. With a shard of granite, he began to peck the rock. He hit it over and over again while walking back to camp.

"What are you doing?" Rebecca asked.

"You never peck a rock before?"

"Nope." She held out the spindle. The tips were rounded and smooth.

"Looks good," Micah said. "To peck a rock you need one that is solid that does the pecking and one that is softer that does the giving. But you want to be careful. If you use some of that clay or sandstone that's down in the valley, it'll give way and break, and you'll have to start all over."

As he spoke, he realized how much he knew about this particular skill. And that he'd learned it all from Foster. A skill that now, most didn't need or use. How long would this talent of making a fire with a bow drill survive in a world that didn't need it? Probably not long at all.

That made Micah sad. It wasn't useless information. In fact, it could be extremely valuable, lifesaving even. But who would teach it? Who would want to learn it? No, sir, that skill wouldn't last another century, of that Micah was certain.

"Do you know how to prepare kindling?" Micah asked. Rebecca nodded and went about gathering twigs, leaves, and dried grasses. She put them together and built a tepee around the pile. Foster had taught her that, too.

After half an hour of pecking, Micah had made a good indention. He let Rebecca try it. It didn't take her long to find the rhythm.

"Now, you want to smooth it out. The smoother the better. So rub your finger over your face, then rub it in the groove you've been pecking. There's oil on your face. That oil will coat that groove." They both did and the indention smoothed. "Behind your ears. In your ears is the best. Your nose too. Your neck."

They were ready.

Micah showed Rebecca how to position the plank so that he could step on the edge as he knelt. The spindle fit nicely into the bowl Rebecca had carved. He wrapped the yucca rope, strung between the bow, around the spindle, then positioned the rock on top and applied pressure with his palm.

"Now the fun begins." Micah pushed the bow then pulled it back, churning the spindle. The whole thing collapsed at the awkwardness of his motion. He laughed lightly. "We'll need to do this a few dozen times until I find my groove and the pieces all figure out how to work together."

He tried again. It collapsed.

He made some adjustments to the string's tautness, to his kneeling position, to the string's placement on the spindle, and to the downward pressure from his palm, and suddenly it began to spin, longer than one or two or five motions. It kept spinning and spinning with the pulling and pushing.

Several minutes later, Micah's shoulder burned. He hadn't used these muscles in ages. "Here, you take a spell."

Rebecca positioned herself as he had and struggled to get the motion. All the forces, if not calibrated, worked against one another. Micah gave her some pointers, and soon she found the rhythm as she had with pecking the rock.

"Foster ever tell you how he learned the bow drill?"

"Nope."

"He said he was six or seven, and his father had taken him into these mountains to hunt. It was Foster's job to make the fire —they weren't going to have fire unless Foster could do it. His father gave him the spindle but let Foster prepare everything else. After a week of eating cold food and freezing at night, his father showed Foster how to make the spindle. Told him that the one he'd been using all week was green."

"Green wouldn't work. It's got to be dry, right?"

"Right. When Foster carved his own and knew it was dry, it took him just a couple minutes to get the embers together. His father told him that he had to build the muscles first, so he had Foster practicing on green until he was strong enough."

Micah took over again, knowing Rebecca was feeling the burn from the repeated motion. As he pushed and pulled, so many memories of his mentor passed through his mind. That old Apache had saved his life more than once, and not a day went by that Micah didn't use something Foster had taught him.

And now he was gone. Why had Micah not reconciled with the bastard? But how could he have if Foster never apologized?

That anger seeped out from under his bed again. He used it. He used it to push through the burn in his shoulder, the stiffness in his neck. Faster he went. Harder. Sweat blurred Micah's vision. He plunged forward, harder still.

The bastard. All he had to do was apologize. Say he was sorry. Micah would have forgiven him. They could have continued the relationship they'd once had instead of the mess it became.

Smoke tickled Micah's nose. He was close now. A few more pushes and pulls.

"Pass me that nest," he said, but Rebecca had it ready. The embers had fallen out the notch, black and red on the dirt. Micah pushed them with a stick into the nest, folded it in half, and held it up. He blew, softly at first, then harder as the nest glowed red and ignited.

He sat the fireball in the base of the tepee of kindling Rebecca had constructed. Minutes later, they had a sustainable fire.

They sat in silence, Micah enjoying the fire, the jerky, the hardtack, the smooth-tasting water of the creek, not like that piss he drank from his own well. He didn't get away enough. Probably because it all reminded him of Foster.

"Did you hate him?" Rebecca asked.

"Foster?" Micah considered the question. "No. I didn't hate him."

"He thought you did."

Her words tore at him like that bullet so long ago. "And if I did? He was a worthless drunk." As the words left him, Micah knew he shouldn't have said them.

"He wasn't," Rebecca blurted. He heard the sadness in her voice. "Worthless or a drunk."

"I ... I didn't mean nothing ..."

"He felt sorry, Micah. Real sorry. He didn't drink since."

Micah didn't believe that for a second. "Sure."

"He didn't. In fact, that's why they killed him. They asked him for a drink, and he told 'em he didn't have any alcohol, that he'd never touch the stuff. Devil water, he called it. They killed him 'cause they thought he was lying."

"Really?"

"Yeah, really. He told me that stuff had cost him his family and his best friend, and he wouldn't touch it as long as he lived."

"If that were true, why didn't he apologize to me?"

"He did."

"No, he didn't."

"Yes, he did so. I took the letter myself."

"Letter? What letter?"

"Several, in fact, that I know of. We'd give 'em to Jenkins who'd come by once a week."

"That bastard." Jenkins was a thief. He'd usually comb through the post for valuables or letters holding information leading to valuables, like shipments and travel plans. He'd feed that news to men like the Chacon Gang for a commission. Micah had tried to out Jenkins a few years past, and the two nearly went to bullets. Since then, Jenkins wasn't about to do Micah any favors. No wonder Micah hadn't received any letters.

"What did they say?" Micah asked. "The letters. You ever read any?"

"No. That's private."

Dammit. He'd been a fool. Both of them had. The letters probably held an apology and a request to meet. That would have been awkward but knowing himself and knowing Foster, the two would have embraced and resumed their friendship.

"What are we doing here?" Micah thought aloud. "What am I doing? This is a matter for the authorities, not some rancher and a girl."

"I can fight."

"That's not what I'm saying. These are dangerous outlaws. Killers. Foster would be downright pissed at me for bringing you along on this fool's errand. I don't know—I suppose I'm chasing after them out of guilt."

"Guilt?"

"Regret, then. Foster raised me. He was sober when I was with him, but he started drinking when I went to fight with the Rough Riders. When I got back, he was a mess. I always wondered if he knew it was me when he shot me. I don't think he did. It was the booze doing the shootin'. Not Foster."

"He didn't know."

"Yeah." Micah nodded. "I don't suppose he did. Say, did he ever teach you how to trap?"

"Yep. Figure fours and all that."

"There are many others too, you know."

"I know."

"Grandchildren, I mean. Foster took in many a stray."

"I know," Becky said again.

"So that makes us, what? Cousins?"

"Foster cousins, I suppose."

"What happened to your parents?" Micah asked.

"Some white men killed my dad because he was Indian. And

they killed my mom because she married one. How about your parents?"

"Geronimo. He hit our wagon. Would have killed me too if Foster hadn't been passing by at the time."

The two sat in silence. Micah's mind drifted to the violence that dotted his life. He'd seen killing. He'd known meanness and hatred. He'd seen firsthand the destructive powers of vices. He'd let anger rule his actions, but what good had come of it? Any of it? It wasn't hatred that brought peace. It was love. Foster had loved him. Foster had loved Rebecca.

As he stared at the fire, the flickering flames and the dancing shadows, Micah had an epiphany. One that had been there stashed away under that mattress with all that other stuff. There were two forces in this world, both fueled by choices. One good and one bad. At the end of the day, Foster had made mostly good choices but some bad ones, and still he suffered a violent fate. But that wasn't fate at all, was it? No. Rather that was the result of a bad choice of another, someone who probably had made some good choices in his life, but mostly bad.

Because of Foster's kindness, he'd taken Micah and Rebecca, and many others, out of terrible situations stemming from the evil of other people. He'd provided for them. He'd raised them. Taught them things, like the bow drill. And because of it, despite the violence in their lives, they'd been shown kindness and goodness and love.

Good could counter the effects of evil. Micah didn't know if good would always win, but fighting evil with hatred and anger didn't make any sense. There were more important things in this world, like helping others. Teaching others. Passing on what had been taught to him. Everything else seemed so trivial now.

Micah had a choice to make, but he'd already made it. Hearing about Foster's letters didn't release the anger from under the bed. It took the entire bed away, the anger, and the shame. It quenched those feelings like water on a campfire. And what remained was the warmth of peace.

To choose good or bad. Love or hate. Selflessness or selfishness. To mentor or to destroy. His existence boiled down to that. And Micah knew what to choose. He'd had a good teacher.

"Get some shut-eye. Tomorrow, we'll report the murder to the sheriff and get some supplies for you in town. Then I'll figure out how to add a bedroom to my little shack."

"And Dodee and Gomez?"

"Foster wouldn't want us to waste another second on them. They're bad men doing bad things. You and me, let's be different. Let's do good things."

"Like what?"

"I'll teach you the bow drill for starters."

"I'd like that."

"Maybe you could brush me up on trappin'. It's been awhile."

Later, nestled in their bedrolls aside the glowing embers, Micah reflected on how his life had changed over the last twenty-four hours. He hadn't expected to become a mentor, and he hoped he'd be a good one, like Foster had been to him.

"Micah?"

"Yeah, Becky?"

"If I live at your place does that mean I have to drink your nasty piss water?"

About the Author

Jace Killan lives in Arizona with his family, wife, and five kids, and a little dog. He writes middle-grade fiction, thrillers, and soft sci-fi on the side. He has an MBA and works in finance for a biotechnology firm. Jace plays and writes music and enjoys everything outdoors. He's also a novice photographer. For more information about Jace Killan and his writing visit jacekillan.com.

DREAM GIRL

KITTY SARKOZY

I saw you for the first time in my favorite coffee shop. You looked so sad with your rumpled hair and equally rumpled suit. It looked as if your body was trying to slither out but couldn't find an exit from the hot, itchy wool, or whatever suits are made of. You looked tired and stressed.

I thought about talking to you right away, but I was learning to knit that day. Orange and pink fuzzy yarn tangled around my fingers, soft butterfly-leg fibers caressing my skin. Sadly, the bamboo needles were silent. I had hoped they would click with each stitch. Maybe the clicking was something you developed over time; if so, I would totally get it.

I was concentrating on my knitting, trying to grow a super funky scarf from the single line the sweet old lady at the knitting shop had cast on for me. I wasn't unhappy that day. Maybe I was a little lonely, the way you get when you sit alone in a café watching all the sad people with their sad lives—all of them pretending to not be alone by traveling in pairs, holding hands, or talking excitedly into expensive phones.

The Smiths were playing in my earbuds; they always make me feel better. Their songs are dark yet catchy, perky and alive.

They remind me that no matter how bad things get, you can always smile and dance.

You were talking on your phone when you came in, but you didn't have a happy phone face on like the three people who came in before you did. Your face was real—real sad, real disappointed. I don't know what you were talking about. I tried to read your lips, but I don't actually know how to read lips. I should learn; that would be awesome.

You sat at a table in the corner and ordered several refills of coffee, which can't have helped your stress level. You had a laptop that, against all reason, made you even more stressed-looking. You ran your fingers through your hair over and over. No wonder you are such a rumpled teddy bear. I feared you might start pulling it out. I had totally decided to come talk to you as soon as I finished the row I was on when you abruptly slammed down the screen of your laptop and stormed out.

That's when I knew how badly you needed my help. I gathered up my knitting as fast as I could, but balls of yarn are wiggly. By the time I got outside, you were gone. I ran around the building hoping to see you, but I guess you drove. I don't drive, so I sometimes forget that other people do.

I was sad for a while. I cried a bit, sitting alone on the cold metal seats outside the coffee shop, shivering because I had left my coat inside. You needed a kind word or a smile. I let you down. I had been selfish and not listened to the call of fate. I vowed that day to follow the signposts of the universe and be true to what I knew was right.

You can't imagine how happy I was when the cosmic spirit of the universe said "You have work to do!" and brought you back to me less than a week later.

I was at the park on Tuesday; I think I was listening to Regina Spektor. She's just awesome, right?! I was singing along, but it was okay, because it was early, before kids start having recess, so I had the swings all to myself. I love swings; if I close my eyes, it's like flying. My whole body tingles with the falls and soars with each rise. I close my eyes, and I'm a dragon or a seagull. Thankfully I didn't have my eyes closed when you walked past, your gaze on the ground, shoulders slumped.

I leapt into action right away, which was great, because the swing was at the perfect height for it.

I followed you for a few blocks. Putting the Smiths playlist on Spotify, obviously. I was dancing a little, you know, to look casual, like I wasn't following you. I was just a regular girl walking around. You went into a FedEx. I sort of hung around outside near some bushes that smelled like Froot Loops.

When I saw you at the register, I got into position a few yards away, then I walked quickly back toward the doors. The universe timed it all perfectly, and I bumped into you as you came out, causing you to drop all your papers.

"Dammit!" you growled.

"Oh, God! I am so, so sorry. Let me help you," I said, hurriedly picking up papers.

It was so weird. As you looked at me and our eyes met for the first time, the song changed. Right as I was thinking about how tired you looked, I realized what song it was. As I picked up papers, half of them résumés on linen paper and half of them "Wanted: Roommate" flyers, I figured out what you needed from me. Maybe it was later that I knew for sure, but the idea entered my head then, even if I didn't realize it consciously at the time.

"Asleep" is our song, chosen for us by destiny.

You were mad at me about the papers, but you were madder at life. I offered to buy you a coffee. You looked at me and said, "Sure."

Maybe you agreed because I had worn my favorite headband that matched the pink highlights in my hair, or maybe you said yes because I was wearing a super cute sundress with long striped socks and the fabulous orange-and-pink scarf I had finished knitting the day before. Or maybe you wanted a cup of coffee. Either way, fate brought us together. We went back to the shop where I first saw you.

This time you were not alone at that little table. This time, instead of being angry at your phone and laptop, you were with me. I made you laugh. I told you fun stories about all the great things I have been doing. I showed you pictures of my kitten. I supported you by listening to your seemingly endless list of problems, but only while we were at the coffee shop.

I spent the rest of the day with you, on the condition that you not think or talk about your girlfriend dumping you, your father being disappointed in you, or how you didn't think you could pay the rent alone. I told you that today was your day off from being you. I even picked out a new name for you. I called you "Luke," like from *Star Wars*. Boys love *Star Wars*.

We walked around the city, and it was like you had never seen it before; all of it was new and shiny. I picked the first bright dandelion of spring and put it in your hair, but it refused to stay, so you put it in your pocket for safekeeping. I let you wear my scarf. We watched the swans in the lake and fed the ducks. We went to my favorite diner and had banana waffles for dinner.

When it got dark, we danced to the music in our souls in the empty parking lot of an abandoned, dilapidated shopping center. At one point I waltzed while you did something like a cha-cha. Then you spun me around, and we laughed as you held on to me to keep me from falling. The stars in the sky danced with us. You told me it was the most wonderful day of your life.

When we slow danced, you cried a single tear. I kissed the salty drop away from your cheek. Then you kissed me. Your kiss was tender, in a way that others might not have expected from your angry, stressed exterior. I wasn't surprised. I knew Mr. Angry wasn't the real you. The real you, the person you should have been, was in that sweet, innocent kiss. I was honored you shared yourself with me in a perfect moment of clarity.

We went back to your place. It was a gray and dreary place.

The ghost of the relationship you'd had with your ex haunted every room, every inch, dusting every surface with the ash of "What should have been?" and "What went wrong?" It would take a hundred perfect days to clean that ash off your soul. I don't know if it could ever be cleaned from your apartment.

You still had a picture of her in the living room. She was one of *those* girls. Her hair dyed the same color of blonde as every other girl like her. She had a name-brand purse and brand-new matchy-matchy clothes, a forced smile, and empty eyes. She was the type of girl who wanted a successful man, an expensive engagement ring, a white picket fence, and 2.5 kids. Maybe if you had never dated her you wouldn't have come to me so broken, so tired. Or maybe you dated her because you *were* broken, worn down by a lawyer father, a conservative family, and social expectations.

You and Ms. Name-brand might have broken each other, enforcing the rigid lives that had been handed to each of you. But I had touched your soul and knew the real you. Had things been different, you could have been so much more. You were a good person, your hands strong, your lips so very gentle.

I went to your bathroom to pee and had a look in your medicine cabinet. As I looked at all the bottles, our song played in my head, and I knew why I had been led to you. My heart broke, and I cried for you, for us. If only we had met earlier, before empty-eyed girlfriends, before itchy suits, before gray ash and shattered everything. You could have seen the beauty in the world, in yourself. We could have loved each other and created joy.

I got in your ceramic bathtub, which was so cold it burned my skin. I wrapped my arms around my legs, hiding my face in the brightly colored cotton dress. I cried for what had been done to you, for the shame and expectations that had been piled on, crushing you stone by stone. I cried for the person you could have been and for who we could have been together. I cried a salty ocean for all that was lost. When I could cry no more, I washed away my tears, put on fresh purple eye shadow and a happy smile.

You had lit candles while I was gone, giving the whole place a warm glow that almost hid the ash. Exactly how your smile and excitement almost hid the crumbling person inside. Sometimes, when I dance alone in that empty parking lot, I wish that it had, so I could have ignored the truth.

We made love that night, tender and passionate at the same time. We drank bubbly Moscato, and you drank me in. You filled all the holes that life had made in your soul with the clean, cool water of my love. You were complete that night for the first time in so long. I was happy to be with you, the real you.

We made love for hours.

I poured you a drink—whiskey, I think. It smelled bad, like medicine. You were already sleepy, but after you drank it, you got much sleepier. I had a moment of doubt looking at your peaceful face, but it went away when you looked at me, pleading, with tears in your eyes and said, "Stay. Please. I don't want to wake up alone anymore."

I tried not to cry. I didn't want to mar your perfect day with my own selfish desire. But it was all too much, and I couldn't hold back. I kissed every part of your face, stroked your hair, and whispered, "I promise you will never have to wake up alone ever again."

I lay there with you as you fell asleep, and I listened to your slow, steady breathing. I held you as your breathing became less steady. I cried harder, with my whole being, as you went completely still with a small smile on your lips. I said, "I love you," and I kissed you. I wanted to stay there with you forever, frozen in our perfect day.

A few hours before dawn, I pulled myself away from you. There were things I needed to do before I could leave. I put the whiskey bottle on your nightstand with the pill bottles. I scattered the few remaining capsules around. I broke the picture of your ex-girlfriend on the corner of your nightstand, the glass raining down as shining glitter. I washed the champagne flutes and put them away. I blew out all the candles and took the empty Moscato bottles with me. I locked the dead bolt from outside with a spare key from your junk drawer.

Leaving you there, alone in that sad apartment, hurt. I felt horrible doing it, but I had to. You weren't really there anymore, but it still felt wrong.

I sometimes wake up at night, and I see you lying there in your gray room, your gray bed, your cold skin covered in a thin layer of dust and ash. I take a few breaths and remind myself that you are free, that I did the right thing, before snuggling my kitten and going back to sleep.

I miss you and wish you hadn't been broken beyond repair. I wish I had met you before it was too late, so I could've fixed you.

I put orange and pink flowers on your grave every Tuesday.

About the Author

Kitty Sarkozy is a speculative fiction writer, actor, and robot girlfriend. She is an Associate Editor at Pseudopod, an award-winning weekly horror podcast in the Escape Artists network. Several large cats allow her to live with them in Marietta, GA, where she enjoys tending the extensive gardens into a perfect, tranquil place to hide bodies. For a list of her publications, acting credits, or to engage her services on your next project go to kittysarkozy.com or follow her on Twitter @KittySarkozy.

WHITE SAILS AND STORMY SEAS

M. ELIZABETH TICKNOR & REBECCA E. TREASURE

Gwen flipped the comm-chip across the backs of her knuckles, watching four-year-old Asher build a block tower on the Prussian-blue woolen carpet. She'd already slid a matching chip into the tiny port behind her left ear, ready to connect to the other—to connect her to Asher. She lifted a cup of breakfast tea and sipped the bitter liquid without looking away from her son.

Sunlight streamed in the window of their 45th-floor apartment, deceptively thin on what was sure to be a sweltering August day. Asher sprawled on the floor, in the center of the pool of sunlight, wearing his favorite red jumper and boots with cartoon rockets emblazoned on their sides. He placed each new block just slightly to the right of the previous one without disturbing the leaning tower. Alternating red and blue blocks, the tower would appear on the verge of toppling, but it always ended up connecting with the wall. Asher had done it a dozen times just this morning.

The comm-chip in her hand weighed more than it should. The tiny piece of metal and plastic, crammed as full of data as she dared while leaving space for the program to grow and learn, pressed into her palm. Each of the four sharp corners punctured her skin. She could swear a hint of electrical zing radiated from the inert chip.

The chips would save them both. She could go back to the programming work she loved, and Asher could go to school and share his genius with the world. With the chip, Asher would be able to speak to her, to fully communicate with her. He'd been her inspiration since before he was born, but now he would finally know—now he would finally understand how much she loved him.

We're ready.

Asher finished his tower. With a wordless howl of joy, he flicked the bottom block away. The next block dropped onto the rug, but the tower held firm. He flicked again and again until the last block was back in the box. Then he started over.

This child isn't acceptable to the school system? The thought had been running through her mind since she'd received the flash-mail two weeks earlier. Asher had been denied entrance into the virtual public school system and required to attend physical classes. Gwen scowled. Her fingers curled around the comm-chip. Junia's son, Kevan, spent his days playing VR on his chiplant and couldn't even spell his name, and he attended VPSS. Asher would be fine.

"We're sorry, Mrs. Turing," the administrator had said when she'd called to complain. "Asher's verbal and interpersonal scores are well below those required for VPSS. He will thrive in our physical schools, with children like him and teachers trained to accommodate his needs."

Children like him. The thought chugged around Gwen's mind like a polluted tugboat, leaving a tainted wake behind. *There are no children like him.* The physical schools were underfunded and filled with mediocre teachers. Worse, the aura of not having qualified for VPSS would follow Asher his whole life.

Asher's rebuilt tower connected with the wall. Despite Gwen's frustrations, she smiled in anticipation of the joy he found in collapsing it, block by block, back to nothing. She flipped on her chiplant recorder and saved the file. Sometimes she'd watch them when she couldn't sleep.

Gwen shifted forward on the sloping chair. "Asher, baby, come here."

He ignored her, as he had every day of his life. She kept talking to him, though, hoping that someday, somehow, her words would reach him.

At thirty-six, Gwen had decided she wanted to be a mom after all and applied for insemination. Her pregnancy had been perfect. When Asher was born, she'd been ready. She'd read all the books, and had prepared the nautical nursery with a 3-Decal that showed a white-sailed ship on a smooth sea. She'd stay home with him for a year, and then go back to developing chiplant programs.

She'd turned off the decal before Asher was a month old. Nothing but rough seas with Asher.

She set down the tea and pinched the chip between her forefinger and thumb. Today she would reach him. Today he would understand. "Asher. Come here."

Flick. *Thump.* Flick. *Thump.* Flick. *Thump.* Flick. *Thump.*

"Asher, come here!" She winced at the edge in her voice. A deep breath settled her rising agitation. *It's not his fault. There's no use getting angry.* "Asher." The singsong falseness of her voice stung worse than the anger. Asher didn't know it was fake, but Gwen did.

She took a deep breath in, let it out slowly, and walked over to him. After settling cross-legged on the floor in front of him, she reached out and touched his soft cheek. Finally, he paused his rebuilding, humming under his breath.

When she leaned forward to insert the comm-chip, her elbow bumped the tower. It fell with a *clatter-thwomp* onto the carpet. Asher began screaming and hitting her, angry tears running down his face. She knew he wasn't purposefully attacking her, but the tight fists flailing through the uncaring air still collided with her arm, shoulder, and jaw.

"It's all right, you can rebuild it again," she soothed, stroking his hair. "Calm down. Deep breaths."

Asher didn't react except to start kicking his legs. The frustration, that useless, hateful, ugly rage at being unheard and misunderstood, swirled up in her chest again. She *knew* it wasn't his fault, *knew* he couldn't help it, but that hot, bubbling desperation to reach him felt as uncontrollable as his own outburst.

"If you'd just listen to me, this would all be over! I'm trying to help us." Gwen grabbed his wrists and held them, sobbing with him and trying to keep him from smashing his head against the scattered blocks. At the same time, she pushed back against that eruption of fury with all her weary might. She didn't want to feel that way—not now, not ever.

Asher finally settled when Gwen used her chiplant to play his favorite song. The stomping chant of Oompa Loompas set her teeth on edge, but his kicking slowed to match the rhythm, so she was able to get behind him and access his port. Trembling, she held up the comm-chip. It caught the empty sunlight from the window.

She bit her bottom lip. It would work. It had to work. She slid the chip into Asher's port, closed her eyes, and initiated the program.

The world blurred, stretched, *shifted*. For a moment, Gwen swore she saw a murky impression of her own face against her closed eyelids. But that was impossible. The program allowed two-way communication, but Asher shouldn't have control. She should be the one initiating any communications.

The image faded; the universe snapped back into place. Gwen opened her eyes cautiously. The world seemed brighter, louder—a common effect of sensory-enhancement chips, the basic program template she had extrapolated from in order to create the comm-chip.

Asher stared up at her, wide-eyed. She smiled and focused her thoughts, reaching out to him with her mind.

Hello, Asher.

Asher screamed.

Confusion and terror slammed into Gwen like a tidal wave. She couldn't focus—she couldn't *breathe*. She recoiled, panting, as she tried to get her emotions under control. But they weren't hers to control—they were Asher's.

Asher, who was running full tilt toward the apartment door.

Gwen scooped Asher up just as he reached the door, weathering the inevitable swath of kicks and punches. "Asher, sweetheart, it's okay. Asher!"

Asher bit Gwen's arm just below the wrist, hard enough to draw blood. Gwen yelped. Her grip loosened. Asher wriggled free, arched up on tiptoe, and slapped his palm against the biometric lock-pad that kept the door sealed.

Only Gwen was authorized to open the bio-lock—except in cases of emergency. The lock's sensors automatically registered Asher's pulse and body temperature, analyzing the potential threat level.

The pad lit up neon-green. The door swished open. Asher charged out the door and tore down the hallway toward the quartet of elevators.

"Asher!" Gwen lurched after him, heart racing.

Halfway down the hall, Asher ducked between the legs of a bulky man in an ill-fitting tracksuit. The man yelped and stumbled, bracing both arms against the walls in an attempt to maintain his balance.

Gwen tried to avoid the man, but she was too close and moving too fast. She slammed face-first into his chest. The two of them fell to the ground in a tangled heap.

The man helped her back to her feet with a grunt. His brow furrowed. "You shouldn't be running in the halls. It's not safe."

Gwen squeezed past him, eyes darting back and forth in search of Asher. "I need to find my son!"

Asher was gone. The right-most elevator was descending, dragging Gwen's heart along with it. Flashing numbers indicated it had just passed floor thirty-seven.

Gwen hammered on the down arrow. No good. None of the other elevators were anywhere close to the 45th floor.

The man drew alongside her, his brow knitted with concern. "That was your son?"

Gwen nodded. She rocked back and forth on the balls of her feet, studying the elevators' floor numbers with frantic intensity, trying to predict which would arrive first. The flickering lights of the elevator indicator pulled at her, and for a moment she fell into them completely. Anticipation of the next *flip* of the digitized number swelled and fell within her like a soothing tide.

"How old is he? He should know better. That kind of behavior is dangerous."

The man's voice jarred her so badly that the hairs on the back of her neck stood on end. She shook herself and glared at him. "Are you a father?"

"No—"

"Then you can't understand. You don't know me or my son. You have no right to lecture me."

Asher's elevator touched down on the first floor. Gwen got a flash-impression of elevator doors swishing open, of scrambling out just in time to avoid a swarm of people who seemed impossibly tall.

The vision passed as quickly as it had come. Gwen shivered and massaged at the chiplant site behind her left ear. What had happened? Was she really feeling what Asher felt, seeing things through Asher's eyes? That wasn't supposed to be possible.

The second elevator from the left arrived with a *ding*. Gwen gasped with relief, slid inside, and slammed her thumb against the button for the ground floor.

The big man stepped into the elevator beside her and cleared his throat sheepishly. "I'm sorry. I didn't mean to come off as rude. I'm just concerned."

Gwen bristled and looked away. "Everyone is always concerned. Everyone always thinks they know best. But they don't, they *can't*. I never knew how difficult raising a child would be until I had Asher. I love him, I *adore* him, but sometimes it's just so *hard*—" She cut herself off, biting at the knuckles of her right hand to choke off a frantic sob. The last thing she needed to do was admit her fears and anxieties to a stranger.

The man fell silent; his brow furrowed in a deep frown. Gwen couldn't tell if he was sympathizing with her plight or judging the weight of her failures. She turned away, but felt his eyes on her back all the same.

The elevator plunged downward. Gwen's stomach lurched. A fresh jolt of fear pierced her abdomen, fed through her chiplant. She chewed on her lower lip, tasting a burst of copper in her mouth as she worried for Asher's safety.

The elevator stopped three times during its descent. By the time it reached the ground floor, Gwen was pressed behind half a dozen bodies. She shouldered her way out, ignoring the protests of her fellow passengers, and held her breath as she scanned for Asher.

The ground floor of the apartment building was covered in 3-Decals that portrayed the illusion of a gold-gilt, cream-white lobby. The ceiling appeared to be fifty feet high, arched like a Greco-Roman cathedral, but Gwen knew better. A ceiling that high would have eaten up at least three floors of living space.

Asher was nowhere to be seen.

Gwen rushed up to the harried-looking woman who worked the front desk during the day. Gwen had only seen her twice before; staff turnover at the apartment complex seemed high.

"Excuse me. Did you see my son come through here? Dark-haired, wearing rocket-boots and a red jumper, about two and a half feet tall." She gestured with her hand.

The woman frowned. "I think he ran outside a minute ago."

Gwen's breath lodged in her throat. "You *think*? Why didn't you stop him?"

"I was speaking with a tenant. By the time I noticed him, he was already halfway out the door."

Gwen ground her teeth and took deep breaths to keep her temper under control. "Do you know which way he ran?"

The woman grimaced and shook her head. "No. Sorry." She continued speaking, but Gwen's attention was abruptly drawn inward.

An intersection. Asher was standing at an intersection. 3-Decals advertising soda danced through the air. Both Gwen and Asher cringed away from the assault of tap-dancing fuchsia and green flowers. The crosswalk sign blared orange: Do Not Walk.

Street signs, was there a street sign? There, across the road—Rigel Avenue.

The crosswalk flared white, the walking man.

Rough hands touched Gwen's wrist. She jerked away with a yelp, her vision once again her own.

The desk worker tilted her head, brow furrowed, lips pursed. "Are you alright, ma'am?"

Gwen shook her head. "I've got to go." She dashed out of the building toward the intersection of Rigel Avenue and 12th Street.

Gwen leaned against the smooth concrete of the light post, breathing hard. She'd been chasing flashes of Asher for eight blocks, and she wasn't used to the exercise. Fear pulsed with her heartbeat, images she couldn't contemplate flashing in her mind: a line of crystals in a gray field, ripples of matte black, a roaring tiger in a 3-Decal, terror in a stark line of light and dark.

Gwen willed her breathing to slow. She had to find Asher. He couldn't navigate the city. Street signs and autos would be a mystery, the 3-Decals layering confusion over a chaotic world. The river wasn't so far away, and Asher—who loved water— couldn't keep his head above it. At least the auto-drivers would avoid him if he stepped in front of them. *Probably.*

She debated on reaching out to Asher again, but memories of the panic caused by her initial attempt stopped her short. She shook off the echoes of fear that rippled through her mind and heaved herself back into her search.

Another flash: green and brown, a whiff of hot dogs. Gwen's head jerked up. *The park.* She often took Asher there in the after- noons, when the sun wasn't too hot and she was up for it—which wasn't as often as it used to be, if she was being honest.

Asher liked the sandbox by the primary-colored playground designed for the littlest children, sifting sand through his fingers for hours, smiling and humming wordlessly. A safe place.

Gwen sprinted into the street and—

—a car slammed on its brakes in front of her. The startled occupants looked up from their screens and stared at her as the car waited for her to clear its path. Her breath came in gasps, and she tried for an apologetic smile as she sprinted the rest of the way across the street.

Sure enough, as she rounded the corner toward the park, Asher's presence filled her mind. Her fingers curved as though gripping the fine crystalline grains of sand flowing through Asher's hands. Her mouth curled up in a wide smile. The sand felt so *good*, both smooth and rough. She felt the dryness in the air washing away any hint of other children's odors, and heard the almost imperceptible *swish* as the sand met itself and unified.

Gwen realized she'd been standing still, one foot on the curb, for a long moment. *What's happening?* She felt another flash of fear, more confusing than the pulsing terror that had gripped her thinking of Asher wandering the streets alone. Her stomach clenched so hard it hurt. She tightened her fists, somehow feeling rough grit between her fingers as she did, and forced herself back into a run.

The park glistened in the hot afternoon sun, the verdant oaks and elms incongruous against the riot of colors from the 3-Decals that adorned the city. Gwen wiped sweat from her eyes and headed toward the path leading to the playground. The shade called to her. Part of her mind saw the black lines on the concrete where the sun's brightness died before it met the ground, having been absorbed by the leaves instead. She pulled up short.

Her mouth dropped open. She would get so angry at Asher when he pulled away from her at the edge of the park. "You love the park, Asher, stop fighting me!" She'd start calm, but by the fourth time she repeated it, her words would hiss, slapping the concrete and the leaves.

It scares him. The change scares him. How did I not realize?

She'd spent every day of his life studying him, in turn infuriated and mesmerized by him, and she'd never recognized that the shade frightened him. The realization of how little she truly knew her son made her heart ache. She didn't know how to remedy that, but damn it, she was going to try.

A force pushed into her mind, making her feel faint. Gwen's body disappeared, and she was lost, adrift in Asher's mind. The sandbox fell away and she—no, *Asher*—ran into the woods, screaming. A small conscious part of Gwen's mind recognized the concern on an unfamiliar woman's face as Asher tore past her, but her mouth moved meaninglessly. Asher pushed the stranger away, clawing and tearing at the fear and containment and confusion.

Gwen's experienced mind translated the feelings and jumbled chaos.

Leave me alone! Who do you think you are? This is wrong wrong wrong wrong wrong.

Asher, I'm here. Gwen tried to push through the scattered images and emotions and fear, but he didn't slow his run—and she couldn't find her way back to her body. *Where am I?*

The chip should have given her access to Asher's communication centers, his visual cortex and auditory processors, but it wasn't supposed to go the other way. She'd wanted to communicate with him, but this was too much. How had he looped back into her mind? Her plea didn't even make sense to her own mind; it was all just noise and intrusion and *wrong*.

The distantly awake part of Gwen's mind saw the ripples of water, the glistening sunlight, and joined the panicked screaming that dominated all else. *Not the pond, Asher, stop running, stop!*

Fear pulled her back to herself. Images of Asher's body floating still and limp—imagined now, but with a prescience that chilled her—forced her eyes to focus. She retched, but pounded into the park toward the pond.

Gwen found Asher huddled under a park bench, soaked from the waist down and muddy from the waist up. She fell to her knees, barely processing the sting of rough gravel amid the waves of relief she felt. She'd been trying to reach Asher for so long, trying so hard to free a mind she could see had brilliance within, that she'd never considered he might not be in a prison at all. To Asher, the world was a thrashing hurricane and his mind was a safe port against the unrelenting storm.

Tears streamed down her face as she scooted toward him. She still hoped the chips would allow them to connect, at least in their minds.

Asher rocked back and forth, humming a monotone buzz, hands pressed over his eyes.

Gwen reached out to touch him but stopped when her hand was inches away from his shoulder. Her own skin writhed with horror at the thought of an unexpected caress. That would only panic him further, and this level of fear—this heart-pounding, heavy breathing, tears-behind-the-eyes fear—had nearly driven Asher to drowning. She'd been so distracted that she'd run into the path of an oncoming car. There had to be some way to bring the two of them more in sync, some way to reach an equilibrium.

Gwen could feel Asher's emotions, but he couldn't understand her words. Maybe he could understand her emotions if she focused them in his direction.

She took deep, calming breaths and visualized Asher's blocks, the leaning tower in alphabetical order, connecting with the wall. Flipping the blocks free one by one. Building the tower again.

The rocking slowed. The humming stopped. Asher peeked at Gwen between splayed fingers. His eyes sent a jolt through her like a spray of cold water—they looked right at her, holding her gaze.

Gwen smiled and opened her arms wide. With feelings, not words, she projected herself toward him: the swell of love in her chest, the calm that came from having found a safe place to relax, the soothing warmth of every hug she and Asher had ever shared.

Asher smiled shyly and climbed out from under the bench. He crawled into Gwen's arms and knelt in her lap, pressing his face against her chest. Despite the wetness of his clothes, Gwen felt an echo of warmth in her soul that complimented—no, magnified—the feelings she'd sent toward Asher. He was responding in kind, and the love that poured from his heart burned hotter than any flame.

Gwen spent the next week working on a new version of the comm-chip. She debated removing the prototype, but every time she thought about it, Asher burst into tears. Once the shock of the increased connection faded, he'd reveled in being able to express himself.

Even though it wasn't the way Gwen had expected them to communicate, she relished it too. Asher experienced everything so *keenly*, with a fervent intensity the likes of which Gwen had never felt, even as a child. By the time the week was out, she barely felt the need to speak—emotional symbiosis was so much more primal and evocative. Asher's presence, their level of connection ... This was what she'd imagined when she'd brought him home from the hospital. No more confusion. No more barriers.

She stared at the new comm-chips for hours after she finished them. She'd programmed the emotional communication to be more distant, more controlled, so they'd be better able to distinguish their thoughts from one another. The chances of losing herself in Asher's mind would be far slimmer.

But was that really what she wanted? Was that what *Asher* wanted? Gwen's original plan had been to make Asher understand her, but she'd come to understand him instead. Now that they weren't fighting to communicate, the input from the chip was much easier to process. Her focus still shifted in odd ways sometimes, but she hadn't lost herself in days.

Asher tugged on her pant leg, then tilted his head and sent her the feeling of warm sand trickling through his fingers, of the weight of blocks and the tickle of paper between his fingers as he turned the pages of a book.

School! It was time to go to school. This would be Asher's second day attending physical classes. The first had gone better than Gwen could have hoped. The teachers were kind, gentle, and understanding of Asher's needs, and even at a distance, Gwen could be there for Asher. They were together now.

She'd helped him understand the shoving of a toy toward him was an invitation to play, not a threat, and encouraged him to redirect from his favorite blocks to the new experience of listening to a story on a circular rug. He'd enjoyed the soothing cadence of the teacher's speech; perhaps, in time, he might learn to recognize the words.

Gwen took Asher's hand with a smile. She threw the fresh pair of comm-chips into the trash bin and started the compacting cycle as they left the apartment. They walked in tandem down the hall, into the elevator, and out the front door to the bus stop.

In Asher's room, a ship sailed on fair seas, a summer breeze billowing white sails.

About the Authors

M. Elizabeth Ticknor has been previously published in two anthologies: *Heroic Fantasy* and *Epic Fantasy*; she also received a scholarship for the 2020 Superstars Writing Seminar. She shares a comfortable hobbit hole in Southeast Michigan with her husband and their twin baby dragons. An avid reader of science fiction and fantasy, Elizabeth also enjoys well-written horror. Her other interests include drawing, painting, and tabletop roleplaying. Visit her at ticknortales.com or on Twitter @lizticknor.

Rebecca E. Treasure grew up reading science fiction in the foothills of the Rocky Mountains. She received a history degree from the University of Arkansas and a Master's degree from the University of Denver. Her writing appears in the anthology, *A Dying Planet*, and she was a 2020 recipient of the Superstars Writing Seminar scholarship. She currently resides in Texas Hill Country with her family. Visit her at rebeccaetreasure.com.

CHECK YES OR NO

MELISSA KOONS

4/28/1987

Jeanine—

I had a really great time on our date Saturday night. Thanks for letting me take you out. You looked really nice, and I'm sorry I tripped and splattered your milkshake all over your jean jacket. You still looked pretty. I guess you really can pull off anything.

I wanted to buy you flowers to go with this note I stuck in your locker, but I don't have the money right now. They wouldn't compare to you, anyway. You're prettier than any flower and smell twice as sweet. I hope that's not weird to say.

I'd like to take you out again, if you're still interested. Maybe I'll be a little less nervous this time.

Check Yes or No

Matt

4/28/1987

Claire—look what Matt left for me. I can't tell if it's sweet or creepy. He stuck it in my locker while I was in chemistry. It's cute ... but the date last night was a disaster. We met at the mall food court, for starters, and not only did he trip and splatter my milkshake all over my fave jean jacket—you know, the one with the rhinestones on it—he dumped our food all over the floor. AND he didn't have enough money to buy it again, so I had to pay for us.

The conversation was so awkward. He kept stuttering and messing up his words and was so obviously nervous. He could barely string two words together. I've never seen a guy so tongue-tied around me—but I'm sure that's something you're used to. It was weird, though. Most guys talk to me really easily—then again, that's because they typically just want to find out if they have a chance with you. Haha! Matt struggled with making conversation, but he listened really well. It was kind of cute. Or is it creepy? I don't know. He *was* sweet. What do you think I should do?

—Jeanine

4/28/1987

Jean,

Girl, like, I've been on some bad dates before but none of them spilled a milkshake all over me. I love that jacket of yours! It's so choice. I hope it's not ruined. I wanted to borrow it for when I go bowling with Jack this weekend. Oh, wait, I didn't tell you? He asked me out! Hopefully our date goes waaaay better than yours did.

He called you a flower? I dunno ... that seems kinda creepy.

He's that lame, quiet guy in your lit class, right? The one who got all weird when you had to work with him on that book report thing and wouldn't make eye contact with you? Yeah, that dude is a spaz. You're probably better off, but it's up to you Jean-Queen.

I'll tell you all about my date with Jack on Sunday!

Claire

4/29/1987

Matt—Okay. But no milkshakes.

—Jeanine

4/29/1987

Dude! She said "Yes!" Where do I take her?

She said no milkshakes. That means she's mad, right? I know the mall wasn't the most stellar option, but it's all I could think of in my price range. I'd seen her and her friends hanging out at the food court before, so I figured she'd like it. Obviously not. What do I do?

Matt

4/30/1987

Bro, chill. You got this. You got her to agree to a second date so clearly you must be doing something right. I bet it was your flower talk. Girls love that crap. Write her some more of that. It's cheaper than chocolates and actual flowers, right?

And yeah, the mall was a bad call. Girls don't want to go on a date where they go all the time. They want something new and exciting. I know your dad is out of a job right now and you're pickin' up the slack at home, but that doesn't mean you don't have options. Take her to the skate park or something. You'll figure it out. Just DO NOT take her back to the mall.

Derek

4/30/1987

Jeanine—

I'm looking forward to our date tomorrow night. I get off work at 8:00 and figured I could pick you up around 8:30? I have a plan but bring a jacket. It might get chilly. Have you been to Forest Park? It's really pretty at night, and you can see tons of stars. I thought you might like it because your eyes always sparkle like stars whenever you talk about astronomy—I remember that's one of your favorite subjects.

It makes me think of that poem we read in class by John Keats: "Bright Star."

"Bright star, would I were stedfast as thou art—"

I don't totally get it, but I like the way it sounds.

See you tomorrow night.

No milkshakes this time, promise.

Matt

5/1/1987

Claire—He's taking me stargazing. In Forest Park. That's romantic, right? Or is it creepy?

—Jean

5/1/1987

Jean-Queen,

Could go either way. I mean, you do love the stars. And he quoted poetry to you? I dunno. But it's obvious he's hella into you. It's cute, I guess. Jack hasn't quoted any poetry to me. He just tells me I should prepare to get my butt kicked when we go to the alley tomorrow. It's starting to feel a lot less romantic compared to your date. Let me know how it goes! Call me right when you get home. I don't care what time, my parents have their poker night so they'll be out until way late and the ringer won't wake anyone.

Claire

5/1/1987

Jeanine—

I'm writing this before our date to give to you to read after it, so I'm really hoping it goes well otherwise I'll probably just throw this away so no one else will ever see it. Okay. Here goes nothing:

The stars seem dim
compared to the twinkle in your eye
when you smile
talking about them.
Your whole face lights up
like the sun
which is also a star
but closer.
You're radiant.

Oh, God, I hope you like this and don't think it's stupid ...

Matt

5/4/1987

Claire—I tried to call but the line was busy. All weekend. Did your sister make up with Frankie, again? Whatever. We both know how that's going to end.

But Claire. CLAIRE. It was the sweetest date. Matt took me to the park, and we hiked not far to this nice little clearing where you could see the stars. It was perfect. He still smelled like french fries, but at least he'd changed out of his work uniform. He told me how he picked up the extra hours because his dad got laid off a couple months ago and can't find work so all the money from Matt's paychecks goes to helping his family. He's got two kid sisters—twins! They're, like, ten years younger than him because his parents didn't plan on having more. Can you say, "Whoops?" Talk about a mega surprise.

Want to know the best part of the whole night? After actually TALKING with him (he was still so nervous, but he managed to get words out and string sentences together this time), he walked me to my door and slipped this note into my hand. He was all blushing and shy—it was legit adorable. It was a poem, Claire. He wrote me a poem about how I was like the sun. It was ... not good ... but so sweet!

I think I'll let him take me out again.

How did your date with Jack go?

—Jean

5/4/1987

Derek, dude, it worked! I don't know how, but it freaking worked! I took her stargazing, and we had just the best night. She's an only child, which is why she spends so much time with her friends.

That girl you're into—Claire, I think? Anyway, she's Jeanine's best friend since preschool, and they basically grew up together. She said they're like sisters, which makes so much more sense to me now. No offense, dude, I know you like that Claire chick and you say she's rad, but she comes off as kinda full of herself, to me. Which is why I was so confused that Jeanine was tagging along with her because Jeanine isn't like the rest of Claire's ditzy side-kicks who hang around her trying to soak up the extra attention.

Man, it was a huge relief to find that out. I was able to chill out and give her that poem I wrote. I almost threw it away because I was worried she'd think it was a horrible joke or something that she was going to laugh about with Claire later, and I so don't need that right now. Not that I ever need something like that. A girl isn't worth public humiliation.

My dad is on my case again about school. He was so pissed that I went out after work. I lied and told him it was for an astronomy assignment to get him off my back. Not having a job has him freaking out about me getting a scholarship for college in the fall. Man, he'll flip if he finds out about Jeanine.

It might not matter for long, anyway. I chickened out and didn't kiss her when I walked her to her door. I just kinda threw the poem at her and ran. I gotta come up with a plan to take her out again. Any suggestions?

Matt

5/4/1987

Dude. Bro. Claire is majorly bodacious. You're just too shy to be attracted to a girl like her. But that's okay, Jeanine is pretty radical, too, and hella into you if she is still agreeing to date you. It's probably good you didn't go in for the kiss—a girl like that isn't going to go for it on the first decent date.

She's got class so you gotta do something classy. How did all those poet guys you're reading get their girls? Or did they never get any girls and that's why they wrote poetry? I don't know. I didn't actually do the reading. That reminds me, can I see your essay before it's due on Friday? Just to get some ideas for my own ... I won't copy this one. I swear!

Thanks, man!

Derek

5/4/1987

Queen Jean!

Oh, my God, the date with Jack was just AWFUL! He was so competitive. He didn't let me win or anything. I kept trying to get him to show me how to bowl, you know, to get him all close to me and whatever, and he just kept saying he wasn't about to "lose his winning streak."

Ugh. So lame.

When he won, he pointed at me and called me a loser in front of the whole alley. Then, when he took me home, he had the NERVE to try to kiss me. Narbo. I don't feel even bad about jabbing my forearm into his throat to get him to back off. He was fine, just choked a little. He was breathing again by the time I made it to my front door. Won't be seeing him again. Warped weirdo.

But your date sounds amazing! Girl, I cannot imagine getting surprise twins. That would be the WORST. Wow, I had no idea he was doing that for his fam. That's a good guy. I feel kinda bad about making fun of him all this time for working in the food court. So where's Lord Byron taking you next?

Claire

5/5/1987

Jeanine—

Shall I compare you to a winter's moon
You illuminate the darkness
and make the frozen world
warmer in your presence
although the moon casts no heat and it's all symbolic

If you're free, I'd really like for you to meet me at the park, Saturday at 6:45 PM. Don't be late, show starts at 7:00. I'll bring the blanket.

Check Yes or No
Matt

5/5/1987

Matt—The sun and now the moon, huh? I'm digging these astronomy metaphors. (It's okay that they aren't scientifically accurate, I like the imagery you're creating.)
Check Yes. See you there. Do I need a jacket?

—Jeanine

5/5/1987

Claire—What is happening in the park Saturday night? Do you know?

—Jean

5/6/1987

Derek,

I know you're BFF with Matt so I gotta ask, what's the dish? He's taken Jeanine on a couple dates now, and he's planning something in the park on Saturday. Be real with me, do I need to be worried about this guy?

He seems genuine and sweet, but I just want to make sure he's not about to hurt my homegirl. He's no secret serial killer or heartbreaker, is he? You can't tell with the quiet ones ...

Claire

5/6/1987

Hey there! Claire, you got nothin' to worry about. Matt's a stellar guy. Promise. He's quiet and shy, but he's not mental. He just has a lot of family pressure to focus on his studies so he can get a scholarship, otherwise they can't afford college for him. He's taking a big risk on Jeanine. His old man can't know they're dating, otherwise he'll make him break it off. He doesn't want Matt to have any distractions.

That's probably what you're picking up. It's a little weird but, like I said, he's a good guy. If you're worried about it, wanna meet up with me Saturday night and we can make it a double date?

Derek

5/7/1987

Derek,

Not a chance.

Claire
P.S. Does Jeanine know Matt has to hide the fact that they're dating from his parents?

5/8/1987

Jeanine—

I just got this huge project assigned in history, and I have a double shift at work tomorrow. I'm going to try to get it all done before I meet up with you, but I wanted to give you a heads-up in case I'm late.
I'll be there. Promise.
No milkshakes. Double promise.

Matt
P.S. Yes, bring a jacket.

5/11/1987

Claire—It was Shakespeare in the park. He took me to Shakespeare in the park! We missed the first act but that was okay. He said his dad wouldn't let him out of the house until he finished that big history project we got assigned on Friday. I don't get it—it isn't even due for another week. His dad sounds like a spaz. Whatever.

It was amazing, Claire! The show was fantastic, and the actors did so good. It was totally different to see it than to just read it. I had no idea Shakespeare was so funny! I didn't get all the jokes, but luckily Matt didn't either, so I didn't feel like a total airhead.

He gave me another poem at the end of the night, and then he kissed me. It was so sweet. And he didn't try anything more! Just a kiss. He walked me to my door and handed me the folded poem. He was all nervous—I knew what he was about to do, but I just let him take his time and go for it his way; I didn't want to embarrass him—and when I thought he was about to chicken out (again) he went for it.

And he missed!

Got my cheek. So I turned my head and kissed him. It was really cute, and he's a surprisingly good kisser! Then he got all shy and left.

How many dates do you go on before it's considered going together?

You gotta read his poem, Claire. He's getting better.

—Jean

Attached poem:

I don't know as many words
as Keats;
I don't have the brilliance
to make up my own like Shakespeare.

I'm not as smooth as Byron,
nor as skilled as Tennyson
to bring all the thoughts I have

about you onto paper.

Without all the flowers,
the metaphors and similes,
I adore you
You make everything greater.

5/11/1987

Jean-Queen!

Oh, my God. That is the most fantabulous thing I have ever read. Aw, I'm getting goose bumps just reading about it. How romantic! What an excellent date. Way to go, Matt! Homeboy has game, I'll give him that. It's awkward game, and I don't think it would work on anyone but you, but he has it, and it seems to be paying off for both of you.

His dad IS a total spaz! Matt's BFF, Derek, was telling me how Matt's dad can't know you're dating or he'll flip. Ugh, it's super harsh you have to deal with this. I'm glad Matt told you about it, though. It would have been all kinds of messed up if he didn't clue you in by now. Bright side, you just have to keep it a secret and deal with his mental dad making Matt late to your dates until that scholarship comes in. He's a mega nerd, I'm sure he'll get one by June.

Also, girl, Jack has not let up. As if jabbing him in the throat wasn't clear enough, he keeps pestering me for another date. I can't tell you how many times I've turned him down. I just rejected him during passing period in front of all his friends. He was super pissed.

Claire

5/11/1987

Claire—What's this about keeping our relationship a secret from his dad? You better spill next class.

—Jean

5/11/1987

Hey, Claire! It sounds like we missed a most triumphant time at the park on Saturday. What if I took you to see the new play they're doing this weekend? I know I'm not as smooth as Byron, nor as skilled as Tennyson to bring all the thoughts I have about you onto paper, but I think you're pretty fly.
     What do you say? Pick you up at 6:00?

Derek

5/11/1987

Derek,

Still no. And that was a line from Matt's poem! I have the original to compare. So lame that you stole it. And you didn't even make it better!

Claire

5/12/1987

What do you mean? "Fly" is totally better than what Matt wrote.

Derek

5/12/1987

Matt—What's this about your dad not wanting you to date me? I am not okay being your little secret. Figure this out. I don't want to go on any more dates until you do. With or without milkshakes.

—Jeanine

5/12/1987

Derek, Jeanine is hella angry with me. I don't know how she found out about my dad, but now she doesn't want to date me if I have to keep it a secret. I didn't want to keep it a secret, I just didn't want to advertise it, either. How do I fix this? I don't think a poem will cut it this time.

I don't want it to be over. I like who I am with her. She makes me feel like I'm more than just the nerd that everyone else sees. She makes me want to speak up and say what I think about things. She cares about my opinions and ideas—even if it's only in really bad poetry.

How do I get her back?

Matt

5/12/1987

Dear Mr. and Mrs. Flyworth,

I am writing home with the notice that your son, Matthew Flyworth, has been suspended from Sunset High School for engaging in a physical brawl with another student, Jack Wyant, in the cafeteria on Tuesday, May 12, 1987. Matthew will hereby be suspended from classes and campus for one week. He may return for final exams on May 19, 1987, and he may appear at graduation on Saturday, May 23, 1987.

A parent, classmate, or otherwise appointed individual may drop off any final assignments that are due prior to his return.

We do not tolerate any physical violence on school property, and please rest assured that the other student involved will be equally reprimanded.

We are disappointed that Matt will be concluding his senior year this way, but our policy is in place for the safety of our students and we cannot make exceptions, even for a first offense.

Sincerely,
Principal Collin Grady

5/13/1987

Jeanine,

I am so sorry! I have no idea how Jack found the note. He must have gone through my locker or maybe it fell out of my purse in class, I don't know! Oh, my God. I'm a total ditz. I can't apologize enough. Please talk to me!

There was no way I could have known he would do something like that. I mean, yeah, he was pissed when I rejected him in front of all his buddies in the hallway—and everyone else who was in the hall eavesdropping—and yeah, he's crazy competitive, but I never would have guessed he'd steal that note and do that.

God, I can still see him standing on top of that lunch table reading Matt's poem to the whole cafeteria. It was heinous. And everyone laughed! They're losers; they don't get it. Matt's poem was so romantic.

And then Jack called Matt out because he thought Matt wrote it for me and it was all so totally mental! You know Matt and I are super not a thing, right? (I mean, yeah, of course you do. He's so not my type.) But then he stood up in front of the whole class and made that big deal about writing it for you ... It was pretty sweet. Quiet Matt stuck up for his girl and declared his love for you to the whole world. Or at least the cafeteria. Same thing.

But I had no idea Jack would get like that. We only had the one date.

Stupid Derek! If he hadn't asked me out and copied Matt's poem and then tried to make it better (but he totally didn't), I never would have had all those notes together for Jack to be able to connect the dots like that.

Please talk to me!

Also, I never in a million years would have expected Matt to get into a fight like that. I had no idea the guy had it in him to fight Jack. Well, kind of fight Jack. Really just that one shot. Jack really clobbered him, huh? Have you heard from Matt since his suspension? Is he hurt?

I'm so sorry! Please talk to me.

Claire

5/14/1987

Claire—It's fine. I know it's not your fault. I was just really upset about the whole thing and needed to cool off. His dad won't let me see him. I called, and he hung up on me. He told me it was all my fault. If Matt hadn't been chasing me none of this would have happened and Matt could have gotten into a good school. His dad said I ruined Matt's life. He won't tell me how he is.

I'm so upset. I haven't had a chance to tell Matt I forgive him! He made it wonderfully clear he doesn't want me to be his little secret, and what he did—God, that was so humiliating, but he did it for me! I can't believe a guy who could barely talk to me on our first date yelled at the school's top jock and picked a fight with him just to prove his feelings for me.

—Jean

5/15/1987

Jeanine, hey. I went over to Matt's house yesterday to pick up his homework to turn it in for him, he gave me this to pass on to you. Sorry his dad is such a dick. Dude needs a major chill pill.

Derek

Attached Note:
Jeanine—

I am so sorry for how my dad spoke to you. I overheard just the end of it, and I swear I saw red. I've never lost it like that before, but it was not okay for him to say those things. You didn't ruin my life. No one has. I get to come back in time for finals, and I can still walk at graduation. Any school that won't take me because I gave Jack a black eye isn't a school I want to go to, anyway.

It was worth it so that the whole school knows you and I are going together. It's not how I would have liked for it to have been made official ... I could have done without the very public humiliation ... and Jack reading my terrible poem that I wrote just for you ... but that's okay. Provided, you still want to date me at all? No milkshakes, promise.

Check Yes or No

Matt

5/15/1987

Derek—please give the attached to Matt when you see him next.

—Jeanine

Attached Note:
Matt—Check Yes. Also, I noticed your last note was missing my poem. Did Derek steal it again? He's got to know Claire isn't ever going to go for him.

—Jeanine

5/18/1987

Jeanine, don't be like that. You don't know that!
Here's your poem from Matt.
Derek

Attached poem:
Cheaper than jewelry.
Longer lasting than flowers.
Sweeter than chocolates.
Yet words still don't come close
to being the treasure that you deserve
because you're the ultimate gift
and nothing I give you
can begin to compare
or accurately show you
how happy you make me.
Are you happy, now?

Matt

5/18/1987

via courier Derek:
Matt—Check Yes.

—Jeanine

8/24/1987

Jean-Queen!

First day of college classes. I can't believe we got into the same school! I know you've already left for your 8:00 AM class, you overachiever, so I'm sliding this under your door for you to find when you get back. I hope your roommate doesn't throw it away like she did the last one. Space cadet.

I was hoping to see Matt around—where is he? I thought he was coming to Portland State, too?

Let's meet for lunch. See you at the student center at 1:00 PM.

Claire

8/24/1987

Claire—I'd love to do lunch! But I have class MWF at 1:15 PM. Tomorrow?

Matt didn't get a scholarship for Portland State, so he took the one for Oregon State University. It pays 50% of his tuition, and he couldn't turn that down. It's a long drive, but we meet up once a month. Now that he's in school his dad has chilled and doesn't seem to hate me so much. Thank God. He's still a spaz, though.

See you tomorrow!

—Jeanine

4/30/1991

Matt,

Hey, man, how you been? I'm sorry it's been a couple years since we were in touch. I'm glad you were listed in the Yellow Pages so I knew where to mail this. Are you still over at Oregon State? I made it a couple years at Portland State and then dropped out. I moved to LA—it's a wild town. I'm working on a studio lot. Just security, but it's cool to see all the Hollywood stars.

I was just back to visit the folks when I ran into that chick we went to high school with, Claire Underhill, on Saturday night, and she mentioned she just had dinner with you and Jeanine.

How's that going? I haven't seen her since I moved away. You guys still doing the long-distance thing?

Let's catch up some time. My phone number is below, give me a ring.

Derek

5/15/1991

Jeanine—

I am the luckiest man in the world. It's been two years since you transferred to Oregon State to be with me. I never thought I would find a woman so incredible that she would want to do that for me. Per our anniversary tradition, I have a special poem for you to celebrate our four-year anniversary. I'm sorry I haven't gotten better, that one Liberal Arts poetry class could only teach so much.

Blue eyes, ocean deep
with all the love you hold.

Heart so full, I can swim in it,
never reaching the bottom.

Smile bright, sunshine blinding
illuminating everything with your joy and happiness.
The world is lighter, because you help me carry it,
with you beside me, there's nothing I can't conquer.

Ocean deep, is my love for you.
Sunshine bright, is my life with you.
Please be my wife?
I propose to you.

Check Yes or No
Matt

5/15/1991

Matt—Check Yes.
—Jeanine

About the Author

Melissa Koons has written and published one novel, multiple short stories, and poetry. She has a BA in English and Secondary Education from the University of Northern Colorado.

A former middle and high school English teacher, she now devotes her career to publishing, writing, and various other pursuits in education hoping to inspire and help writers everywhere achieve their goals. When she's not working, she's taking care of her two turtles and curious cat.

DON'T IGNORE IT

TANYA HALES

T he old pickup truck rattles along the dusty road, never peaking above thirty miles per hour. My grandpa hunches over the steering wheel, looking almost as much a part of the car as any of the warped leather seats. I glance idly out the window at the plowed farmlands that stretch on for miles, then back at my phone.

"It's faster to get onto the highway and then loop back from the Redwood exit," I tell him. "It would save us seven minutes. Google Maps says so."

Grandpa says nothing for a minute, staring ahead from beneath bushy, curling brows. "This is the shortest path between us and your uncle's house," he finally tells me. "Saves gas. Besides, I like the scenery."

I gaze out at the unremarkable rows of fruit trees. We make this trip multiple times a week, so saving seven minutes each way seems like a big enough deal to me, but going the slow route through the farms keeps him happy, so I don't press the issue.

Grandpa has always been particular about the way he does things. On our last trip to Walmart, we went over to the travel section so he could grab a dozen of those really small tubes of toothpaste.

"Why don't you just get a big one?" I asked him.

"The paste gets stuck in the bottom of the big tubes," he said as he threw two more travel-sized tubes into the cart for good measure. "It's more convenient this way."

I checked the price and grimaced. "You'd save a lot of money."

"Eh," he shrugged. "I'm not hurting for money."

That's the way he's always been.

He'll eat Raisin Bran from a cup, explaining, "We have more cups than bowls. Besides," he says, raising the mug he got from Disneyland more than two decades ago, "I like Mickey Mouse."

Tonight, I'm holed up in my room, leaning over a report that is due tomorrow for Mrs. Breagan's class. It's almost midnight, and I'm supposed to be writing my opinion on some of Plato's philosophies. It's not going well.

Grandpa knocks on the door and enters my dimly lit room. Before I can demand why he's barging in at 11:52 when he normally goes to bed by 9:00, he motions for me to follow him.

"It's a cloudless sky. The Leonids should be visible tonight."

"Leonids?" I ask him. I'm confused and annoyed, and I really don't want to lose my train of thought for the thesis of this paragraph.

"Meteor shower," he tells me. "Come on. Let's go sit on the patio."

I tap my pencil impatiently against my desk. "I need to finish this report," I tell him. "It's for school."

He waves his hand dismissively. "The report will still be here when you get back. Come on. This will be good for you." And then he leaves.

Over the next fifteen minutes, I try to regain my focus. But I keep glancing out my dark window and imagining my grandpa sitting alone on the patio. Finally, I stand up and make my way out of the dark house to join him on the back porch.

He's sitting on the patio swing, gazing up at the sky. He has a blanket over his shoulders and a Donald Duck mug of hot chocolate in his hand. Beside him sits another folded blanket and steaming mug.

I settle down next to him and turn my face to the sky. The blanket staves off the autumn chill, and the hot mug feels comforting in my hands. I only have to look at the sky for half a minute before I see the first shooting star streak past.

Grandpa settles back and sighs. "You know," he tells me softly, "this is the way we are meant to live." We watch as four more stars stream past in quick succession. "When you find something that makes you happy, don't ignore it."

And for the first time, with stars flashing overhead and the crisp, chilly air of an autumn midnight bringing goose bumps to my arms, I think I understand what he means.

About the Author

When Tanya Hales was a baby, she enjoyed books by chewing them to pieces before eventually moving on to the higher art of reading. Tanya splits her time between her work as a writer, an illustrator, and a mother, all of which she loves intensely. She now lives in the Utah Valley with her family, constantly daydreaming about imaginary worlds.

ADDITIONAL COPYRIGHT INFORMATION

ABOUT THE EDITOR

Lisa Mangum has worked in publishing since 1997. She has been the Managing Editor for Shadow Mountain since 2014 and has worked with several *New York Times* best-selling authors.

Lisa is also the author of four national best-selling YA novels (The Hourglass Door trilogy and *After Hello*), and several short stories and novellas. She has edited six anthologies about fantastical creatures. She graduated with honors from the University of Utah, and currently lives in Taylorsville, Utah, with her husband, Tracy.

IF YOU LIKED ...

If you liked *Hold Your Fire*, you might also enjoy:

Dragon Writers
Edited by Lisa Mangum

X Marks the Spot
Edited by Lisa Mangum

Monsters, Movies & Mayhem
Edited by Kevin J Anderson

OTHER WORDFIRE PRESS TITLES EDITED BY LISA MANGUM

One Horn to Rule Them All

A Game of Horns

Dragon Writers

Undercurrents

X Marks the Spot

Our list of other WordFire Press authors and titles is always growing. To find out more and to see our selection of titles, visit us at:
wordfirepress.com

 facebook.com/WordfireIncWordfirePress

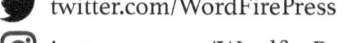 twitter.com/WordFirePress

instagram.com/WordfirePress